S0-BHZ-725

STAND LIKE MEN

Also by James Sherburne

HACEY MILLER

THE WAY TO FORT PILLOW

James Sherburne

STAND LIKE MEN

a novel

BOSTON
HOUGHTON MIFFLIN COMPANY

Second Printing w

Library of Congress Cataloging in Publication Data
Sherburne, James, 1925– . Stand like men.
I. Title.
PZ4.S5498St [PS3569.H399] 813'.5'4 72-12399
ISBN 0-395-17117-2

Printed in the United States of America

To Dyne Englen, Joe Benge,
Bill Nave, and Jim Tuohy

. . . Stand like men, and linked together —
Victory — for you'll prevail;
Keep your hand upon the dollar,
And your eye upon the scale.

— *The Miner's Lifeline*

Contents

STAND LIKE MEN

Prologue

The Name

ALMOST A HUNDRED YEARS before Breck Hord was born, a dog appeared by a nameless branch of Poor Fork, which is one of the three sources of the Cumberland River.

He was an old hound of indeterminate breed, with a grizzled muzzle and sad, weak eyes. He was sick and starving, and his back legs trembled uncontrollably as he climbed down the bank and drank from the clear, cool stream. He lapped the sweet water thirstily. It was early spring, and the woods around him flamed with redbud and dogwood; the sarvis trees on the hills glittered with white blossoms like frost crystals in the sun.

After a while the old dog lay down beside the creek and closed his eyes. The bank was dappled with shade, and there were cardinals and woodpeckers and a pair of indigo buntings in the trees. It was a good place to be — no other would ever be better.

Throughout the long afternoon he died.

For the next day or two, he looked as though he were sleeping, so he was not molested. But by the third day his lips had pulled back from his teeth, and a line of ants moved busily between his body and a nearby hole.

The big birds discovered him soon, and opened up his belly and stripped out his entrails. They did their usual thorough job; his ribs, arching together like the fingers of an old man's folded hand, shone white and clean, as did his pelvis. With his body undisturbed above and below the belly, he looked like a man dressed in a jacket and boots, but naked in between.

After that he was left alone. As the mountain seasons changed, his hair and skin and flesh fell away, until nothing remained of him but bones.

Nimrod Hord found the bones when he was scouting up Poor Fork for a place to build a cabin. He liked the looks of the little creek, and he told his wife that night, "I found me a pretty place, up the hollow on that Dead Dog Branch." From then on, the creek had a name.

Nimrod Hord raised his family on Dead Dog Branch, and was joined by some of his kinfolk. (Those who could spell spelled their names in a variety of ways — "Hord," "Hoard," "Harde," and sometimes even "Howard" — but it was all the same name.) They lived there through the nineteenth century. The Civil War came and went, but aside from laying the groundwork for a few feuds, it didn't change much. Nothing changed much, until coal was discovered in Harlan County.

A group of Harlan businessmen persuaded the railroad to come into the county in 1910, and from then on coal was everything. In two years there were fifty mines operating, fifty great tipples crouching over fifty grimy railroad spurs like gigantic praying mantises. And more came later.

The mine on Dead Dog Branch was formally named "Excelsior No. 2," but it was popularly known as "Dead Dog." The company that owned it was controlled by a Michigan automobile manufacturer who believed he knew best what was good for his employees, and preferred them not to join unions. The company required each miner to sign a contract promising never to become a union member. In the parlance of the time, these agreements were called "yellow-dog contracts," and workers who signed them were known by staunch unionists as "yellow dogs."

During the nineteen twenties, when the United Mine Workers of America began recruiting in the unorganized mines, an antiunion miner named Fraley had his brains blown out on the banks of Dead Dog Branch.

From that time, the mine was no longer called either "Excelsior No. 2" or "Dead Dog." It was called, inevitably, "Dead Yellow Dog." And so it is called today.

Chapter 1

The Hollow

BRECK HORD could just barely remember the days before the mines came to Harlan County. The family had lived in a comfortable and well-built cabin a half mile up the hollow. It sat with its back against the rising ground, three rooms wide and a loft above, with a front porch facing the creek, and a side porch for sitting when the front porch was in the sun. A few hogs were kept in a stone pen on the other side, for fresh meat and to keep the snakes down. There were also a cow, a horse, chickens, and dogs for all purposes.

In those days Breck had a twin brother named Andy, tow-headed and snub-nosed, whose mercurial temperament made Breck seem stolid and slow by comparison. The two boys prowled the woods and splashed in the creek together, hunted ginseng to sell to the pharmacist in Harlan Town, searched the hills for blooming linden trees with their pungent linden honey. They set traps for beaver and cony, fished for hornyheads and suckers and eels. They were inseparable from breakfast to bedtime.

Breck also had another brother, Claiborne, and a sister, Phoebe. Claiborne had been born in 1900, which made him six years older than Breck and Andy, so that whatever the twins could think of to do, Claiborne had already mastered; if there was a Forbidden Forest, they could be sure Claiborne had already been there, and blazed a trail through the virgin timber.

Phoebe was a year younger than the boys, a skinny, big-eyed little thing distinguished by her inscrutable silences and unexpected tenacity.

One memory Breck had of those days concerned a conversation with Andy and Claiborne, which began with bees, focused on the reproductive habits of bees, and moved to reproductive habits in general. They lay in the grass under an old oak tree, and Claiborne elucidated the Mystery.

"Girls are fractious as a moony horse," he said, with his bony freckled face composed into a grave pedagogical expression. "It's all a man can do to handle them. But I'll tell you one thing for certain, though."

"What's that, Claiborne?" asked Breck.

"The best time to get them is when their folks is in church. In the Holiness Church, I mean."

"How come is that?" Andy demanded.

"When they're standing outside, listening to that singing and hollering and carrying on, it gets them all hotted up. Especially when their folks is talking in tongues inside, or handling the serpents. That gets them hotted up the most. There ain't hardly no way to keep them from crawling into the bushes then."

"You ever done that, Claiborne?" Andy asked, big-eyed.

"Why, God dog, boy, what do you think I'm telling you about? Course I have — you couldn't count all the times. Hundreds, I reckon."

Andy squirmed excitedly. "What's it like, Claiborne?"

"Fine as frog hair," the older boy replied complacently. But when his brothers begged him to describe it, he reproved them: "Now what would be the point of that? You two ain't *equipped* to understand. It would be like a bird trying to tell a catfish about flying." He yawned smugly. "No, you just hold your horses a few years, and think about growing up to be like your old brother Claiborne. Your time will come, I promise you."

Breck and Andy looked at each other resignedly; they had heard *that* before. The conversation veered back to the Holiness Church people. Breck asked what it was like when they handled the serpents, and Claiborne told them, very graphically, with gestures, picking up imaginary rattlesnakes and copperheads and draping them around his arms, head, and shoulders. Andy said in a tone of dismissal, "They must not have good sense."

Breck was fascinated. "How come they don't get bit and die, Claiborne?"

"Because the snakes is Satan, and if you ain't afeared of Satan, then God gives you the strength to overcome him — that's what they say."

"Do you believe that?"

"I don't believe it or not believe it — I just go over there to get me a girl. But this here's a fact: there's plenty of them that's been bit lots of times, and there ain't none of them died from it. At least," he amended, "not since old Anse Burkett died two years ago."

"How come he died?" Breck asked.

"I guess 'cause he didn't trust God enough." Claiborne lowered his voice and leaned closer to Breck. "It was bound to happen — there was a bird flew into his house a couple of days before. From then on, it was only a matter of time."

Breck glanced apprehensively over his shoulder at the mention of this fatal omen. Some things were not for conversation, even on a sunny spring morning. But Andy threw back his shock of tow hair and laughed scornfully. "I don't believe none of that superstitious stuff. It's all made up to scare kids with, ain't it, Claiborne?"

"If you say so, Andy — with all your experience and all," his older brother said mockingly.

There was a moment of silence as each boy thought his own thoughts. Then, with a sudden whoop, Andy threw himself on Claiborne's back and called to Breck to help pin him down. The three of them wriggled like seined minnows in the tall grass.

*

Every spring Breck's father, Jubal Early Hord, would hitch old swaybacked Glory to the bull-tongued plow, and plant his two acres of bottomland. Most of it was in corn, but he kept small plots of hemp and tobacco as well, and a stand of sugar cane along the creek provided him with the sorghum that he mixed with honey to make the "long sweetening" that served the family in place of sugar.

Except for the spring plowing, Glory's leisure generally went undisturbed, unless Jubal Early decided it was time to visit the Cleggs in Perry County. When that mood came over him, it was a bad day for Glory, for it meant pulling a wagon full of people all the way up and over Pine Mountain.

Breck and Andy loved these visits to the Cleggs', because they gave them an opportunity to listen to Great-Grandpa Jewett Clegg tell about the French-Eversole War. As a young man Jewett Clegg had been a partisan of Fulton French's in that legendary mountain vendetta, and he could recount its culminating engagement, the Battle of Hazard, with almost total recall. "Lord God Almighty, how we poured it on them!" he chortled, his dim eyes slitted as he fired an imaginary rifle. *"Whang! Whang! Whang!* It was like to deafen a man." He paused to spit. "They was down in the courthouse, in town, and we was up the hill in the graveyard, behind the gravestones. We had to shoot low, on account of being above them like that. We'd aim down around their knees, and that would put the ball into them right in the middle of their bellies. *Whang! Whang!*" (Spit!)

"How many did you kill, Gray-gramp?" asked Andy, his eyes glittering.

"Honey, I'll tell you the mortal truth — I just plain lost count. But they was dropping like flies!" He stopped to savor the never-to-be-forgotten exaltation of that morning. His jaws worked rapidly, and his hands trembled with excitement.

"Was that the end of the war?" Breck asked.

Slowly the light died out of the old man's eyes. He looked at Breck with dull resentment. "Oh, it went on awhile after that, but never amounted to much no more. Just petered out. People forgot about it, unless something reminded them." He looked at Andy, who was his favorite, in a way that was almost beseeching. "It's peculiar, how things peter out like that, ain't it?"

Breck Hord never forgot those stories as long as he lived.

*

All Breck's memories of the old life were set in the years prior to 1916, for that was the year when the happiness of his youth was blighted, and his personality turned in upon itself, and he began to appear closed and unapproachable to others.

One hot afternoon in July, little Phoebe complained of a stiff neck and a sore back. Her mother felt her forehead, and put her to bed immediately. By the time Jubal Early and the boys came home for supper, she was nauseated and burning with fever.

Jubal Early rode off for the doctor with his supper wrapped in a red bandanna and tied to the ring of his old McClellan saddle. It was full dark before he returned, with the doctor riding beside him. The doctor spent a half hour with the patient, and then told her parents that Phoebe probably had either influenza or infantile paralysis. He described the symptoms of each illness and explained what to do if these symptoms appeared, for he couldn't promise to be back before three or four days.

Phoebe had infantile paralysis. When her fever broke, she had almost no sensation in her right leg. Everyone in the family took turns exercising her leg muscles. Once when Breck was working with her, she said flatly, "All this don't make no nevermind."

"What are you talking about, Phoebe? Doctor said this will fix your leg up as good as it ever was."

She looked at him almost compassionately. "Oh, I reckon not, Breck. I reckon it ain't never going to be like that again — not to look at, nor to walk on neither."

He kneaded the unresponsive thigh muscle fiercely. "You shouldn't say that, Phoebe."

"Why not? It's my leg, ain't it?"

The doctor came back, examined the patient, shook his head, prescribed continuation of the exercises, accepted two dollars from Jubal Early, and rode off. At the insistence of his wife, Hannah, Jubal Early summoned Aunt Cloa Burkett to look at Phoebe; Aunt Cloa, the widow of Holiness saint Anse Burkett, was the best-known midwife and granny-woman on Poor Fork. Aunt Cloa prescribed a poultice of cornmeal, whiskey, and tobacco, to be held in place from hip to thigh by a splint secured with soft deerskin. She also accepted two dollars for her services.

The two treatments were equally effective.

Two months after she was stricken, Phoebe was able to take a few steps, aided by a cane. She wore a brace on her knee. As she grew older, she continued to improve slowly, until she was able to walk fifty feet at a time. But it was a victory of spirit rather than flesh, for the leg shriveled and the muscles turned to suet.

One day in the fall of that same year, Breck and Andy were playing in a cave they had discovered back up Pine Mountain. They considered it their private hidy-hole, and probably no one else in Harlan County knew it existed; the Indians who would have remembered it were all dead. The boys were playing their favorite game, French-Eversole War; Andy, as a French adherent, was escaping from the Hazard jail to join his allies in the graveyard. He burst from the cave mouth at a dead run, peppering Breck with buckeyes as he came. His ankle turned on a rock. Feeling himself falling, he tried to recover his balance by throwing his weight to one side. This increased the distance of his fall, and his body arched more than eight feet before his head cracked against a limestone outcropping.

In later life, nothing ever muted the harshness of the details in Breck's memory. He could close his eyes and feel the weight of Andy's limp body on his back as he stumbled down the hillside, with Andy's feet dragging over the rocks behind him, and Andy's head bouncing against his neck. He could feel again the overpowering weariness that made him leave his brother under a silver maple and stumble the rest of the way to the cabin for help. He could remember the laying-out, with Andy's body washed and rubbed with lotions, the eyelids weighted with coins, and the mouth tied closed with a dark blue cloth; Andy dressed in his best clothes, the Sunday suit he had worn only a half dozen times, his thick tow hair brushed back from his unlined brow, and a pillow under his head. That night a group of men from the nearby hollows had sat up with the corpse till dawn; a few hours later another group dug his grave in the Hord family cemetery on the hillside overlooking the creek. In the afternoon, the service: "The Old Rugged Cross" and "In the Sweet By and By"; the Scripture; the lowering of the box, with Andy's head to the east. The cadaverous old man sprinkling dirt on the coffin, and the funeral over, except for the neighbors who stayed behind to shovel the grave dirt back.

Everyone in the family was affected by these two tragedies, but Breck and his father were affected the most. In Breck's case, the result was even more laconic speech and reserved behavior than before; he ceased volunteering information, preserved a dead-level temper, and showed as little spontaneous emotion as possible. Jubal Early's reaction was more drastic: bent under the weight of the double tragedy, he signed away his land.

The war in Europe had increased the demand for Appalachian coal substantially. Large northern and eastern corporations formed coal mining subsidiaries, and competed briskly for Harlan County mineral leases. When a company acquired a lease, the railroad immediately built a spur to serve the prospective customer, a tunnel was sunk into the hillside, and a tipple arose over the tracks to convey the new-minted black wealth to the apparently insatiable mills and munitions factories.

Jubal Early was approached by agents of three different corporations. At first he wouldn't talk to them, feeling that even to discuss selling Hord property would be disloyal to the family, past, present, and future. But then one of them made him understand that the corporations only wanted to buy the rights to the minerals *under* the ground — that title to the surface land would remain with the Hords.

"You're fixing to pay me five dollars an acre just for what's underneath?" Jubal Early asked incredulously. "I own title to upwards of forty acres, you know."

"I know, Mr. Hord," said the agent, a lawyer from Harlan Town. "I'm fixing to pay you two hundred dollars in hard-cash money for the right to dig out some coal which we may never even get around to digging, while you keep hold of your good bottom land same as you always did."

Disheartened by the death of one child and the crippling of another, Jubal Early signed the lease, and Hannah signed her name next to his. The agent took a fat wallet from his hip pocket and ran his thumb across a sheaf of bills with a sound like the shuffling of playing cards. He counted out ten twenty-dollar bills, congratulated them on their business acumen, sympathized with them over their sorrows, thanked them for their courtesy, and left.

What Hord had signed was a broad-form deed, which guaranteed the lessee the right to all mineral substances under the ground. In addition, it authorized him to excavate for them, to build roads and structures on the land as he saw fit, to harvest the timber for mining props, and to divert and pollute the water in any way necessary or convenient.

Within a month a railroad gang was building a spur up Dead Dog Branch, and a mining gang was blasting out what would become the driftmouth of the main shaft, slanting down and back into the hillside. Excelsior No. 2 was under way.

Breck spent most of his free time watching the progress of the work gangs. Work stopped when the snow came, but started again in the early spring. The railroad spur crawled along beside the creek where the sugar cane had been, and the tipple rose in spidery dominance over the empty cornfield. From foggy dawn to smoky dusk, the noise was incessant; whistles and hammers, black powder and dynamite, ripsaws and band saws, shouted orders and angry complaints — there was no end to it until sundown, but then there was a complete end, for the birds didn't nest along Dead Dog Branch that year.

In the evenings, Breck sat on the front porch listening to his father and his brother Claiborne arguing. Already remorseful over signing the deed, and uncomfortable with the changes it had brought, Jubal Early was ready to move the family away from Dead Dog. Claiborne advised a wait-and-see policy, pointing out that the mine would be operating in a month or two, paying wages of seven dollars a day.

Jubal Early was incredulous. Seven dollars a day? Seven dollars a week, more likely. "They're getting it, Pa," Claiborne assured him. "Over to the mines in Lynch and Wallins Creek, they're getting that, and more. Forty dollars for a week's work, one feller got, and he was back home eating his supper by full dark every night!"

Listening to their argument, Breck would hug his knees and say in silent prayer: *Don't let Pa move us away from Dead Dog! We can't leave Andy up on the hill, with nobody around but strangers!*

The question was resolved one rainy afternoon, as the runoff from the growing slag heap coursed blindly down the red clay hillside into Dead Dog Branch. "I ain't going to watch no more of this," Jubal Early announced decisively. "Going to pack up the whole kit and b'iling and move out of here." He had made up his mind; the family would move to Leslie County, where there was an empty cabin available. It was on land owned by the Allardyces, Hannah's people. Better than an acre of cleared bottom land went with the house.

"You won't make no seven dollars a day there, though," Claiborne said moodily.

"That's a fact — but you might hunt a varmint or catch a fish without it wasn't scared away or poisoned first," his father answered.

"A man can buy a lot of fish for seven dollars."

Over their heads the rain pattered down on shingles which had been rived by Nimrod Hord almost a century before.

During the hectic days of moving, Breck was weighed down by a sense of guilt. He was almost sick with shame at leaving his brother's grave behind. The only thing that gave him comfort was planning his return to Dead Dog Branch. *Once I'm grown, nothing can keep me away,* he told himself. *Claiborne wants to come back, and I can come back too!*

On their third trip over Pine Mountain, with the last of their possessions in the wagon, Breck and Phoebe sat on the tailgate and looked back at Harlan County. It was early morning, and heavy fog lay in the valley. As they neared the top of the mountain they came out into sunshine. Other mountaintops were suddenly visible to the east and south and west. It was as if they were bugs on the rim of a green bowl almost filled with steamy hot milk.

"It's right sad to be leaving, ain't it, Breck?" asked Phoebe.

Breck glanced at her leg, rigid in its homemade brace, thrust stiffly out from the wagon, and realized that her need for reassurance was even stronger than his own. He told her it was going to be great fun, moving close to all their mother's kinfolk. It was going to be like joining up with a whole new family, he predicted with assumed confidence.

They sat in silence, swaying with the movement of the wagon. They reached the crest of Pine Mountain and started down the other side. Phoebe said, "I do wish Andy was with us."

"I do too, for a fact," Breck replied. She touched the back of his hand gently, and after a moment he clasped her hand in his own.

Chapter 2

Coming Back

DURING THE MISERABLE two and a half years Breck lived in Leslie County, his appearance and his personality took the shape they would bear for the rest of his life. His brow was wide but low, his eyes small and deep-set, his nose short, his mouth wide and almost lipless. His squarish head sat firmly on his muscular neck. His shoulders were unusually broad, and his chest unusually deep. Although certainly not handsome, he would have been pleasant-looking enough, except for his characteristic lack of expression. As it was, he impressed people as being either careful or dull, depending on their own bias. The closed quality of his appearance was reflected in his speech, laconic and unemotional.

He found the neighboring Allardyces to be clannish, and he made no friends in school. Also, there was never as much to eat as there had been on Dead Dog Branch. In later years, it seemed to him that the family had survived mostly on dried persimmons. His longing for companionship became acute when, late in 1917, Claiborne joined the army.

The day before he left for camp, Claiborne told him why he had enlisted. "God dog, little brother, it's the only way I see of getting out of this worthless damn hollow! If I stay around plowing these hills much longer, I'm going to have one leg that's a foot longer than the other!"

"After the war you're coming back here, ain't you, Claiborne?"

"Why, no. If I come back to Kentucky at all, I'll get me a job in the mines. A man can make some money there—enough to dress up his wife good, and eat beefsteak off a china plate, and buy a bottle of red whiskey, if he has a mind to!"

"What about Ma and Pa? It'll about break their heart if you don't come back."

"Look, Breck," Claiborne said quietly, his thin, bony face expressing unusual seriousness. "Pa knows they're paying good money at the mines. If he don't want to take advantage of it, there's nothing I can do to help him. A man owes it to himself to do what he wants to do, and go where he wants to go. We're a long time dead in this world."

Breck thought about Andy and didn't say anything. Claiborne went on, in a lighter tone: "Tell you what I'm going to do for you. You behave yourself, and I'll bring you back one of them German officer's helmets, with a spike on the top. I'll kill me one dead as a doornail, just so you can have it. How about that?"

For a second Breck's face lit up with sudden animation, before returning to its usual impassivity. "I'd like that, Claiborne, if it wouldn't be too much bother," he said politely.

His older brother looked at him quizzically. "Well, be careful you don't fall over dead from excitement," he said.

When Claiborne came back a year later, he didn't bring a German officer's helmet, because he had never gotten overseas. He brought a wife instead. Her first name was Joicy, her maiden name was Creech, and she had been born and raised in a hollow off Troublesome Creek, not twenty-five miles from Dead Dog Branch. Claiborne, however, had never set eyes on her until he bought her a drink in a Louisville saloon. She had arrived there by a circuitous route that had begun when she ran away from home with a hardware drummer, and had continued through a series of relationships of greater or lesser duration — but never for only a single night, not even in her hungriest days. Joicy was a tall woman, thin through the arms and shoulders but with surprisingly large and upstanding breasts. She had a long, oval face, coarse black hair, and a big mouth which she painted bright red. Claiborne tried to treat her with an offhand male-possessive attitude, but it was obvious he found her overwhelmingly desirable.

Claiborne and Joicy had no intention of remaining in Leslie County, even for a few days. There was too much money to be made in the Harlan mines for that. They intended to get themselves a piece of that seven-dollars-a-day money. "And you know where we're fixing to live, Pa?" Claiborne asked, with a trace of impudence in his expression. "The name of it is Excelsior Number Two — but folks call it the Dead Dog mine."

"Our hollow, you mean? Hord hollow?" Jubal Early asked in surprise.

"Leastways, it *was* our hollow. There's a good-sized camp there now, I hear. Better than thirty cabins along the creek-side, real nice places, all painted up slick, with big porches and flowers growing around."

"Them cabins is for the miners?" his father asked.

"That's right, Pa. And they got them a commissary store, right there in the hollow, that sells anything you could think of — all kinds of food, meat and beans and flour and coffee, furniture —"

"Lamps made out of colored glass, so the light comes out of them all different colors, like a picture," Joicy interrupted eagerly.

"— all kind of clothes, men's, women's, children's — they even got baby clothes," her husband went on. "I tell you, Pa, you wouldn't believe all the truck they got to choose from! Anything you want, you just tell them to put it on the bill, and you pay for it at the end of the month, when you settle up!" Claiborne and Joicy grinned at one another in anticipation of their rich and easy life together.

Hannah Hord spoke for the first time, quietly, without looking up from her mending. "There's more to life than lamps made out of colored glass," she said. "Sometimes folks don't find that out till it's too late."

A few days after Claiborne and Joicy left, Breck and Phoebe were sitting together on the rickety porch steps. He happened to mention Joicy in conversation, and was astonished when Phoebe hotly described her new sister-in-law as no-account trash. When he objected that Joicy had behaved in a friendly manner toward her, she explained that the woman had only wanted to get on her good side. "I can tell," she said positively. "She only married Claiborne to get all them fancy things at the commissary store, only he's too simple to know it."

"Simple? Claiborne ain't simple!"

"He is about women — all men are." Phoebe tossed her head haughtily. "It takes a woman to understand another woman."

"Well, *you're* no woman, Phoebe!"

"I'm a darn sight closer than *you'll* ever be!" she replied with triumphant logic.

Breck often thought about the coal camp Claiborne had described on Dead Dog Branch. He tried to imagine how it must look, with the bright new houses lining the creekside, tree-shaded and cool in the long summer afternoons. He pictured children playing beside the water, splashing their store-bought clothes unconcernedly, while their tolerant parents watched from their porches and the smell of frying pork floated on the air about them. And up the hillside, in the little graveyard, was Andy.

By the fall of 1919, Jubal Early had come to the end of his two hundred dollars' lease money, and the family entered a bleak winter. The snap beans ran out first, then the sweetening, then the coffee. By spring the family was subsisting on a plateful of pinto beans a day, cooked with the last chunks of hog belly and sopped up with fried cornmeal. They just about didn't make it.

One old, sunny day in March, Jubal Early and Breck walked through the cornfield, kicking at patches of unmelted snow. The red clay dirt was still half-frozen. "Damn old ground just keeps holding on to winter," his father said morosely. "And then, when it ain't too hard, it's too sticky. If it don't break your bones, it sucks you up like a hog wallow. A man can't live on it."

"We got through all right, Pa," said Breck.

"Yes, we did — and all of us looking like the back wheels of bad luck, too." He shook his head sadly, acknowledging an error he still couldn't understand. "No, boy, it's my fault. I never should have signed that paper. I bear witness, I traded your birthright for a mess of pottage. Maybe I should have moved us back to the hollow, along with Claiborne, when he went back last fall. We couldn't have been no worse off, that's for certain."

The beginning of hope began to grow in Breck's heart, but he kept silent for fear of scaring it away. They reached the end of the field and stood looking at the cabin of their nearest neighbors, some of the unfriendly Allardyces. The sight of the neat tarpaper roof and the snugly smoking chimney seemed to help Jubal Early reach a decision. "Ehh-yuh, I reckon it's time for us to go. Up stakes and out of here, and back to Dead Dog. I've made up my mind."

"Yes, Pa." It was all Breck could do to keep from smiling.

*

The mining camp on Dead Dog Branch didn't look like Breck had imagined it. The cabins didn't nestle in the shade, because there wasn't any shade in the camp, except the skeletal shadow of the tipple on the hillside. Children in store-bought clothes didn't splash unconcernedly in the creek; there were plenty of children, but they wore bib overalls and linsey-woolsey dresses, and no child in his right mind would want to play in the rust-red, sulphur-smelling water of Dead Dog Branch. Nor were there many flowers growing from the slate and coal dust around the front porches.

But there *was* the smell of frying pork in the evening air, and after dinner neighbors sat outside, talking quietly and sometimes laughing, watching the dusk deepen into night. And there *was* the commissary, stocked with an assortment of food and clothes and furniture such as Breck had never seen before.

And there *were* seven-dollars-a-day wages. Not for Jubal Early at first, because he was new to mining and didn't know how to get the coal out. But for the other miners, including Claiborne, the seven dollars was there to get, and most days they got it.

Claiborne and Joicy lived three houses down the creek. Their cabin was furnished as handsomely as any in the camp. Their living room boasted a dark green mohair sofa and matching chair, a wingback chair, a lamp with a colored glass shade, a picture of a clipper ship under full sail, and a seven-by-ten rectangle of red-and-green plaid linoleum. For sitting on the porch, there were two cane-bottomed straight chairs and a rocker. On warm evenings Claiborne and Joicy sat there, Joicy in the rocker because she was pregnant, and Claiborne deferred to her more than many husbands would. They talked about things they wanted to buy.

Until school started in the fall, Breck found the days long and hard to fill. He spent much of his time upstream of the camp, roaming over Dead Dog Branch and the hills that flanked it. One afternoon the notion came to him that he would like to see the old cabin, deserted since the family had left it four years before.

It was in poor shape. A hole in the roof let sunlight in; one of the porch-roof poles was gone, causing the roof to sag like a heavy eyelid over a bleary eye; animals and people had left many different kinds of waste on the floor. But it was shadowy and quiet, and there were birds nesting in the trees outside. Breck sat on the floor, a half smile on his lips, remembering the summer days of his childhood.

He heard a rifle shot outside, then, rapidly, two more.

Curious, he looked out of the window. As best he could judge, the shots had been fired from a point halfway up the slope, near where his and Andy's cave must be. He stepped out of the cabin and entered the underbrush, following the half-remembered and almost invisible trail. He climbed for two or three minutes. Suddenly another shot sounded directly ahead of him, and he thought he heard the passage of a bullet over his head. "Hey, you there!" he called out. "Watch it, you got company." He pushed aside a branch and walked out into the clearing below the cave mouth.

It was still early in the afternoon; the bushes and trees cast their shadows directly down, so the greenery seemed to float, shimmering, in the sunlight. A stillness lay over the hillside, for the rifle shot had startled the birds, and they had stopped singing. Breck's breathing sounded loud in his ears, and he drew a deep breath and held it.

For there, standing before the cave, cradling a rifle in one arm, and brushing his tow hair back from his eyes with his hand, was his brother Andy.

Or so it seemed for one stunning moment. Then, in the space of a delayed heartbeat, his mind registered half a dozen differences between the remembered brother and the boy in front of him. This boy was stouter than Andy would have been, and stood with his weight on one foot and the other foot turned out, in a posture Andy had never assumed. His forehead was narrower than Andy's, his ears flatter against his head, his nose longer and straighter. In fact, the only real similarity lay in the hair color, and even in that, Breck realized, Andy's had been a touch lighter. And yet the sense of recognition had been overwhelming while it lasted.

The boy with the rifle spoke first. "What the hell's the matter with you? You want to get a bullet right spang between your eyes, coming up on a man when he's hunting? Ain't you got no sense?"

"I heard the shooting. I wondered who was doing it."

"No skin off my ass if a feller wants to get himself shot," said the other with a shrug. "I ain't never seen you before. You live around here?"

Breck explained that his family had just returned to the hollow, and had moved into Dead Dog camp. This caused the other to curl his lip contemptuously. "We wouldn't never live in no mining camp," he said. "We live down the road a mile, in our own house. What's your name?" Breck told him, and asked him his in return. "J. C. Stackpool," was the reply.

"What's J.C. stand for?" asked Breck.

"Just never you mind. You want to shoot a few varmints with me?"

For the rest of the afternoon, the boys tramped the hills together, trying out their marksmanship on squirrels and rabbits. Breck learned that J.C.'s initials stood for Jesse Champe, not, as a tiresome parade of jokers had claimed, for Jesus Christ. He was the fifth of seven children, and the oldest still in school. His three older brothers worked with his father in Excelsior No. 2. School played a decidedly minor role in his life. As he proudly explained to Breck, none of the men in his family had gotten past the Fourth Reader, and between the four of them they made better than a hundred and twenty dollars a week. "Hell, we got two cars in the family now, and we're fixing to buy another. Why in the world would anybody waste their time going to school when you can get that kind of money in the mines?"

During the weeks that followed, Breck and J.C. were constant companions. They hunted, fished, swam, explored, and loafed together. To their families and their neighbors, they seemed inseparable friends. Yet sometimes Breck wondered if he even liked the other boy at all.

J.C. was both arrogant and wheedling; to get his way, he would plead, cajole, or threaten, often all three in succession. He lied easily and without compunction when it suited his purpose. His sense of humor generally fed on the discomfort of others. He showed an ugly temper when it was safe to indulge it.

And yet — sometimes when he was with J.C., Breck wasn't lonely for so long at a time that he almost forgot what loneliness felt like. How much of this was due to J.C.'s own personality, and how much to his superficial resemblance to Andy, Breck couldn't have said. But the fact remained: he had a friend, and his leisure hours were full and bright where they had been empty and drab before.

Chapter 3

One Way to Find Love

WHEN THE UNITED MINE WORKERS of America began to organize the Harlan County mines, the union was initially successful: nearly 40 per cent of the working miners signed up. But in the early nineteen twenties there was no pinch of economic necessity, and, after the first flush of enthusiasm, the new members began to allow their dues to go unpaid. By the middle of the decade, less than 5 per cent of the Harlan miners were still active union members. Who needed a union when the times were so good a bachelor miner might buy a twenty-dollar silk shirt and wear it underground, because he couldn't think of anything else to do with the money?

One who remained in the union was Claiborne Hord. The birth of three children had sobered him considerably, and he felt the UMW offered added job insurance that a family man needed. He often tried to persuade his father of this, but Jubal Early would shake his head and say he couldn't see the point of handing over a piece of his earnings to some fellow in an office in Middlesboro.

"Pa, just because times are good now is no reason they'll be that way tomorrow," Claiborne argued.

"Well, that's as may be." The older man would wet a finger and rub at the imbedded coal dust on the back of his hand. "You got any of them Two Black Crows phonograph records we ain't heard, son?"

Breck didn't pay much attention to their discussions, because his mind was on other things. He was seventeen, and randy as a jack rabbit. He spent most of the long summer evenings with J. C. Stackpool, racing up and down the roads to Harlan Town in one of the Stackpools' three secondhand cars, looking for girls who were looking for boys.

They found enough — but these encounters rarely worked out well for Breck. Squeezed into the rumble seat of a Model T coupé with a girl he didn't know how to talk to, or groping awkwardly for an immature breast as he lay in the deep grass overhearing J.C.'s success ten feet away, he often lost the necessary singleness of purpose.

One night, as the boys drove homeward after what had been, for Breck, a particularly unrewarding engagement, he suddenly remembered what his brother Claiborne had once told him about the way to get girls.

He interrupted J.C.'s detailed description of his night's mating impatiently. "Listen, J.C., you know any girls whose folks go to the Holiness Church up on Beech Fork?"

"I reckon. Why?"

"Never you mind. Just put your mind on it."

J.C. considered a moment, then named five or six girls in quick succession. "Come to think of it, I know a mess of them. Now, why?"

Breck quickly explained Claiborne's theory. J.C. was fascinated. "You mean they get all hot and bothered watching the serpents, and that makes them want to go into the bushes?"

"That's what Claiborne said."

"Goddamn!" J.C. whooped. "Hey, old buddy, let's you and me do some churchgoing."

It was eight o'clock the next Tuesday evening when Breck and J.C. drove up beside the unpainted wood-and-tarpaper building on Beech Fork. A service was going on inside; the door was open, and the congregation was singing "Devil in a Box" to the accompaniment of two guitars and a tambourine. Outside the door, four teen-age girls lounged against the building, talking to two boys. A number of smaller children were playing a game of tag around the parked cars in an adjacent field.

J.C. walked confidently up to the group by the door, with Breck behind him. "Howdy, Geneva," he said to the girl he recognized, and, to the other three, "Howdy there, you pretty things."

"Howdy yourself, J.C. Stackpool," said the girl named Geneva. The other girls smiled; the boys with them scowled. "What you doing hanging around here?"

"Old Breck Hord and I figured on watching them handle the serpents."

"Well, you're out of luck. Better come back some other night." She tossed her head and yawned impudently.

"When you reckon would be a good time?" J.C. asked.

"No way of telling. Generally it's on Friday nights they get the snakes out, or pass the hot coals, or drink the strychnine."

Breck, feeling awkward, cleared his throat and said, "Do they really drink strychnine? I mean, real poison strychnine?"

Geneva glanced at him condescendingly. "Why, sure. Some of the saints drink it down like soda pop. Old Anse Burkett done it a lot."

"Didn't it never do him any harm?"

"Why, no. Old Anse died of a copperhead bite, didn't have nothing to do with drinking strychnine. You can ask

Bonnie Brae, here — she's kin to him. Ain't that right, Bonnie Brae?"

Bonnie Brae Burkett, a pale, pretty fifteen-year-old with straw-blond hair and milky blue, slightly protuberant eyes, spoke shyly. "That's right. He just didn't have the strength to wrestle Satan that day. He was under an omen."

Breck remembered. "A bird — it flew into his house a couple of days before. How come he kept on handling snakes after that? Seems like it was only a matter of time then."

"Once you're a saint, you just don't stop being a saint whenever you feel like it," Bonnie Brae explained. "Being a saint is for good. It's the Lord's will if He wants to take away His power — it ain't up to you."

Breck found himself interested enough to ask more questions about the Holiness Church, but J.C. was impatient to go. "We'll be seeing you around," he said curtly. "Come on, old Breck, let's find us some action." But if there was any action around, they didn't find it. Breck climbed into bed a little before midnight, and dreamed vividly.

They went back three times, and each time found no serpents in evidence. But the fourth time there was an electric presence in the air when they walked up to the church entrance. The group of youngsters standing near the door was larger than usual, and they were whispering nervously and peering into the building.

"Hot damn, I reckon tonight's the night!" said J.C., with a satyr's grin. Breck suddenly found himself short of breath.

At the front of the church was a row of wooden boxes, open at the top and covered with wire screen. Inside were the snakes, copperheads and timber rattlers. The sound of their restless movements was audible throughout the room. The congregation, neatly dressed and subdued in manner, sat on unpainted benches, the men on one side of the center aisle, the women on the other. A few of the women had babies in their arms. The preacher, a muscular man in a tight-fitting black suit, almost bald, stood meditating before the only decorative article in the church, a wall calendar with a garishly colored picture of Christ on the Cross.

J.C. positioned himself beside Geneva and began an intense whispered conversation. Breck stood beside Bonnie Brae Burkett. He slipped his hand under her upper arm, and she pressed it tight against her side. Her eyes were wide and excited. "When are they fixing to start?" he asked softly, very much aware that the tips of his fingers were touching the side of her breast.

"Soon as Reverend Marcy feels the spirit," she answered. "I'm glad you could come, Breck."

At that moment the Reverend Marcy turned away from the Savior and faced the congregation. "Good evening, honey," he cried out in a deep harsh voice, as though he were alone with each person in the room. "The Lord welcomes you here tonight, amen."

"Amen," the congregation answered.

"Welcome to the Lord, honey," the preacher repeated, embracing an old man in the front row. "Amen! Welcome to the house of God, brother!" He moved across the front of the church, hugging each front-row worshiper in turn, first the men, then the women. "Hallelujah, sister! Praise the blessed name of Jesus!" he cried.

"Amen! Amen!" the congregation answered. In the moments between the preacher's exhortations, the scratchings and rattlings from the boxes grew louder.

The Reverend Marcy finished greeting the saints along the front row, and, crouching like a boxer, turned his back to his audience. Then he whipped around with one arm extended. "Is there anyone here who don't remember the words of the

Savior, that burn away the power of Satan, and cast him back into hellfire where he belongs? Say them with me, honey — shout them out:

> *And these signs shall follow them that believe; In My name shall they cast out devils; they shall speak with new tongues; they shall take up serpents; and if they drink any deadly thing, it shall not hurt them; they shall lay hands on the sick, and they shall recover.*

Amen, brothers and sisters, amen to the mighty word of God!"

"Amen! Amen! Amen!"

The preacher closed his eyes and began to sing:

> *Just as I am, without one plea,*
> *But that Thy blood was shed for me,*
> *And that Thou bidd'st me come to Thee —*
> *O Lamb of God, I come, I come!*

"Come up, honey, oh, won't you come?" he called softly. "Won't you come now? Won't you come, brother? Oh, sister, won't you come to Jesus?"

The congregation continued to sing, "O Lamb of God, I come, I come!" as he begged and pleaded for sinners to accept salvation. Beads of sweat appeared on his brow. "Don't fight it, don't fight the everlasting joy! There's a saving grace you'll find with your Redeemer, you won't find it no place else — not in whiskey, nor gambling, nor sinful lust. No, Lord, only with the Lamb of God. Oh, won't you come? Oh, won't you come to Jesus?"

A fat, middle-aged woman in the second row stood up and began to testify that she had made her body into a vessel for the lusts of men. As she began to describe specific instances, the woman beside her fell to her knees and started crowing and pecking at the floor like a rooster. A man across the aisle began to jerk uncontrollably. From the back of the church, an old man with a white beard cried out a description of an encounter with the Devil. "He tried to bugger me, Lord, and it felt like a red-hot iron!" A half-dozen other men and women broke out in shouted confessions.

Breck felt Bonnie Brae's body trembling. The blood pounded in his ears.

The fat woman in the second row suddenly began talking in tongues. "Mmm-waa laa-laa laa-waa mmh-huh!" she shrieked, her eyes staring blindly ahead. "Mwanf! Mwamfa-maa-waa! Mmm-mmm wa-la mwala mwa-huh!"

"Oh, honey, won't you come to Him now?" called the preacher over the bedlam of voices.

A man in the front row started for the wooden boxes, crying thanks to the Lord for giving him the faith to take up the serpents. He dropped to his knees in front of a box, ripped off the wire screen, and thrust his arms inside. He pulled out a five-foot timber rattler, which writhed furiously around his forearm, its rattles buzzing. "Oh, bless You, sweet Jesus, bless You for this happy hour." He groaned ecstatically, holding the snake at arm's length above his head, then lowering it until it was draped around his neck, its blunt snout only inches from his face, its mouth open and fangs exposed. "Bless You, bless You, Jesus!" the man sobbed with joy. The snake struck him on the cheek once, then again, then a third time. "Thank You, God, bless You, Jesus, bless Your holy name!" A thin trickle of blood started down his chin, and in his rapture he rubbed his face against the snake's body, and a crimson smear stained the umber-patterned scales.

"Oh, my Lord!" Breck gasped to himself. His arm was tight around Bonnie Brae's body, and she was twitching and panting as if on the verge of climax. He saw J.C. and Geneva stumble away from the church wall and into the surrounding bushes, their hands already pulling impatiently at each other. But Breck could only stand and watch, as if rooted to the earth.

Other worshipers joined the first man at the boxes. Snakes were all over the front of the church, writhing over bodies and crawling on the floor. Most of them moved in a hypnotic, rhythmic sway, as if charmed by the cries of "Hallelujah!" and "Amen!" — but here and there one spat and struck.

Preacher Marcy, a copperhead in each hand, crooned to the reptiles like a lover. His eyes were shut tight, and his body was as wet under his black suit as if he had just been baptized.

The handling of the serpents lasted for less than ten minutes. Gradually the hysteria subsided, and the worshipers looked around blankly, as though emerging from a dream. Very carefully they began collecting the snakes and replacing them in their wooden boxes. Breck realized that he and Bonnie Brae were the only ones who had kept their places by the front door through the whole service. A few moments later, as he said good night to her, he was glad he had watched the ceremony — but he was also nagged by the worry that she might not think he was as much of a man as J.C. and the others. He resolved that the next time snakes were handled at Beech Fork, he and Bonnie Brae would be in the bushes, too.

*

That summer was the best Breck ever spent in Dead Dog camp. His relationship with Bonnie Brae progressed; the next evening when there was snake-handling at the church, he didn't stand rooted at the front door again. With energy and tenderness, he began a long, sweet season of lovemaking. Bonnie Brae was a willing partner, and many nights they lay lip to lip and thigh to thigh on the cool, matted grass, while the Holiness congregation sang "Ring Them Bells of Love," or handled serpents fifty yards away.

And the money stayed good. The family had everything anybody could think of — a car, plush furniture, vacuum cleaner, wringer washer, china dogs and horses, good dress-up clothes, a .30–'06 rifle, an illustrated Bible, an ice-cream freezer, and a chrome dinette set. Breck's after-school job of cutting timbers, while not paying anywhere near as much as underground work, allowed him to clear between five and ten dollars a week on top of his commissary bill. If he wanted to drive into Harlan Town on Saturday night and drink bootleg liquor, there was no reason he couldn't.

Jubal Early was, in a curious way, content. Although he knew he had made the great mistake of his life by leasing away the mineral rights to his land, he nevertheless felt pride in himself for learning the trade of coal mining as a middle-aged man, and for being able to use this knowledge to provide for his family. Once when his wife was lamenting her lost garden — for nothing but weeds would grow beside Dead Dog Branch — he said humbly, but with a touch of sly satisfaction, "I done ruint us, and that's a fact. But I reckon there's worse ways to be ruint than this."

Claiborne and Joicy had another child, a girl, making a total of four. Claiborne's worried expression deepened until he began to look like a hunted man. He continued to talk about the need for Harlan County miners to join the UMW of A, but times were too good for men to pay much attention.

Phoebe, who didn't miss much, noticed and commented on Breck's activities one night. "I declare, I don't see how you find the strength to get up in the morning, the way you carry on all night," she said tartly, as the two of them sat on the porch watching the full moon rise like an unnaturally round pumpkin. "I think it's a shame and a scandal."

"Phoebe, what in the world are you talking about?"

She turned to him, suddenly furious, her large eyes gleaming with reflected moonlight. "Don't you pretend to me! Why, all summer long you and that J. C. Stackpool have been prowling the roads like two tomcats, and some nights when you come home it's a wonder you can climb the front steps! Don't tell me you ain't been loving some gal half the night!"

"Doggone it, Phoebe, hush up!" said Breck nervously.

She glared at him a moment, with her mouth open, ready for more outraged comments. Then she looked away, and there was silence between them. When she spoke again, the anger had left her voice. "What's it like, Breck, being loved real good? Is it enough to make up for all the other things a body has to put up with in this world?"

He didn't need to look at her to know she was staring at her withered leg, thrust stiffly in front of her and held straight by its brace. "Oh, I don't know," he said evasively.

"No, but tell me, Breck. I got as much right to know as anybody else. Please – I mean it!" There was supplication in her face. "Elseways, how'll I ever find out?"

"Well, it's –" Breck cast about for something to say, and remembered an expression of Claiborne's. "It's as fine as frog hair."

"Go on!" she urged, as he paused for thought.

"It's like eating something you like, and tasting it all over your body," he said carefully.

Phoebe's lips were parted, and her eyes shone. "Yes!" she whispered.

"It's like being filled up with fizz, like a pop bottle, when you put your thumb over the top and shake it up —"

Jubal Early Hord stepped out on the porch. "Eee-yeh, that's a courtin' moon, for a fact," he said, closing the front door behind him. "You all don't mind, I think I'll sit me a spell before I go to bed."

Without a word, Phoebe got up and went into the house. Jubal Early looked inquiringly at Breck. "Something eating on her?" he asked. Breck replied that he couldn't say. "She does seem a mite notional lately, for a fact," the father said musingly.

They sat on the porch until the orange moon blanched, and shrank, and climbed halfway up the sky. There was so much sweetness, quietness, loneliness in the night that Breck hated to go to bed.

That night marked the end of Breck's childhood. The next morning Jubal Early was crippled beneath a two-hundred-pound rock that fell from the roof of Dead Dog mine.

Chapter 4

Boy into Man

WHEN HIS FATHER was carried from the mine entrance on a blanket, face contorted with pain and mouth bright with blood, Breck was waiting silently on the slope beside his mother and Phoebe; Joicy was a foot or two behind, with her baby in her arms and the three older children hanging onto her skirts; around the family crowded the silent and motionless women of the camp. The sun had just cleared the hilltop above them, and the hollow was bathed in fresh morning light.

Breck left his mother's side and took his place beside his brother Claiborne, carrying the blanket. The men brought Jubal Early down to the creekside. The company doctor met them there, and motioned for them to put the injured man down on the ground. He squatted beside him for a brief examination.

"At least two ribs broke, maybe penetrated the lung. Possible injury to the spine. No way of telling what else. I reckon he'll live, God willing. You all got a place where he can lie quiet, without twenty kids climbing all over him?" the doctor asked Hannah. When she nodded, he ordered the blanket men to take Jubal Early home. "I'll be there directly," he called after them.

Breck walked carefully over the irregular ground, watching his feet to avoid stumbling. *Things are going to be bad from now on,* he told himself bleakly. *Poor Pa. Nothing's going to be the same.*

The accident altered the Hords' finances suddenly and dramatically for the worse. Until the extent of his injuries was known, Jubal Early would receive no money beyond his earnings up to the time of the accident. Later, he would either be offered compensation of between a hundred and five hundred dollars, or go back to work with obviously reduced capabilities. Claiborne, supporting a wife and four children, could hardly contribute enough to fill the gap.

Without discussing it with any of the family, Breck approached the mine foreman, a long-jawed, speckled man named Jeems Maggard. When Breck asked to take his father's place underground, Maggard began listing objections. Breck answered a number of them before he realized that the foreman enjoyed the exercise of his authority too much to give a quick answer; he wasn't an especially mean man, but, when he had an edge, he figured it was against reason not to use it.

Breck cut into his list of reservations: "Well, you decide, Mr. Maggard — I ain't about to beg you." Maggard glanced at him quickly, and saw something in his eyes that was harder than anything he had expected to see.

"Well, I guess if your brother Claiborne's willing to wet-nurse you, I don't give a damn one way or the other," he said irritably. Breck nodded and turned away. Maggard called after him, "Tell Slemp at the commissary you'll be working inside — he'll give you the supplies you need and put it on your account."

"I know," said Breck without looking back.

The next day Breck waited on the porch drinking coffee until Claiborne came by. They walked together up the slope to the wash shanty, where they changed into their work clothes — Breck's clean and new, Claiborne's veneered with coal dust and stiff with sweat. They put their good clothes in wire baskets, ran the baskets up to the ceiling, and snapped their padlocks on the chains, so nobody could rob them while they were working. Then they hooked their carbide lamps to their caps, picked up their lunch buckets, and walked to the "Toonerville Trolley" which would take them and the other miners into the earth.

Well, here I go, thought Breck, as the train began its clattering progress into the tunnel. *I only hope I'm man enough.*

"I'll tell you something, little brother," Claiborne said encouragingly. "No matter how low-down, awful, rotten things get down here, there's one thing you can count on." He paused until Breck turned his head to glance at him questioningly, then said, "They can always get worse!" He grinned at his brother for a moment, enjoying his joke, before adding sympathetically, "No, I'm just joshing, Breck. Once you get the hang of it, it ain't bad at all."

"I aim to do my best," Breck said.

They sat silently as the train moved into the heart of the mountain, following the fifty-four-inch seam of bituminous coal that was Excelsior No. 2's reason for being. At the entrance to each side tunnel to the right and left, a single weak light bulb tried and failed to penetrate the surrounding darkness. The lights were fifty or a hundred yards apart. As the electric motor pulled the slowly swaying cars down the main tunnel track, the miners who had not already done so ignited the carbide lamps on their caps. At the beginning of the trip there was a strong, steady breeze from the blower at the tunnel entrance, but as they went deeper into the mountain the movement of air became less noticeable, until there was no feeling of evaporative coolness as the sweat stood out from their pores.

The train moved for a quarter of a mile without stopping, passing areas emptied of coal, where the seam had been worked until it narrowed and finally disappeared in the slate. Then the engineer began stopping beside each lighted side tunnel. The number of miners remaining in the cars dwindled as the train neared the front tunnel face, the slowly advancing limit of the mine. The train made its final stop, and Breck and Claiborne got out, together with eight or ten others.

The Hords were working with Sam Troutman and Loyal Stackpool. Troutman was burly, slow-moving, and powerfully muscled, with an oddly high-pitched voice and deferential tone; Stackpool, one of J.C.'s older brothers, was slight and feisty. Troutman uncoupled a car, and the four men manhandled it along the track that ran through the short side tunnel and into the great forty-foot-square area, where they would work for the next ten hours.

This area had begun as a single tunnel five feet wide, curving out, around, and back on itself. The outer wall had been mined until the tunnel no longer looked like a tunnel at all, becoming instead a great open hall surrounding a single column of coal and rock ten feet square, with upright timbers adding support to the top every few yards. The men were working the far wall, following the narrowing seam into the mountain.

"It'll peter out in two weeks or so, and we'll start out on another side tunnel," Claiborne explained to his brother. "Here, let's see what old Duffy done for us today." Francis Duffy was the shot-firer of Excelsior No. 2. Each evening after the other men had left the mine, he placed explosive shots in all the working faces where the miners had drilled holes, and detonated them. This loosened the coal for the next day's work. The shot-firer had done his work well, for the harsh light of their carbide lamps showed the gleaming black vein of coal well broken up and ready to be loaded. "Nothing wrong with that," Claiborne said. "Reckon we might as well get to it, little brother." He lifted his pick and sank its point into the soft black coal. A moment later, Breck followed suit.

All during that first day, Breck felt the strangeness of working underground. A man's lamp barely poked a hole in the enveloping darkness, so even though he worked with the sound and smell of other men around him he always felt alone. It was the dark, and the stale, dead air, and the incessant sound of water dripping somewhere; it created a loneliness so dense that not even the voice of a friend or brother three feet away could penetrate it.

At the end of the day, muscle-sore and bone-drained, Breck left the strange public darkness of the mine for the equally strange public exposure of the wash shanty, where forty-odd men crowded together, naked and wreathed in steam from the communal shower, with the water running dark gray off their glistening bodies.

"God dog, don't that water feel good, though?" Claiborne cried happily. "Whoo-eee! That's what it takes to put the sap back in a man!"

Breck soaped himself silently with the gritty lye soap, thinking, *Tomorrow'll be a whole 'nother day of it, then the next day, and the day after that. Wonder if I can keep going.* He pressed his hand against his biceps muscle, searching for weakness. *I expect I can,* he thought.

Breck was a quick learner, and before the month was out he was loading more cars each day than his father ever had.

Claiborne had to push himself to keep up, and Stackpool complained that the way Breck was going he would make the rest of them look bad. For Breck moved like a machine, speaking only when necessary, establishing a rhythm and never varying it. Each day he worked straight through the morning without pause. At lunchtime he laid down his tools, opened his bucket, and ate, exchanging few comments with his fellow workers. When he finished, he stretched out on his back and was immediately asleep. He slept for fifteen minutes and awoke when the others were ready to resume work. He stepped a few feet away from the working face, urinated, then picked up his tools and began digging and loading coal again. He continued without stopping until quitting time.

Jubal Early recuperated slowly. It was months before he was able to walk along the creekside, visit the commissary, and ride with Breck and Claiborne into Harlan Town on Sundays. When spring came he began to work at odd jobs around the tipple, for a few dollars a day. He never mentioned going underground again. Breck knew for certain then what he had suspected before: that he himself was in the mines for good.

*

Every fall the meager social life in the hollows along Poor Fork reached its yearly peak, with assorted stir-offs, apple-peelings, and dances at the high-school gym. One Saturday evening Breck and Bonnie Brae joined fifty other couples at the gym for a harvest dance. The orange and brown crepe-paper festoons that hung from the walls, and the cornstalks and gourds in the corners, did little to soften the room or disguise its purpose — the smell of mixed sweat and varnish was unconcealable. But Breck was proud and happy as he circled the floor with Bonnie Brae on his arm, nodding to acquaintances and receiving envious glances in return. Bonnie Brae had the milky, almost transparent skin that often accompanies light blue eyes and straw-blond hair; when she was upset, blood flushed her skin in angry blotches, but when she was happy it suffused her face with a radiant glow. This night she was happy.

The music began. The fiddler was a well-known local performer of "Devil Ditties," as the Holiness people called all nonreligious songs. He was accompanied by a spirited group consisting of a banjo, dulcimer, and two guitars. They began with "Lord Lovel" and "The Dying Knight's Farewell," and then swung into "Sourwood Mountain":

My gal lives on Sourwood Mountain,
Hey diddle, diddle de day,
She won't see me 'cause she's poutin',
Hey diddle, diddle de day . . .

Breck thought no girl had ever danced with more grace and spirit than Bonnie Brae. Her lips were as bright as holly berries, and her hair shone around her shoulders like sunshine. "Oh, Breck, I'm so happy! Ain't you happy?" she whispered in his ear.

The temperature in the gym began to rise, and the sweat-and-varnish smell increased, augmented by the reek of corn whiskey, which came indoors with some of the men who had stepped out for a breath of air. Breck saw Claiborne deep in an animated discussion with another man, but ignored his brother's summoning wave, rightly concluding the men were talking union. He felt too good to waste his time that way.

The first fight took place at nine o'clock, and, by the time

Bonnie Brae was ready to leave, there had been two more. It was that kind of night.

Breck pulled the borrowed Ford pickup truck off the road near an abandoned cabin, put his arms around Bonnie Brae, and kissed her. She responded eagerly, but when she felt his hand begin tugging her skirt up, she seized it and held it captive against her thigh. "Don't, Breck — there's something I got to tell you first." She hesitated in sudden alarm, her eyes as big as jackrocks. "Say you're going to be glad, hon — say you're going to be tickled!"

Breck felt a sudden chill ripple through his body. *Somebody just stepped on my grave,* he thought. "All right — I'm going to be tickled. Now, what?"

"We're going to have to get married. We're going to have us a baby."

Breck's first reaction was that he couldn't let her see how he felt. He kept his face expressionless, hiding the wave of shock that hit him like nausea. Her eyes searched his face. "You *are* tickled, like you said, ain't you?" she asked uncertainly. For answer, Breck took her fingers in his hand and kissed them. "Oh, Breck," she cried, pulling him to her and covering his cheek and neck with rapid little kisses, "this is the happiest day of my whole lifetime!"

Breck kissed her on the mouth, and after a moment slipped her skirt up over her hips. *I guess I've got a right to it now,* he thought, with a kind of ironic lechery. *Might as well get my fill.* He made love to her as though he were two people, the distant and uninvolved one watching the other accomplishing the act. She had two orgasms before he achieved one. Oddly, it was the most satisfying sex he had ever known.

Bonnie Brae and Breck were married at her family's cabin three weeks later. They spent their first legal night together cramped into a three-quarter-size cherry bed that had come over Cumberland Gap in 1807. The next day they drove to Dead Dog Branch to receive their guests at the traditional second-night wedding feast, called an "infare."

Most of the twenty-odd guests were family. One of the few outsiders invited was J. C. Stackpool. But by the time the last of the other guests had left, J.C. still hadn't made his appearance.

He chose to arrive two hours later — and he was not alone.

Breck and J.C. hadn't seen much of each other in the past few months, and, when they had happened to meet, they had both been a little edgy — J.C. a bit too boisterous, Breck a bit too noncommittal. The truth was, they were growing away from one another. Breck invited J.C. to the infare hoping it would help to reestablish the familiar relationship between them, which, to Breck at least, still had a special value.

Breck and Bonnie Brae had made love in a bed that was big enough for the two of them, and were asleep in each other's arms, when a furious barking of dogs called them back to consciousness. A moment later an offkey voice began bellowing "The Tailor Boy," with lusty thumps on a washbasin substituting for the censored words.

Oh, listen to me, you married men, if you travel from town to town,
You'd better keep your wife chained up, you better tie her down —
And if you do not heed me, why, as sure as you have a wife,
Oh, she'll be having a [thump! thump-thump!] *most every day of her life!*

Many other male voices joined the singer to repeat the last line:

Yes, she'll be having a [thump! thump-thump!] *most every day of her life!*

There was a great pounding on the front door, and the agitation of the dogs increased.

"Glory, hon, what in the world is that?" asked Bonnie Brae fearfully.

"Shivaree," Breck answered. He threw back the covers and put his feet on the rough plank floor. "Some of the boys wanting their share of the fun." He stood up, broad-shouldered and hairy-legged in his new candy-striped nightshirt. He went to the window and raised it. "Hey, what's going on out there?" he shouted.

Twelve or fifteen men were standing between the creek-side and the Hords' front porch, most of them strangers to Breck. He identified the singer by his washbasin. In the center of the group was J. C. Stackpool, tow hair gleaming like silver in the moonlight.

"Hey, old buddy," J.C. called, "I brought a couple of friends over for the infare."

"You're too late, J.C. The infare's over. Everybody's gone home!" Behind him, Jubal Early and Hannah entered the room, followed a moment later by Phoebe. Jubal Early came to the window, looked out, then turned to Breck with an interrogative expression. Breck shook his head and said in a low voice that he reckoned they were only funning.

J.C. yelled again: "Come on out! Ain't nobody going to hurt you. We just want to make sure you don't disappoint that pretty little gal you got there!"

Breck answered with bogus joviality that he wasn't about to disappoint her, and urged the men to leave him get on with it. The man with the washbasin said something impatiently to J.C., and J.C. answered with a grin. Then he repeated his demand that Breck come out. "You better, Breck, or the boys might get their feelings hurt and come in after you!"

With a sigh, Breck replied that he would be right out. He closed the window, picked up a pair of pants, and pulled them on, stuffing in the tail of his nightshirt. As he started out the bedroom door, Phoebe blocked his way. Framed by her sleep-tousled hair, her face looked thinner than ever, and her eyes were wide. "Breck, don't let them get you outside! Drunk as they are, there's no telling what they'll do!"

He said something meant to be reassuring and stepped past her, crossed the living room, and opened the front door. J.C. was on the porch, flanked by the man with the washbasin and another man who held his hands out of sight behind him. In the light spill from the door, J.C.'s eyes glittered like broken glass.

"Well, if it ain't the bridegroom!" J.C. said, grinning, anticipating unpleasantness which was both sanctioned by tradition and backed by force. "You're going to thank us when you know the favor we aim to do for you, honest to God!"

"And what would that be?" Breck asked, keeping his voice casual.

"GRAB HIM, BOYS!" J.C. shouted. Hands seized Breck's arms and twisted them behind him. The smell of moonshine whiskey was suddenly close and nauseating. He was pinioned, unable to move. "Show him what you got, Cloyd," J.C. said to the man beside him. The man brought his hands into view. In one he held an open can of yellow paint; in the other, a paintbrush. "We aim to paint your pecker yellow, so that little old girl of yours can find it in the dark," J.C. cried. "Get him down there, get him flat! Somebody hold his legs!"

"Goddamned if you will!" Breck roared, throwing his

weight forward and straining his muscles against the grip of his captors. But he couldn't break free; borne down by the weight of many bodies, he crashed to the floor on his back. Eager hands unbuckled his belt, tore open his fly, and jerked his pants down over his knees. Grinning faces crowded close above him. He felt the touch of something cold, wet, and bristly against his penis. He bellowed wordlessly in revulsion and outrage, twisting his arms and legs with all his strength. One leg came free, and he lashed out with it, catching the paint can with his bare foot and splashing most of its contents on J.C. "I'll kill you, J.C., goddamn you!" he raged. "Let me up! Let me up so I can fight him! Let me up, you hear me?"

"Let him up so he can fight," called a voice in the crowd, and the cry was taken up by other voices. One by one, the hands holding him down loosened their grip, and in a few moments he was able to struggle to his feet and pull his pants up. All the buttons were off, but he secured the trousers with his belt. He descended the steps to the bare strip of ground in front of the cabin. J.C. stood facing him, one hand brushing absently at the yellow paint stains on his shirt. Their eyes locked together, and Breck saw an intensity of malice in the other's eyes that startled him.

Residents of cabins on both sides of the Hords had joined the crowd. Claiborne stood tensely in the circle that had formed around the two antagonists, waiting to see if he was needed. Jubal Early watched from the porch. The three Hord women remained inside the cabin, crowded together at the front door. Out of sight behind the door frame, Hannah's hand rested on the muzzle of Jubal Early's shotgun.

Breck and J.C. began to circle, each moving to the right. The hard-packed clay had a surprising texture under Breck's bare feet, and he suddenly realized that J.C. was wearing heavy shoes. *If I want to stay all together, I better keep clear of them,* he thought. A rush of adrenalin prickled through his body like a thousand needles, and everything in his field of vision blurred out of focus except the opponent he was about to meet.

J.C. stepped forward and swung at his head. Breck ducked the blow, and struck J.C. heavily below the arch of the rib cage. J.C. grunted, swayed, recovered, and smashed Breck on the cheekbone. Breck threw his arms around J.C. and tied him up.

J.C. stamped down on Breck's right instep.

The explosion of pain Breck felt was unbelievably intense. Instantly he shifted all his weight to his left foot and raised the other from the ground. His eyes closed as a grimace of agony twisted his face. J.C. hit him twice, first above the heart, then just over the right eye. Breck stumbled backward, forced to put weight on his injured foot to keep his equilibrium. He couldn't see out of his right eye, and realized it must be blinded with blood. J.C. followed him swiftly, lashing at his face until Breck began to fall. Just as Breck's hands hit the ground behind him, J.C. launched a kick at his head. It missed, and J.C. lurched back and suddenly sat on the ground.

Got to get him fast, before he cripples me up so bad I can't hurt him, Breck thought. He got up and wiped the blood from his eye while J.C. struggled to his feet. *Can't stomp the son of a bitch barefoot. Got to do it with my hands.*

The two fighters moved toward each other warily. J.C. feinted, then jabbed; Breck returned a straight blow to J.C.'s jaw. For ten seconds they stood, shod toe to bare toe, hammering at each other's face. *Got to do it with my hands, got to do it with my hands,* Breck chanted to himself. Then, as he missed with a swing which carried him forward until his head was behind J.C.'s shoulder, the voice in his mind cried exultantly, *Or some other part of me!*

He butted J.C. with his head, a shattering blow that caught the other under the ear and dropped him to the ground with the finality of a fallen tree. Breck reeled and almost fell beside him, then stood swaying and trying to see through the spinning red shapes that blurred one eye and the blood that blinded the other.

I done it! he thought. *I done it barefoot!*

He felt an arm wrap around his waist, and Claiborne's voice sounded close by his ear, above the babble of the bystanders. "All right, you wanted to see a fight, now you seen one. Go on home now, and take your friend here with you, and let this boy go to bed with his bride like he's supposed to!" Gently Claiborne led Breck through the excited laughter and congratulations of the crowd, and up the porch steps.

"Reckon you're going to do her any good tonight, Breck?" shouted a neighbor from down the creek.

Claiborne answered, "Hell, yes — he's my brother, ain't he?" He helped Breck into the house. "You done just fine, little brother. I'm proud of you," he said in a low voice. "Bonnie Brae, you get this boy to bed, and let him sleep as long as he can. Tomorrow he's going to feel like twenty-five-dollars' worth of pure disaster."

Bonnie Brae helped Breck to bed, assisted by Hannah and Phoebe. Claiborne lingered on the porch a few minutes, watching the last members of the shivaree group help a groggy J.C. Stackpool into a waiting car. Jubal Early sat beside him in a cane-bottomed chair. The lights in the cabins to the right and left winked out. The night air was sharp with the edge of approaching winter.

"Best fight I seen in years," Jubal Early said judiciously.

"It was a dandy, all right. That's a good boy, that Breck," Claiborne answered. "I feared for his life, when I seen he didn't have no shoes on."

"Us Hords could always fight," said Jubal Early.

They looked out into the night together for a minute or two, neither with anything to say, but enjoying each other's kinship and company. Then Claiborne left, and Jubal Early went to bed.

Breck slept for eighteen hours, and, when he got up, he walked with a limp that lasted three months.

Chapter 5

Dead Dog Gets a New Name

WHEN W. F. TASKER, manager of the Excelsior No. 2 mine, announced a ten-cents-per-ton reduction in the price paid to miners for a ton of coal, nobody was too worried. The second reduction, four months later, wasn't so bad either. But the third one hurt; people found they couldn't afford the luxuries at the commissary whenever they were in the mood for them, and sometimes even the necessities took some thinking about. New men weren't being taken on at the employment office. The miners began to notice that the weighman was crediting them with less coal and more slate, but the new tight-lipped atmosphere around the camp didn't encourage them to question the change in public.

In private, the talk was more and more about the union.

Listening to the talk, Claiborne decided the time had come for a new organizational drive in Harlan County, and wrote a letter to District 19 headquarters of the UMW of A, asking that an organizer be sent to Dead Dog.

At the same time, the board of directors of the Fairleigh Automotive Corporation agreed with founder and board chairman Amos Fairleigh that the time had come to insulate the miners against the blandishments of outside agitators. "Damn unions are always fishing in troubled waters," the old white-haired inventor growled. "We've got to protect our boys from themselves." He urged that individual employment contracts be introduced in the "captive" mines of Fairleigh's wholly owned subsidiary, Wolverine Sheet and Tube. The board of directors concurred.

The UMW organizer and the yellow-dog contracts arrived at Dead Dog camp the same week.

Claiborne and nine other members of the UMW met the organizer in a cabin five miles from Dead Dog. The organizer was a stocky red-haired man named Sizemore, with a twitch that twisted his left cheek and eye into the parody of a wink. "I got me twenty different mines to cover, boys," he told them, "so it's up to you to line the men up. I'll help you any way I can, but you got to do most of the work yourself." He pointed out the need for secrecy during the opening months of the drive. He warned them not to put anything down in writing, for any list of union members or sympathizers that fell into the hands of the Operators' Association would result in the blacklisting of every man on the list. "Use a code, or keep them in your mind, or whatever," he advised. "But don't leave any names get out till we have sixty per cent of the men along Poor Fork ready to join up."

Excited and strengthened, Claiborne went home planning his campaign. But the next morning, before he had a chance to approach a single miner, he was summoned to the office of mine manager W. F. Tasker. Fearing that somehow his attendance at the meeting with Sizemore had become known, he entered the small office warily. The clerk in the front room gestured toward the closed door at the rear. Claiborne knocked on it, and a vigorous voice inside told him to come in.

Willis Fenton Tasker had two passions in his life, and neither his wife, Henrietta, nor his mistress, Amy Herron, was included in them. They were his future with the Fairleigh interests, and his pack of coon-hunting dogs. Unlike his women, both passions were lean and hungry. Since his graduation from the university, in Lexington, where he had studied engineering and geology, and his return to the mountains of his birth, he had moved steadily upward in the Fairleigh-Wolverine empire. Still in his thirties, he was in complete charge of a small mine, and expected to exchange it soon for one of the vast black Fairleigh labyrinths that honeycombed the land around Wallins Creek.

The walls of his office were covered with photographs of hounds.

Tasker greeted Claiborne warmly, asking about his family, and particularly about his brother — "A real piss-cutter, they tell me." His narrow gray eyes crinkled at the corners, and Claiborne felt more wary than ever. He sat with his back straight and both hands resting on his knees, and answered "Yessir" when expected. The mine manager leaned forward over his desk, signifying that the small talk was finished. "Claiborne, you may not know it, but there's a lot of men in this mine that look up to you," he said crisply. "It just might be that you could save them a mess of grief, if you had a mind to."

"How's that, Mr. Tasker?" Claiborne asked.

"Look — I know you signed up in that damfool union right after the war. But what the hell, so did a lot of other people. It never did any harm, and, if you wanted to pour your money down a rathole, it's a free country." He looked at Claiborne for agreement, and Claiborne said, "Yessir."

"So you know how plain worthless the union is," Tasker continued. "But some of the younger fellows, they don't have the benefit of your experience. If the union was to try to come back to Harlan County again, they might make the same mistake you did, and pay their good money to join up. But this time, the mistake would be a lot more serious. In those days, it was live and let live, plenty of money for everybody, and no hard feelings afterwards. But, buddy, those days are long gone." He took a cigar from the walnut humidor on his desk and offered the box to Claiborne, who took one and tucked it into his shirt pocket. Tasker lit his and shook out the match. "There's hard times coming for people who don't play it smart," he went on. "You've seen the cuts in the price per ton. There aren't the jobs there were — nobody's hiring any extra, and some are laying off. The market up east is going to hell, and the freight differential is killing us. Thirty-five cents a ton extra! No wonder we can't compete!"

"Don't all our coal go to Detroit to make Fairleigh cars?" Claiborne asked.

"Yes, so what?" Tasker frowned through a blue haze of smoke.

"Well, if our coal is all spoke for, and they're going to keep on making cars with it in Detroit, then why do they need to cut our wages?"

"Jesus Christ, Hord, we're not on a desert island here! Coal is coal! When the price falls in Pittsburgh, it falls everywhere else too! When they lay men off at Wallins Creek, it means they'll be laying them off here soon, as sure as fate! It's a buyer's market, for God's sake!" He paused and shook his head ruefully. "Well, I'm not about to give you a lesson in economics, Claiborne. Just take my word for it, this is a bad time for a man to start playing around with any union foolishness. It could get him fired, and once he's on the outside looking in, he'll play hell finding another job in Harlan County. Understand?"

Claiborne understood. He also understood the printed

sheet of paper Tasker picked up from his desk and held in one hand as he continued: "We feel we have a duty to the men, to keep them from hurting themselves and their families. So we're going to ask every miner at Excelsior Number Two to sign one of these individual employment contracts. What it says is that anybody who works for us will keep his God-given right to make his own decisions, and not let some union grafter make them for him."

Claiborne's fingers tightened on his bony knees. *Son-of-a-bitching yellow-dog contract is what it is,* he thought furiously. Silently he reached out his hand, and after a moment Tasker placed the contract in it. Claiborne's mind raced behind his impassive eyes as he read the legal phraseology without comprehension. *What do I do with this thing? If I sign it, and they find out I'm in the union, will they put me in jail? A man can't walk far with four young ones!*

"I told you what it said," Tasker said impatiently. "Unless you went to law school, you're not going to learn any more by reading it." Claiborne nodded and picked up a fountain pen from the desk. Slowly he signed his name to the document. Tasker gave a little sigh. "Well, all right!" He took the paper and put it in a desk drawer. "Thanks, buddy, we appreciate it! Now talk it up with the men, hear? Tell them how it will protect their jobs and all."

Claiborne rose. "I'll surely do that, Mr. Tasker. I'll really talk it up." As he put his hand on the doorknob, the mine manager said solicitously, "Remember me to your daddy, hear?" When the door had closed, W. F. Tasker permitted himself a slight smile.

That night Claiborne reported the incident to Sizemore, and the UMW organizer assured him he had been right to sign the yellow-dog contract. From now on, it would be easier to talk to the men without arousing the suspicions of management, he thought. "They'll think you're a good, loyal yellow dog now. Only — be careful."

Claiborne was careful. During the next few months, as every miner in Excelsior No. 2 signed a yellow-dog contract, and as another cut in the price of coal was announced, Claiborne quietly sounded out each of his fellow workers. By a running inventory he kept on the back of a calendar on his bedroom wall — rows of upright lines, no names — he reached the point where he calculated he could promise the union over fifty votes whenever an election took place. There were almost that many more who, like his brother Breck, were friendly but refused to commit themselves.

Then Claiborne approached a miner named Fraley, a loud Irishman from West Virginia, who, to hear him tell it, had been king of the hill in every mine he'd ever worked. At the beginning, Claiborne had been leery of him, but after three months' worth of stories about foremen who had come a cropper when they crossed Fraley, and crooked weighmen who rued the day they ever lied to Fraley, and commissary managers who pleaded for mercy after they cheated Fraley, Claiborne persuaded himself the newcomer would prove an asset to the union. One evening he drew him aside as they walked down the slope from the driftmouth, and the two men talked for twenty minutes.

That weekend Claiborne drove into Harlan Town to shoot some pool and share some bootleg whiskey with a few congenial spirits. It was nearly midnight when he turned off the Poor Fork road and started up Dead Dog Branch. Two hundred yards up the dirt track the way was blocked by a fallen tree branch. He got out to push it aside and a flashlight blazed in his face, blinding him.

"That's him — drunk as a skunk," said a voice he couldn't identify.

"Ain't it a crime, driving when you're drunk? A man could have an accident that way," said another voice, this one familiar.

"God dog, boys, get that light out of my eyes before you drive me stone blind," Claiborne complained, pantomiming comic discomfort. "I can't see no better than a yard up a black cow."

Something heavy hit the side of his head, and he fell to the ground. Other blows landed on his face and body, and a foot kicked him savagely in the side. "Union son of a bitch, maybe this will teach you a lesson!" screamed the unfamiliar voice ecstatically.

Instinctively, Claiborne sought to escape from the light. He pulled himself into a ball to reduce the damage to his face, belly, and groin, and kept himself rolling toward the vegetation at the side of the road. After what seemed like hours, but was only seconds, he bumped against a tree trunk and scrambled upright behind it. It took them a few moments to locate him, and during that time he found a sturdy forked branch. He broke off both forked ends short, leaving wicked splintered points. When the first of his assailants charged at him, he drove the points into the man's face, twisting his wrist as he did so. The man screamed and fell back. Claiborne followed him, jabbing and turning the branch with all his strength. He felt something tear, and the man fell to the ground. Claiborne pivoted and struck the second man across the face with the branch, and then, with another blow, knocked the flashlight out of his hand. He flung his weapon at the black bulk in front of him, turned, and sprinted down the dirt track toward Dead Dog. In the light from his car's headlights he could see the tree branch blocking the road, and he leaped it and continued running, guided down the darkening twists and turns by memory.

He brought back reinforcements from the camp. They found the windows of his car had all been broken, the tires and upholstery slashed, and the wiring ripped out. "I'm glad we got back here as soon as we did," Claiborne said to Breck. "If we'd have given them any more time, them boys might have done some damage."

On Monday Claiborne learned that his employment at the mine was terminated, and that he was to settle his commissary bill and vacate his house immediately, on pain of arrest for violation of his employment contract.

It was Saturday of that week before he had a house and a job to move to. Since most of his savings were used to square his commissary bill, he had to find an employer who would extend him credit until his first payday. The only mine interested was the Little Aleck, an independent off Clover Fork, with a poor safety record. The cabin that went with the job was small, and in need of repair.

*

Claiborne had his second and last load of furniture piled in a borrowed Dodge pickup. The green mohair sofa, which had always seemed sumptuous to Breck, looked unexpectedly shabby in the outdoor light. Joicy and the children were waiting at the new cabin, and Claiborne was making the last run alone. He drew Breck aside.

"Little brother, I reckon now you see what I've been telling you for the last three years," he said seriously.

"You mean about how being in the union will get you beat up and fired and driven from your home?" asked Breck.

"It weren't the union that done it. Never think it was. It's the union that's going to stop it." He put his hand on his brother's shoulder. "I wish you favored the union more. There's things you could give that would make a difference."

Breck shook his head. "I'm comfortable going my own way," he said.

"Sometimes that ain't enough. Well, we won't argue. Only promise me that, if Sizemore or somebody talks to you about it, you'll think it over real good."

Breck could agree to that, and the brothers shook hands. Claiborne said good-bye to his mother and father, his sister and sister-in-law, and drove away to Clover Fork.

Three nights later, the miner Fraley, who was an agent provocateur employed by an industrial relations counseling firm in Detroit, had the better part of his head blown off by a hollow-nosed rifle bullet. He died with his blood staining the water of Dead Dog Branch, thereby giving the mine and the camp a new and tenacious name.

Chapter 6

The Tightening Vise

BONNIE BRAE'S AUNT CLOA BURKETT was a remarkable woman. The widow of Anse Burkett, late strychnine-drinking saint of the Holiness Church, she had become inactive in the church after her husband's death. Although one of the best-known granny-women on Poor Fork — she had been "cotching" infants up the hollows for fifty years — she found that midwifery didn't consume all her energies; she felt the need for another activity to replace her churchgoing. She chose the labor movement. After one of her nephews had been killed by a rockfall in a substandard mine, and her only brother had wheezed his life away with lungs webbed with silicosis, she wrote her first song about the miner's life. It was sung to the tune of "Barbara Allen":

In Harlan County I will tell
Of miners and their sad plight —
They labor deep inside the earth,
And never see the sunlight.

They breathe the cruel black coal dust
And dodge each falling boulder,
And many a man will rest in his grave
Before he's twelve months older . . .

She called it "Harlan County Miner," and it had fourteen other verses. Two or three ditty singers picked it up and performed it on all three branches of the Cumberland River. When it became popular, particularly with UMW sympathizers, Aunt Cloa decided to write some more. She patterned "Feed the Miner" on "Thread the Needle," "Commissary Man" on "Give the Fiddler a Dram," and created poignant new words for "The Hills of Home." But her greatest success was "Aunt Cloa's Blues," which she wrote after the coal price reduction in the spring of 1928:

Tell me, all you miners, if you can't give your children bread —
Tell me, you brave miners, that can't give your families bread —
Why do you go on living, when you might as well be dead?

Some people in the coalfields thought "Aunt Cloa's Blues" did more for the labor movement in eastern Kentucky that year than the UMW itself, for the union was involved in one of its chronic internal power struggles and had curtailed its organizing efforts.

*

Aunt Cloa went to Dead Yellow Dog to deliver Bonnie Brae's baby. Breck was sitting beside the bed and holding his wife's damp hand patiently. Bonnie Brae's skin was blotchy, and her eyes were wide with panic. "Oh, Breck," she cried in a flat little voice, "I'm going to die, I just know it!"

"That's sure as the Second Coming, unless you mind your business and bear down," said Aunt Cloa harshly, as she bustled into the room. "Get out of here, Breck, and go do some important Man's Work, like crawling under a car."

Aunt Cloa had a grandmotherly dumpling of a face, out of which her hard eyes glittered like polished steel balls. She stood less than five feet tall, and her small-boned rounded body could accomplish anything she asked of it. She carried a hatpin in her hair bun for protection, and a clay pipe in her skirt pocket for relaxation. She hadn't needed the first for years, and rarely had an opportunity to enjoy the second.

She stayed with Bonnie Brae for the better part of three hours. Before she left, she presented the Hord women with a healthy male child, who was immediately named Little Andy. "Don't worry — in this world a good bowel movement is more important than a pretty face any time," she said dryly. "You can pay me my five dollars now, and I'll look in again next time I'm down this way."

Outside the house she cut short Breck's attempt to express his thanks. "The young one ain't what you ought to be thinking about, Breck Hord. Young ones all got the same problems, and the biggest one is getting enough to eat when their daddies are too jellyfishy to join a union, even if their backbones pop out their bellybuttons. When are you going to get up on your hind legs?"

Breck tried to escape in his usual laconic manner. "I've been thinking it over, Aunt Cloa —"

"Well, when do you reckon you'll *stop* thinking it over? When your wife and child got nothing left to eat but bull-dog gravy, and they can't find no more grease for that?"

"Aunt Cloa, you know thing's ain't nowhere near that bad," said Breck reasonably. "We've got plenty to eat, and nobody's running around naked yet."

"And you think it's going to stay like that? Wake up, boy. Last year your ma paid sixty cents a bag for flour at the commissary store. You know how much it costs now? Eighty cents! And fatback that was ten cents a pound, it's fifteen cents nowadays!"

"Well, prices have gone up, that's all."

Her little soft-looking finger poked his chest like a ten-penny nail. "Prices have *not* gone up, is what I'm telling you! Stores in Harlan Town and Evarts and Cumberland, they're still selling flour and fatback for what they was last year! It's only in the commissary stores they've gone up! It's only in the mining camps we're paying more for everything we buy!"

"Don't you reckon that's because we buy with company scrip? I expect it evens out in the long run, or else people would stop trading at the commissary." Breck felt uneasy with the conversation, because food prices were not a subject that should have to concern men.

Aunt Cloa looked at him quizzically, shifting lumps of doughy flesh into new positions around her piercing eyes. "I declare, you don't get around any more than your sister Phoebe, do you? Don't you know what happens to mining people who try to do their buying at other places, instead of the commissary store?" She glared at him, waiting for an answer. When none came, she went on fiercely: "I'll tell you what happens. Over to Black Mountain camp, a woman name of Weed had five young ones and a husband who was ailing with the bloody flux. They was hurting for money, so she went into Evarts to get the most groceries she could, using her cash savings to buy them with. It weren't more than a week later, they got a letter from the company — said that since Black Mountain paid his wages, they expected him to do all his trading at the company store!"

"Well, they got a point there," said Breck, forced by her hectoring manner to play the devil's advocate.

"Sure they have! The point is, they got us where they can squeeze us dry, and there ain't no way we can stop it! You interrupted my story. A month later, this Weed feller and his wife was in Evarts again, and his wife seen some real pretty yard goods in a dry goods store — prettier than anything back at the commissary. She wanted to make her little girls some clothes for winter, so she went in and bought a few yards. That's all in the world she bought. And you know what happened to those people?"

"I guess the man got fired," Breck said reluctantly.

"Fired *and blacklisted!* That was more than a month ago, and he ain't been able to find another job yet! And you can bet everybody else at Black Mountain got the message: You want to work in the mine, you trade at the commissary — even if it costs you every cent you own! Ain't nobody else buying yard goods in Evarts — not with jobs getting fewer, and the price of coal going down to nothing. And it's going to get worse — until boys like you are willing to do something about it!"

Breck looked at the pudgy figure beside him, straight-backed and unrelenting, with her little hands folded over her round belly and her hard slate-colored eyes fixed straight ahead. Hoping to change the subject, he said, "I reckon you're right, Aunt Cloa. About the baby — anything you want me to do?"

"Why, yes, Breck," she said, with a sudden sweet smile. "You should JOIN THE UNION, is what you should do!"

"I mean besides that."

"Breck, don't you care that your brother Claiborne is as respected a union man as there is in Harlan County? Don't what he stands for make any difference to you?"

"I always did think a lot of my brother."

"Talking to you is like whipping a hickory post with a

pussywillow," Aunt Cloa complained. "No, don't bother to walk with me any farther. I'd rather walk by myself — the company's livelier. Go spend some time with your wife, you hear?" She walked away down the creekside, singing her new song:

Oh, scrip, oh, scrip, oh, worthless scrip,
Go see what worthless scrip can buy!

*

When the Great Depression hit the rest of the country in 1929, it was already a year old in Harlan County. The price of a ton of coal, which had been above $10 during the war, had fallen to $1.50. From a peak of 12,000 miners working in 71 mines, employment had skidded to less than 9000 men in 39 mines — and most of these were working two- or three-day weeks.

Other places, it took people a while to realize what trouble they were in.

In Harlan County, they already knew.

As the price of coal fell, the mining practices of the coal operators became wasteful. In mine after mine, only the broad bottom stratum of coal was mined. This "robbing," as it was called, resulted in cheaper coal, which further depressed the market — and, when each mining operation pulled out, the upper strata of coal and slate collapsed downward, dislocating the higher unmined veins and making the remaining coal inaccessible. Throughout 1929 and 1930, deserted mining camps, with disintegrating cabins in the hollows and broken seams under the hills, became familiar sights along the three forks of the Cumberland.

Claiborne's mine was robbed, and, as one of the central pillars holding up the roof was cut, thirty feet of rock came down on the men below. Four miners died; Claiborne escaped by three feet. The operators decided that the coal remaining in the seam could not be mined economically, so the mine was abandoned. The manager and the foremen and the commissary manager moved out of their houses on the hill. So did most of the miners in the cabins below. Claiborne and Joicy stayed, along with a few other families, because they had no place to go.

At Dead Yellow Dog Breck kept on working, if only for three days a week. Jubal Early continued to bring in a few dollars of scrip each payday doing odd jobs around the tipple, so the Hords weren't as bad off as some of their neighbors. Hannah and Bonnie Brae were able to put food on the table every meal, but often there was no meat for days at a time. Fried mush and bulldog gravy was the staple, with whatever vegetables could be found — most often pigweed and turnips. Generally there was coffee.

Prices rose at the commissary, as compared with independent stores. Weighmen at the tipple gave short weight to every car. Wages were paid exclusively in company scrip — it had been months since any family in the camp had received cash money. W. F. Tasker announced a new "cleanup" system, with every miner expected to clear the rock from his working face after he had loaded his last car, on his own time, without pay.

The union was totally inactive. If there were any organizers on Poor Fork, they kept themselves well hidden. Sizemore hadn't been seen for a year.

One day late in the year Bonnie Brae went to the commissary. It was the first weekday of the new month, so she knew that Breck's earnings for the past two weeks would be credited to their account. She took her time making her selection, gossiping with neighbors, enjoying the feeling of having money to spend, and not wanting it to end too quickly. At length she was finished, and Amy Herron, the sharp-faced, big-busted commissary clerk, whom many suspected of maintaining an indecent relationship with W. F. Tasker, quickly totalled her purchases, and transferred the figure to the Hord account slip.

"That's four dollars and forty cents, Mrs. Hord," she said briskly, her full lips turned down at the ends in an expression which, though unconscious, appeared to be a deliberate sneer.

"For all this food?" asked Bonnie Brae in surprise. She had expected it to come to twice that much.

"No — four dollars and forty cents left in your account. You want it in scrip, or you want to let it ride?"

Bonnie Brae's mouth was suddenly dry. In an apologetic tone, as though the fault were hers, she suggested that a mistake must have been made — that her husband's wages for the past two weeks hadn't been figured in. No mistake, said Amy Herron coolly, crossing her arms to bring the palms of her hands up with plaesant pressure under her breasts. Breck's wages of forty-four dollars and seventy cents were credited on the slip. Bonnie Brae realized the miners' wives around her had stopped talking; the sudden quiet in the room was almost shrill. Riley Slemp, the commissary manager, raised his pale, careful, liver-spotted face from his inventory sheets.

Amy Herron smiled patiently. "It's all writ down, Mrs. Hord. Your bill for today is ten eighty. There's thirty-one dollars and fifteen cents in cuts outstanding. That leaves four forty in the account."

Bonnie Brae was stunned. Thirty-one dollars and fifteen cents in cuts? She turned to the woman on her right, seeking sympathy or explanation. "It ain't never been that high before!" she said. The woman didn't answer.

"Now look, Mrs. Hord," Amy Herron said briskly, "you

want to check over your account, you come back this evening, or send your husband over. Right now I've got to take care of these ladies here. Now, were you next, Mrs. Odum?"

Bonnie Brae stood for a moment at a loss, unable to decide what to do next. Then she picked up her box of groceries and walked numbly toward the door.

Breck went to the commissary right after supper that night. Slemp and Amy Herron were alone, except for two boys drinking Dr. Peppers and leafing through pulp magazines with grubby fingers. The older of the two held a copy of *Spicy Detective;* the younger was still willing to settle for *Doc Savage.*

Abruptly, Breck demanded the facts about his account. Before Amy could answer, Slemp moved in smoothly, producing the Hords' account slip and placing it on the counter where Breck could read the penciled figures. "Here we are, Breck," he said helpfully. "This shows that during the last two weeks you made forty-four dollars and seventy cents, besides which you still had a credit of one dollar and sixty-five cents on the books."

As Breck studied the column of figures, the commissary door opened and closed to admit Francis Duffy, the shot-firer of Excelsior No. 2. The old bachelor, dapper in the white shirt and tie he always wore when he wasn't underground, walked quietly across the room and stopped a few feet from the counter.

"Bonnie Brae said the cuts was way up this time," Breck said. "What about it?"

"Here they are, all listed out." Slemp ran the eraser tip of his pencil down the sheet. "Totals up to thirty-one dollars, fifteen cents." When Breck's heavy eyebrows rose in surprise, he smiled disarmingly. "You want to go over them one by one? All right. This first one is a store charge: I recollect your wife come in two weeks ago, got a carton of soda pop, some pinto beans –"

Breck waved his hand impatiently and told him not to bother with food charges. Slemp nodded and skipped down the column. "This five dollars and thirty cents item, that was for a pair of shoes. You recollect them?"

Breck snorted. "I should – I could have bought the exact same shoes in Harlan Town for four dollars a pair." Slemp looked sad, as though Breck's remark was a disappointment to him. He studied the remaining figures, then looked up with a baffled expression.

"The rest of these are your standard cuts, Breck, same as you always pay." Breck said he reckoned they better go over them anyway. Slemp shrugged with a smile. Amy Herron clasped her hands behind her head and arched her back, turning an inscrutable look on Francis Duffy. The old man stared at her breasts and grinned, scratching his smooth, shiny, pink chin. "Lights, dollar and a quarter," Slemp read. "Medical insurance, two dollars. Burial fund, fifty cents. Rent, six dollars –"

"Hold on there," Breck said harshly. "Since when is my rent six dollars? I never paid but four till now."

"Oh, I reckon you didn't hear. There's a notice about it on the board there. The company's had to up the rent from a dollar a room to a dollar and a half. Expenses have gone up, on account of coal prices going down. You can't expect to rent a house in nineteen thirty for what you was paying in nineteen twenty-five, Breck."

At the magazine rack, the boy reading *Spicy Detective* suddenly giggled. Slemp glared at him and raised his voice. "If you're through with them soda pops, shag out of here now, before you eyeball the pictures right off the pages of them magazines, you hear?" The boys gave him hurt looks, replaced the magazines, and left. Amy Herron raised an arm and toyed with the hair on the back of her neck. Duffy made a sound that could have been either a chuckle or a cough.

Slemp continued: "Just three more items – smithing on your tools, four dollars and sixty cents; explosives, seven dollars; carbide lamp fuel, a dollar eighty. Those sound about right to you?"

Breck nodded slowly, and Slemp totaled the column. It added up to thirty-one dollars and fifteen cents, the same figure as before. The commissary manager smiled over his shoulder at his clerk. "Reckon we don't have to fire you, Miss Amy." Amy turned up the corners of her mouth a fraction of an inch. Duffy made his chuckle-cough sound again.

Breck raised his hands in front of him, palms upward, with the fingers spread apart, and looked at them. Then he lowered them, and wiped them downward on his pants, pressing hard against his thighs. "And how much you figure I still got coming, to last me till next payday?" he asked.

"There's four dollars and forty cents due you. Want me to give it to you in scrip, or you want to let it ride on the books?"

Duffy spoke for the first time. "With Fairleigh-Wolverine scrip worth sixty cents on the dollar, John D. Rockerfeller couldn't afford to take it," he said in a high clear tenor lifted by a brogue that was sensed rather than heard. "The only way to make a profit on it is never to have had it to begin with!"

Slemp gave the shot-firer an irritated frown, but answered politely, "I'll be with you in a minute, Mr. Duffy. Let me finish with Mr. Hord first."

"Oh, don't bother yourself about me. I'm sure Miss Amy will do me the honor, once she's finished tidying up her lovely hair."

Amy Herron looked at the old man with dislike, thinking how much he resembled a clever and malicious turtle, with his heavy lids masking the quick, clear eyes below. She asked him what he wanted. "Two cans of them sardines in olive oil," he replied, "and a box of saltine crackers, and a package of orange pekoe tea, please, miss. And two packs of Spud cigarettes, so I can be mouth-happy." He quoted the advertising slogan with an intimate leer.

Breck told the commissary manager to let his four dollars and forty cents ride. He turned from the counter and walked straight out the door. He hadn't gone far when the old Irishman caught up with him. Duffy was smoking a cigarette that smelled of menthol, and carrying his groceries in a little paper bag.

"Ah, it's a clear, cold night," he said conversationally. "The snow will be here before the week's out, freezing us to icicles, damn the luck. Reminds me of the nights in Schuylkill County when I was a boy. That's where I was born, you know." He paused, then repeated the name as if there were a question mark after it. "Schuylkill County?" When Breck didn't reply, he went on: "Do you know, I heard a man say that the mine operators in Harlan County make enough profits through their company stores to pay all their expenses, whether they sell a pound of coal up north or not. Would you guess there was any truth in that, Mr. Hord?"

"What? How should I know?"

"I'd be prepared to believe it. Of course, I've always been a cynical man. Ever since I saw what it was like to be raised in Schuylkill County in the seventies." Again he paused, and when Breck didn't speak, he went on: "Most of the lads there belonged to the Ancient Order of Hibernians, you understand. You've heard of the Hibernians, Mr. Hord? No? But maybe you know them by their other name — the Molly

Maguires." The old turtle eyes glinted as though in appreciation of some secret joke.

He had heard of them, Breck replied without interest. "They blew up mines and bushwhacked the police."

"That they did, that they did. And they paid for it, too," Duffy said. "I remember watching my uncle dance at the end of a rope, and me only eight at the time. He was a bodymaster — a leading man in the organization. I believe he killed three men with his own hands before he was betrayed by his dear friend and companion, who was nothing else but a dirty Pinkerton spy, if you can imagine it. Ah, the duplicity of the capitalist class!"

Breck asked with mild curiosity, "You seen your own uncle get hung? I reckon that's something a man don't never forget."

"I can close my eyes and see him twitching at this moment, and his wife and two daughters standing beside me watching, and not a single tear did they shed. And do you know what his last words were? 'Dynamite's the stuff!' he shouted out, as they pulled the hood down over his face, 'Dynamite's the stuff!' And the words were ringing in the prison yard when they dropped the trap!"

After a moment of silence, Breck said thoughtfully, "I don't see how it does anybody any good to blow up a mine. All it does is fix it so nobody can work there. Pretty soon there wouldn't be any jobs left at all."

"I wouldn't argue with you for a moment," said Duffy. "There's not a bit of sense to it. It's the absolute height of foolishness. But," he continued, leaning toward Breck with a subtle smile, "wouldn't it be a day to remember!"

Breck looked hard at the neat, well-scrubbed old man in his spotless shirt and pre-tied bow tie. Duffy returned the gaze, his smile broadening into a wide grin that exposed unbelievably white and regular false teeth. "Have a Spud," he said, extending a package. "Be mouth-happy."

"No, thanks. This is where I turn off." Abruptly Breck turned away and began walking along the creekside toward home. The old Irishman stood watching him a few seconds. Then he headed toward his cabin and his supper of sardines and crackers.

*

The winter of 1930–1931 was the worst in the history of the Harlan coalfields. Mines continued to close, and miners with jobs were lucky to work three days a week. Those who had been fired were ordered to vacate their cabins, but many families refused to leave, because they had no other shelter to go to. To accomplish their eviction, the operators hired private policemen to enforce the right of property in the mining camps. These "gun-thugs," as the miners called them, were few in number that winter, but they had the authority of the Harlan County Coal Operators' Association behind them, and many were deputized by John Henry Blair, the high sheriff of Harlan County. When the gun-thugs failed to persuade a family to move from their home in the afternoon, the home often burned to the ground that night.

The evicted miners had to take what they could get in the way of shelter. Most moved into abandoned shacks up in the hollows, but some lived in junked automobiles, and a few set up housekeeping in caves. When the heavy snows fell in January and February, women and children kept indoors, huddling close to sooty coal fires. The lack of exercise, combined with wretched diet, brought on pellagra and the "bloody flux" in almost epidemic proportions. The weakest died. The biggest problem was how to bury them in the frozen ground.

Dead Yellow Dog kept working through the winter. As a captive mine, with all its production earmarked for the Fairleigh Automotive Corporation in Detroit, it was less affected by the economic crisis than the mines that competed on the open market. But the Fairleigh factory could satisfy the national demand for its products by operating four hours a day, and, as its production schedule fell, so did its demand for coal.

By the beginning of 1931, two thirds of the miners at Dead Yellow Dog had been laid off. Breck was still working, but only six hours a day, two days a week. The money he brought in — six or seven dollars a week, in scrip — was all the family had, for Jubal Early no longer could pick up odd jobs around the tipple.

Breck refused to allow himself to think of anything beyond surviving the winter. He spent his free time in the hills, hunting. A good return for eight hours of struggling through snowdrifts would be two scrawny squirrels, but he was glad to pay the price, because it kept him out of the cabin and away from Bonnie Brae's frightened questions — "What are we going to do, Breck?" "How long can we go on like this?" — that seemed to reproach him for a guilt he felt but couldn't explain. He was glad to be away from Little Andy, too, with his waxy skin and eyes that seemed to grow ever larger, as though they were parasites living off the rest of his body. And he was glad to be away from Jubal Early and Hannah, both sitting calmly and waiting, beyond even the recollection of resistance. And to be away from Phoebe, as she consumed herself with outrage.

One crisp silvery day in late February Claiborne appeared. He had gotten a ride as far as the bottom of the hollow, and walked on up. He was shockingly thin, but his sunken eyes sparkled in their sockets as he told Breck his news. "The union's coming in for real, boy! Phil Murray's going to be in Pineville for a meeting next Sunday! We're going to sign up every damn miner in Harlan County!"

"Who's this you say's coming?"

"Phil Murray! He's the vice president of the UMW of A — John L.'s right-hand man! God dog, when a man like that comes, you know they're not just screwing around! This time they're in for good, I promise you!"

Breck looked at the snow that still lay over the hills, and wondered if spring was close enough for him to allow himself to think of anything beyond bare survival. He decided it was. "Come in and have some coffee, Claiborne. How you aim to get over to Pineville Sunday?"

"Fellow named Cornett has a Hudson still runs. You want we should come by for you?"

The following Sunday the Hudson appeared on the Poor Fork road as arranged, and Breck, Claiborne, and five other men drove into Pineville to hear Phil Murray urge the unionization of the Kentucky coalfields.

Two thousand miners heard Murray speak; the majority were out of work to begin with and most of the rest were unemployed twenty-four hours later. Spies reported the names of attending miners to the Operators' Association, and they were fired wholesale. At the Insull mine at Black Mountain, for example, one hundred and seventy-five men were told to turn in their tools and vacate their cabins. D. C. Jones, judge of the circuit court, defined union organization as a crime under Kentucky's criminal syndicalism law, and, under this definition, miners known to have been present at Pineville that Sunday were blacklisted through the whole Harlan coalfield.

Judge Jones — "Baby" Jones, as he was called — made an understandable decision, in light of the fact that his wife came from one of the wealthiest mineowning families in eastern Kentucky.

Monday afternoon Breck climbed out of the electric tram at the driftmouth, to find the foreman, Jeems Maggard, waiting with a list in his hand. When he saw Breck, Maggard stuck out his long jaw and tilted back his narrow head imperiously. "You, Hord, come over here. I got something to say to you."

Breck walked over to him, impatient to get under the hot showers in the wash shanty. "What's that?" he asked.

"You thought you was getting away with something, but you wasn't. We know where you went yesterday," the foreman said accusingly.

"If you'd asked me, I would have told you," Breck said indifferently.

"You went to a union meeting, spite of your signed contract. You broke your pledged word, Hord!" Maggard's speckled face was a study in outrage.

Breck pointed out that he had not, in fact, broken any agreement, because he hadn't signed up with the union. Maggard shouted that just going to the meeting showed that Breck couldn't be trusted. "Boy, don't you know it's not smart to bite the hand that feeds you, when there's better men than you out of work all over Harlan County?"

"If you got anything to say, say it," Breck said quietly.

"What I got to say is, bring in your rust, Hord — turn in your tools! You're fired!"

"You miserable egg-sucking son of a bitch," said Breck, hitting the foreman a powerful blow on the side of his head.

Maggard fell backward, down the slope, rolling over once and ending up on his hands and knees, his lank hair hanging down like a fringe over his enraged eyes. "Keep away from me, you hear!" he screamed. "You touch me again and you're a dead man!" He rose to a crouch, and one hand darted to his pocket and reappeared with a large clasp knife, which he jerked open. "I'll let the beans out of your belly, Hord, I swear to God I will!" He was balanced between fear and fury, as dangerous as a threatened copperhead.

"I ain't ever coming near you again, if I can help it," Breck said flatly, his sudden anger gone. "Don't worry — I'll be out of here as soon as I can get someplace to go. But listen, Maggard — you try to use that pigsticker on me, and twelve months from now your wife will have been a widow for a year." He walked past the foreman and continued down the slope without looking back. Maggard swore furiously as he returned the knife to his pocket.

Breck moved his family to an abandoned cabin near Claiborne's, in Aleck's Hollow off Clover Fork. It had been almost a year since the Little Aleck mine had shut down. Many of the cabins had been empty all during that time, although a few had been occupied by families evicted from other mining camps during the winter. The one Breck selected was in the best repair of those available. All the windows were broken out, half the boards from the front porch had disappeared to feed fires in other cabins, a missing leg caused the cast-iron stove to lean drunkenly to one side, surrounded by fallen sections of stovepipe, and the slaty March sky showed through a three-foot hole in the roof. Dried leaves, animal droppings, and wads of yellowed newspaper crowded the corners, half-covered by a ragged blanket of gray snow.

"It's a sorry place, Bonnie Brae," said Breck somberly.

"Oh, it won't look so bad once we sweep it out and patch them holes over," his wife answered cheerfully. Somehow, the disaster of their eviction from Dead Yellow Dog had settled the worries that had been suspended in her mind like a murky cloud; her thoughts suddenly were clear and constructive. "No problem about where to put the furniture — there's plenty of room for everything now." Most of the furniture was gone, sold for a fraction of its worth during the winter, or simply abandoned in the empty house at Dead Yellow Dog because it wasn't worth the effort to move it.

"God Almighty, we was better off back in Leslie County, with all them Allardyces around," said Jubal Early, shaking his head at the irony of the years. But Phoebe, like Bonnie Brae, seemed to rise to the challenge of the ramshackle cabin. "Breck, why don't you and Pa see to that stove? Things will look a sight better when we get some hot food inside us." She directed her mother, her sister-in-law, her husband, and her father through the almost insurmountable problems of getting a meal on the table, while little Andy shrieked in protest at being confined to the back seat of the borrowed Chevrolet.

Claiborne and Joicy and their two oldest children helped with the house, and by the end of the first week it was bearable. The windows were tightly covered with wrapping paper, smoothly greased to let in soft yellow light. The hole in the roof was patched with a yard-wide square of flattened tin cans. The stove was leveled with flat rocks, and the stovepipe reassembled with rags wrapped snugly around the seams. Floorboards had been borrowed from empty cabins to repair the porch. The privy in the back was upright again. The walls and floor of the cabin were scrubbed until the wall paint gleamed and the wood grain in the floor stood out in clean damp detail.

The jagged March wind still found ways through the walls, but nothing short of rebuilding would stop that. The family had three big beds which, covered with their bright, crazy-quilt "kiverlids," offered the surest defense against the last cruel winter days and nights. Jubal Early and Hannah had one bed to themselves, Breck and Bonnie Brae had another, and Phoebe took Little Andy in with her. Then one day the sarvis trees on the hills glittered with blossoms of bridal white. The slopes were sibilant with rivulets of melted snow. Birds sang in noisy excitement. Claiborne took Breck off hunting, and Bonnie Brae sang "The Dying Knight's Farewell" as she did her housework.

Phoebe said laconically, "Well, I reckon we made it through, if we never see the back of our neck."

*

Claiborne and Breck were drinking coffee in Claiborne's kitchen when a Dodge sedan bounced up the pothole-pocked dirt road and stopped in front of the cabin. The car's occupants were dressed in khaki shirts and pants, and had gun belts strapped around their waists. Both had deputy sheriff badges pinned to their shirt pockets.

The man who stamped up the porch steps first was heavy-set, with powerful muscles just beginning to be overlaid with fat. He had a cherubic look, with a pug nose, thick, curved lips, and deep blue eyes that looked sincere. His name was Nugent Emory, and Breck remembered him from school. The other deputy was an older man named Hondell, a thin, angry-looking consumptive, whose brother had once worked at Dead Yellow Dog.

Emory pushed open the kitchen door and entered without knocking; Hondell followed. Claiborne set his coffee mug down carefully, and remarked that he would be dogged if he could remember asking the two deputies into his house. Emory grinned at Joicy, standing by the stove, and ran his eyes deliberately over her body. She looked back at him with an expression that affirmed her own sexuality as it repudiated his. Breck gathered his legs under him. Hondell rested his hand on his gun butt. Claiborne repeated his remark, this time adding the request for an answer.

With his eyes still locked with Joicy's, Emory said, "You ain't got no house to ask anybody into, Hord. This house belongs to the Little Aleck Mining Company. You're squatters here, and the company wants you out."

"The company ain't worked this mine for a year," said Claiborne reasonably. "Why should they care who lives in these cabins? They ain't good for nothing anyway — most of them won't even keep the cold out. What's the company going to do with them?"

Emory looked at Claiborne for the first time. He continued to grin, but with contempt. "It's none of your goddamned business what the company's going to do with them. You just drag your ass out. No union son of a bitch is going to live rent-free in a company cabin! Why don't you go over to Evarts with the rest of the UMW shitheels?"

Claiborne pushed back his chair and rose, followed a second later by Breck. "There's a mite too many 'sons of bitches' and 'shitheels' in this kitchen to suit me," he said. "Unless you're figuring on pulling them big old pistols and using them, I think you better move on out." His hands hung loosely at his sides, Breck's gripped the back of a kitchen chair, and Joicy's held a carving knife and an iron skillet.

Emory said they would leave when they got damn good and ready. The five people in the kitchen stood looking at one another in air so full of hate it seemed to tremble, like heat rising. The impasse was broken by Hondell, who hawked and spat on the floor. As if that act somehow excused them to leave the room, the two deputies turned their backs and swaggered from the house. "You been warned, remember," Emory called over his shoulder. "Anything happens now, it's your own fault."

Claiborne, Joicy, and Breck watched the Dodge sedan roar up the road toward Clover Fork. Joicy spoke first. "What you reckon we better do, hon?" she asked her husband.

He pulled his lower lip downward, exposing yellowed teeth. "I don't see no need for moving yet awhile. It ain't as if we had any place to go. And besides, I've put a right smart piece of work into this house — I ain't anxious to chuck that away. No, I reckon if they really want to get shut of us, they'll come back again, with some kind of legal paper. That's what they do when it's official. Ain't that right, Breck?"

Breck nodded his agreement, and Joicy looked reassured.

Four nights later a fire started in the unoccupied cabin farthest up Aleck's Hollow. A stiff wind was blowing down from Big Black Mountain, and the burning house was at the windward end of the row of cabins facing the creek. The flames leaped from house to house, and in twenty minutes all sixteen houses in the row were ablaze. Five of the sixteen had been occupied, and the five families who had lived in them lost most of their possessions. No one was injured.

Chapter 7

Evarts

EARLY MORNING

MAY FIFTH WAS A COOL, crisp day in Harlan County. The sky was cloudless, and the air smelled as fresh as well water.

Bonnie Brae Hord was the first person to wake up in the shack. As always, it seemed as though she were surfacing in a pool of sleep sounds — Breck's deep, regular breathing, touched with a baritone burr at the beginning of each exhalation; Hannah's thin, resonant snore; Jubal Early's smacking sounds, as his lips and tongue sought tirelessly for his missing teeth; Phoebe's rustling cough; Little Andy's whimper; all their individual sleep voices blending into a kind of nocturnal harmony. And from the next room, the muted noises of Joicy and Claiborne and their four young ones.

Lordy, it's daylight again, she thought. *Pretty soon I'll have to get up. But not just yet — it won't hurt to lie still a little while. I work hard enough the rest of the day — God won't mind if I take a minute off.* She lay quietly with her hands under her head, looking at the dim ceiling and thinking about God. She didn't picture Him as the fierce and unforgiving champion of goodness, as she had in her childhood, when she watched Him visit the Holiness Church to wrestle with the serpents of Satan. Since she had become

Breck's woman, and mother of his child, she hadn't thought about God much at all, and never with the mixed dread and joy she had experienced once. *But it's no disrespect,* she thought. *I know He's there if we need him. Long as we do like we're supposed to, there ain't no reason for Him to show up at all.*

Breck moved restlessly in his sleep, rolling his head from one side to the other. *He's running out of sleep time—pretty soon he'll have to wake up and face the day too,* Bonnie Brae thought, studying the stolid features that were only gentled when he slept. *I wish I could give him longer.*

The pool of sleep sounds around her began to change, rippling nervously, as if the brightening light outside were a wind that was roiling the water. Breck mumbled; Hannah gave a peevish snort; Little Andy cried out suddenly; from beyond the door Claiborne spoke softly to Joicy.

I reckon I can't put it off, thought Bonnie Brae, throwing back the covers on her side of the bed.

*

J. C. Stackpool woke before dawn. He had slept poorly, in spite of the moonshine whiskey he had drunk the night before. He was excited by the prospect of the day ahead. He stood in front of the window and looked out at the mist rising from Dead Dog Branch, thinking that in an hour or less the deputies and the truck would be here, to help him load his furniture and give him an escort to the Black Mountain mine.

Foreman! he thought exultantly. *I'm going to be a foreman! God damn, boy, how about that!* He ran his fingers through his shock of tow-colored hair, and then smoothed it down mechanically. *And in a real mine, too, not a damn rathole like Dead Yellow Dog!*

Behind him his wife shifted in the bed, half-awake, and called out, "J.C.?"

"Oh, shut up, you fat old cow," J.C. said evenly. His wife was eight months pregnant. He hadn't felt like touching her for four of those months, and blamed her for it.

"You ain't no kind of man at all," the voice behind him said, and the mattress creaked as the heavy body searched for a less uncomfortable position.

J.C. continued to look into the mist, as he thought of his life at Dead Yellow Dog. He remembered his family with irritation, his childhood friends with amusement or contempt. He ran over the names of some of the girls he had had. He thought of four years underground, the men on his shift, the jokes, the accidents, the drunks, the fights. It all went past his mind's eye featurelessly, until he came to Breck Hord.

That Breck, that was some old boy, he reflected sadly. *Too bad, what happened when he got married. He just didn't have no sense of humor, was all. He had to take it personal. Things never got back the way they was, after that. Goddamn, but that was some fight, though!* Unconsciously, his hand rubbed over his mastoid bone, where Breck's hard skull had hit him. *Silly son of a bitch!*

His thoughts moved to Breck's discharge from Excelsior No. 2, and Claiborne's earlier. *Damn fools got themselves mixed up with that union crap, they deserved to get the boot. In this world, you take care of your own self, or nobody does. Nobody ain't never helped me out a damn bit, that's for sure.*

A brackish taste of corn whiskey rose to his mouth. He swallowed it, making a face, and then left the window and poured himself a glass of water and drank it. His wife called from the bed, "J.C., hon, will you bring me a glass of water?"

"Get it your own self. Time you got out of bed anyway. Get us something to eat, before those deputies start loading our furniture out from under us." He went back to the window and conjured up the image of the girl he had had the week before, using it to block out his mental picture of the woman behind him.

Then, disquietingly, one unbidden thought wormed its way through his erotic recapitulation: *I do wish we didn't have to drive through Evarts to get to Black Mountain, though.*

*

Sizemore, the UMW organizer, was in Evarts, although he couldn't think of any good reason for being there, and several for being somewhere else.

Evarts was a tinderbox. Because it was the only town in Harlan County with a mayor and a police chief who were sympathetic to the unemployed miners, its population had increased from 1500 to 5000 in a little over a month. Most of the new arrivals were living in tarpaper shacks on a farm on the outskirts of town owned by an ex-miner. There was no sanitation, no electricity, almost no food, and a long walk for water. For medical attention, there was only the Red Cross — and the Red Cross wouldn't help strikers.

And almost everybody in Evarts was on strike, much to the discomfort of Sizemore and the other UMW organizers.

During April, as the number of jobless miners in Evarts had swelled from hundreds to thousands, the demand had grown for the United Mine Workers to call a strike. Sizemore had passed the word up the chain of command, but the answer came back from District 19 headquarters: "No strike!" John L. Lewis was engaged in a bitter struggle for control of his own union with the rebels of Illinois' District 12, headed by Frank Farrington, and was unwilling to spare any effort or energy for sideshows in Appalachia. But the Evarts local, by then both large and desperate, voted to override the national organization — the rank and file declared a wildcat strike.

A few of the smaller mines still operating were shut down by the strike, but the larger and richer mines prepared to continue operations in spite of it. The huge Insull-owned Black Mountain Coal Company brought in armed strikebreakers in sealed boxcars. The number of gun-thugs in the county was somewhere between one and two hundred, all deputized by John Henry Blair; some were assigned as guards at each operating mine, and the rest were organized into flying squads and quartered in the Lewallen Hotel in Harlan. Their salaries were paid by the coal companies, but the county paid them a fee of two dollars for every arrest they made.

In late April there was a steady flicker of shooting, robbery, and arson, like heat lightning on a summer night. Seven stores and commissaries near Evarts were robbed on seven consecutive days. All the houses occupied by strikers at Ellis Knob Coal Company were burned. A group of scabs were badly beaten, and Blair sent armed deputies into Evarts with orders to arrest those responsible; in the ensuing gunfight a deputy and a striker were killed. Snipers bushwhacked guards escorting other scabs to Black Mountain, but there were no casualties.

The Red Cross left Evarts. Sizemore wished he could.

It was not the first time in his life that the pretense of leading workmen had required him to scamper like a rabbit to keep from being left behind. During the past decade it had often seemed more important for a UMW organizer to talk tough than to act tough, which was one reason the union membership in 1931 was less than a quarter of what it had been in 1920. Sizemore understood this policy and even accepted it, with some misgivings. He considered himself a realist, and thought in terms of carts and horses, games and candles, and birds in the hand.

But the morning of May fifth he wished things were different.

He stood on the front porch of a boarding house in Evarts, a cup of sweetened coffee in his hand giving pleasurable heat against the presunrise chill, and looked down the street toward the coal oil lamps that glowed in the strikers' shantytown a quarter of a mile away. His cheek convulsed in a parody of a wink; his tic had gotten worse in the past few months.

What the hell can I say to them? he wondered to himself, thinking about the meeting that the officials of the local had set for nine o'clock in the morning at the local movie theater — against his wishes. *How can I tell them District 19 will pull the union out of Harlan County before it will authorize the strike?*

The door behind him opened. It was his landlady, a round little woman with a birthmark on her throat, shapeless in a blue flowered wrapper. She held a coffee pot in one hand. "I thought you might like a mite more coffee," she said. She was proud of renting a room to an important man like Mr. Sizemore.

"Thank you, ma'am — that's real thoughtful," he said, reaching his cup toward her so she could pour.

She gathered the edges of her wrapper snugly about her throat with one fat hand. "Chilly now, but it looks like it's going to be a real fine day, once the sun gets up," she said.

"It does, for a fact," Sizemore answered, sipping his coffee. "It surely does, for a fact."

*

Amy Herron turned over in her bed to escape the morning light, and slipping one hand between her thighs, cupped it tenderly over her crotch. "Oh, Jesus," she said aloud. She had only been asleep three hours; it had been three thirty when W. F. Tasker drove her home in his Reo-Royale Eight. *It must have been that bottle of bootleg Canadian Club,* she thought, squeezing her eyes shut. *It slowed him down. It's never taken him that long before.* Three hours on the back seat, trying and trying, and then drinking a while, and then trying some more; the regular way, and on the side, and every other way he could think of — and he couldn't get it off, couldn't get the job done, just pushed it in and out like a big goddamned wooden pole. "Oh, sweet Jesus," she said again, "what's the matter with the man?"

*

Phoebe Hord also awoke to thoughts of love.

She had been dreaming of the night last year when a shy, sandy-haired widower named Barrett had taken her to the moving pictures, to see *Our Dancing Daughters.* The dream progressed, as it always did, through the ice cream and cake at the ice-cream parlor next door to the theater, through their discussion of the kind of person the *real* Joan Crawford must be, through her growing joy that Barrett was overcoming his shyness and finding her gay and attractive. Happily inside her dream-self, she left the ice-cream parlor and got into Barrett's old coupé, and rode through Harlan Town and out along the Poor Fork road, chattering all the while. Then

Barrett slowed down and pulled off the road into an overgrown dirt track and turned off his lights. As the blackness of the night rushed in upon them, for a moment she was so startled that she asked, "Why, what in the world are we stopping here for?"

"Phoebe, let's us sit a while and talk," Barrett said, his voice tremulous and unsure. "What did you think of the movie?"

"We already talked about what I thought about the movie."

"You know, I really like you, Phoebe," he gasped, suddenly wrapping one arm around her shoulders and seizing her breast with the other hand. "Don't you like me some? You do like me some, don't you?" He squeezed her breast, hurting her, and she felt the rough skin of his cheek against her lips as he tried to find her mouth with his own.

Her body stiffened, and she pulled her head away. "What are you doing? Stop it, you hear!" She pushed her hands against his chest with all her strength, turning her face to the window and the darkness and the night sounds outside. *My God, he's touching me,* she cried silently, *he's touching me where no man has a right to touch me!* Terror poured into her body as if his hand had punctured her and let the outside coldness in. Her resistance blunted the thrust of his attempt, and he felt foolish and ugly as his shyness returned. But like a gambler calling for double or nothing in an attempt to retrieve disaster, he forced her head around until he could put his mouth against hers, thrusting his tongue against her sealed lips, wedging his knee between her rigid legs — while a voice in his brain droned despairingly, *It ain't going to work, it ain't going to work a bit!*

Phoebe fought back hysterically, scratching and even biting at him until he released her. Now, almost a year later, asleep in her bed in the tarpaper shack in Evarts with the sounds of morning taking root around her, Phoebe remembered the defeat and dejection of the next few moments — Barrett attempting to apologize, to protect the last remnants of the confidence he had so carefully assembled, she crushed beneath the weight of her returning sense of separateness. Then the silent ride back home, and the turning away from one another of two people who would never again be able to remember that evening without pain.

Phoebe opened her eyes and looked blankly into the morning light. *It didn't have to happen like it did,* she thought. *There was a lot of other ways it could have come out. If only things was different. If he'd have been gentler. If I wasn't so scairt.*

She lay quietly for a few moments, then got out of bed and began to help Bonnie Brae with breakfast, such as it was.

*

In the mine guards' barracks at Black Mountain, Nugent Emory awoke to the familiar smell of stale sweat and flatulence that characterizes all barracks, everywhere. He sat on the side of his bed in his long underwear and scratched himself under the overhang of his belly. His sidekick, Hondell, still lay under his gray cotton blanket on the next bunk, his eyes squeezed shut. Emory kicked his mattress. "Get up, peckerhead," he said pleasantly. "Get some of that good breakfast in you. Make a new man out of you. Get the taste of that damn ruckus juice out of your mouth."

Hondell opened his bloodshot eyes and glared sullenly at Emory. "Shit," he said. He got out of bed and stood up uncertainly, then quickly sat down. "Whoo-ee," he groaned. "That little old girl ruint me. I'm lower than a mole's asshole." He started to lie down on his mattress, and Emory kicked it again, harder. Hondell sat back up. "How come you're so bright-eyed and bushy-tailed this morning?" he asked bitterly.

"It's a great getting-up morning. Birds singing, sun shining, all sorts of good things going on, buddy. Come on, get up, now, while there's still some breakfast left!" Grinning sardonically at his friend, he proceeded to pull on his khaki pants and shirt and his shoes and socks. Then he strapped on his pistol belt. While Hondell was dressing, Emory drew his Smith & Wesson Police Special from its holster, broke out the cylinder, ejected the cartridges and looked at each one of them carefully, squinted through the oily barrel toward the light, raised the hammer with his thumb two or three times, replaced the cartridges, snapped back the cylinder, and returned the pistol to his holster. By this time Hondell was dressed, and the two men left the barracks for the chow hall.

Breakfast was fried pork, grits, gravy, pancakes and syrup, and strong, fragrant coffee. Emory loaded his tray; Hondell settled for two pieces of lean pork and a dab of grits. They carried their food to Jim Darling's table and sat down. For the past few days, Darling had functioned as their squad leader, and, in an informal way, they were reporting for the day. He returned their greeting with a curt nod and continued his breakfast. There was little conversation among the seven men at the table until they finished eating and lit their cigarettes. Then Emory asked, "Well, Jim, what you got figured out for us today?"

"I thought it might be nice to take a little joy ride to Evarts," Darling replied. He found a fiber of pork gristle between his two front teeth, and flicked it out with his thumbnail. "It's been a while since we said hello to them rednecks — I expect they miss us."

Emory looked at Darling sharply to see if he was joking, but Darling's pale gray eyes were cold, and the expression on his square, commanding face was mirthless. "I could live without them a while longer," Emory said. "Last time anybody went in there, it ended up with a fair amount of shooting."

"You sound scared," said a guard named Gill contemptuously.

"No, I ain't scared, but I don't see no point in taking foolish chances 'less they're necessary," Emory said reasonably. "When somebody talks about going for a joy ride to Evarts, then I'm interested to know if it's necessary."

"It's necessary," said Darling. "There's a man they're bringing in for a foreman here. Him and his wife and all his furniture's going to be on a truck coming up from Harlan this morning. The company's got a house for him in Kenvir, but he's got to come through Evarts to get there. There'll be some deputies with him, three or four men in one car. We'll meet them the other side of Evarts, and bring them through town and on in."

"So we got through Evarts once on the way down, pick up this truck, and come through again on the way back — is that right?" said Emory. Darling nodded, his eyes expressionless on Emory's face. Emory suddenly grinned, and, turning to Hondell beside him, poked the little man in the ribs. "Hey, old buddy — when we get back, what'll we do with the rest of the day?"

*

Claiborne had been elected vice president of the UMW local in Evarts and had used his popularity to favor the wildcat strike. When he met Sizemore outside the Evarts theater a few minutes before nine o'clock, he was confident that the national organization would authorize the strike.

"Hey, Sizemore, I reckon we'll have every man in the local

here this morning – and a mess of their women besides! God dog, I hope you got some good news for them!"

Sizemore gave a tight smile. His cheek jumped. "Well, I've got the word from District Nineteen, if that's what you mean, Hord. But whether you'd call it good news –"

At that moment a gray-haired woman with a thin, tired face pushed through the crowd around Sizemore and tugged at his sleeve. Claiborne recognized her; she worked in the sheriff's office. "Mr. Sizemore, there's something you ought to know –" Sizemore, glad of the interruption, turned to her swiftly, and she leaned her head close to his ear and spoke in a voice so low as to be inaudible to Claiborne. Sizemore listened, his face impassive. When she had finished, he said, "Thank you, Milly. And thank your friend for me." She disappeared into the crowd, and Sizemore looked off into space, his eyes focused inward.

"What was that about?" Claiborne asked.

"Hmmm?" Sizemore gazed blankly at Claiborne a second, then his eyes narrowed. He hesitated before speaking, as if weighing alternatives. Finally he said softly, "The gun-thugs are coming through here this morning. Three carloads full. They're going down to pick up a scab and escort him back to Black Mountain. Now for Christ's sake shut up about it."

Claiborne's eyes widened. "How in this wicked world do you know that?" he asked.

"Just never you mind how I know it. You just sit on it till we decide what to do with it. You hear?"

The theater was filling up. It was a minute or two after nine when Sizemore, Claiborne, and the other local officers took their seats on the narrow stage in front of the movie screen. The small theater, shabby in the daylight, was full, and men stood in the aisles. Claiborne had a giddy feeling of stage fright, sitting up there exposed to so many people. He looked over the crowd, seeking familiar faces. After a moment he found Breck, sitting next to Sam Troutman from Dead Yellow Dog. Breck gave him a solemn nod. Two rows back, dapper in a white shirt and tie, was Francis Duffy, the shot-firer. The old Irishman caught Claiborne's look, and bobbed his head brightly, like a chickadee picking seeds. A few seats to his left, majestic in a shiny black pancake hat, was Aunt Cloa Burkett. Her eyes were closed, as if she were writing a new labor song in her mind. Beside her was another familiar face; in the row behind, still another. As his nervousness abated, he realized the audience was speckled with friends and acquaintances.

The president of the local opened the meeting and dispensed with all routine business to call upon Sizemore. Sizemore stood up and faced the expectant crowd, his stocky body rigid in his ill-fitting serge suit, his wiry red hair rebellious, his hands half-open, half-closed, curiously ineffectual. He cleared his throat; it was the only sound in the theater.

"Most of you know I've been down to District Nineteen, representing you all," he began. "First off, I want you to know that you Harlan miners are mighty important to the UMW, right on up to John L. himself. They're all watching us, right here, and they're not about to settle for anything that's not in the best interests of every man in this room." He paused, as if debating whether he had made the point sufficiently clear, then went on to reinforce it: "Believe me, the only thing in this whole world John L. Lewis and Phil Murray care about is getting justice for the coal miner. They've spent their whole life fighting the operators that have sweated you and starved you and ground you down into the dirt. Why, they were fighting before most of you boys ever knew what UMW stood for!"

Why don't he just get to it? Claiborne thought. A wave of uneasiness passed over the audience like a collective shudder. Claiborne's eyes moved from face to face in front of him; he saw blank faces, uncomprehending faces, faces beginning to form expressions of surprise, of anger, of disgust. He saw Breck's face stolidly reflecting an inward kindling of rage; Duffy's alert and malicious; Aunt Cloa's serene except for her glittering eyes. Suddenly Sizemore's equivocation seemed unbearable a moment longer. Claiborne cried out, "Well, tell us, goddamn it, just tell us — are they going to authorize the strike?"

Sizemore turned to face him, his expression compounded of hurt and anger. "Hord, you know it's not that easy —" he began.

"Just tell us," Claiborne repeated, raising his voice to a shout to carry above the growing rumble of the crowd. "Are they or ain't they?"

"Are they or ain't they?" called a voice from the audience. Other voices picked the question up. "Are they or ain't they? Are they or ain't they?" Sizemore raised his hands. His cheek was twitching without interruption.

"Listen — it's not the time! It's not the right time for a strike! There's too much at stake! We can't go off half-cocked here in Harlan County, pull all the other locals after us, and start a strike we may not win! Try to understand that! It's not just you men by yourselves any more — you're part of the union now. You got to think of the other guys!"

Claiborne stepped up to Sizemore and grabbed him by the arm, "What do you mean, we got to think of the other guys? A minute ago, you said they was thinking about us! Just what's the goddamned point of joining a union if they tell you to kindly shut up and starve quiet, so's you don't bother the other locals? Is that what I've been paying dues for ten years to hear? Well, listen — if it is, it ain't good enough!"

Sizemore jerked free. "Shut up, Hord — what are you trying to do? Sit down!" He spread out his arms like a Baptist preacher calling the children home. "Listen to me — listen to me!" he shouted. "What I'm telling you is just common sense! Trust the union — the union knows best!"

His voice was drowned under the roar of protest that filled the theater. He seemed to shrink under the force of the crowd's anger; his body sagged, his hands fell to his sides again, half-open, his Adam's apple jerked as he swallowed.

Claiborne waited for the crowd's outrage to peak and start to decline. Then he began to speak to them, as coldly furious and as sure of himself as he had ever been: "Friends, we been sold out! They tooken our money for dues, and let us get ourselves blacklisted, and beat up by the thugs — and all for nothing! We got nothing! That's all we deserve — nothing! Ain't that right? Ain't it?"

"No!" roared the crowd.

"Just nothing! Just dirt! Ain't that the truth? Ain't that what we are?"

"NO!"

"Oh, yes it is! It's got to be" — Claiborne hesitated, prolonging the moment almost imperceptibly before final commitment — "or else, why do them gun-thugs think they can drive right here into Evarts this morning?"

*

In Chicago, on West Erie Street, on the Near North Side, Michael Rogoff was awake and looking out into his air shaft, trying to ascertain what the weather was like outside.

Michael Rogoff had never heard of Harlan County, Kentucky, in his life.

It looked like it might be raining. He thought gratefully that he didn't need to go outside. He had arrived in Chicago a day earlier than expected, he had a loaf of bread, a quarter's worth of bologna slices, a jar of mustard, a copy of *The Theory of the Leisure Class,* and the use of a Crossley radio, which was playing Frank Crummit's record of "Three Little Words."

The hell with it, he thought, lying back down on the irregular bed. *I'll check in at Party headquarters tomorrow. Maybe today I'll go to a movie.*

MIDMORNING

Ten deputies, in three cars, left Black Mountain a little before ten o'clock. Jim Darling was in the lead car, along with Emory, Hondell, and the guard named Gill, who was driving. Darling sat in the back seat, holding a Thompson submachine gun on his lap. On the ledge behind him were a double-barreled shotgun, a sawed-off shotgun, boxes of shotgun shells and .38 and .45 caliber ammunition, and a canvas bag full of tear gas and smoke grenades. All the men carried pistols.

Emory was in good spirits, and he joshed Hondell about his hangover. "Buddy, you look like the feller that come in last in the human race. You better shut your eyes before you bleed to death. You ever see such an awful-looking thing in your life, Jim?"

"He ain't likely to win no beauty contests," said Darling, idly clicking the safety of the Thompson off and on.

"That's a fact," said Emory. "It's really a mystery to me

how women find him irresistible, the way they do. A sorry-looking critter like that, and they can't keep their damn hands off him — while a handsome feller like Gill, here, can't get his end in no ways, no matter how hard he tries."

Gill cursed him, and Darling laughed shortly. "What's the matter there, Gill? He hitting too close to home to suit you?" he asked.

"Aw, hell, I just get tired of talking about pussy all the time, that's all," said Gill, his eyes on the narrow road in front of him. "To hear him go on, you'd think there wasn't nothing else in the world."

"There ain't nothing else as *good* in the world, that's the truth. And you can take it from the man who knows," said Emory complacently.

"Horseshit," said Gill. The four men lapsed into silence, watching the trees go by. Five minutes passed. Then their car topped the last hill and started down into the valley that lay beside Clover Fork. Evarts was before them.

*

The road to Harlan crossed the L & N railroad tracks a few feet from a bridge over Clover Fork. A highway maintenance crew had been working on the bridge. Their truck was still parked beside the road. A little farther on was a stack of railroad ties. The road continued through a cut, the ground sloping up and densely wooded on the right, falling away to the embankment of Clover Fork on the left.

Breck was lying behind a big maple tree on the hill, overlooking the railroad crossing. There were at least thirty other men around him, each armed, each with his own tree for protection. Below, Breck could see other men concealed behind the stack of railroad ties and the maintenance truck. Across Clover Fork was a warehouse, and he knew there were miners at its windows and on its roof. All told, he guessed sixty or seventy men must be waiting in ambush.

He held Sam Troutman's .30 caliber deer rifle in his hands, Troutman preferring to use his twelve-gauge shotgun with the hand-carved curly-maple stock. The rifle looked like a good gun; the bluing was worn from the barrel in several places, indicating it had seen much use. Breck felt comfortable with it.

Claiborne was behind the pile of railroad ties, but Breck had preferred to take his position on the hillside. Now, stretched out with the cool ground under him and the warm sun on his back, he remembered his great-grandfather Jewett Clegg telling him the story of the French-Eversole War when he was a boy. *He must have felt like this, squnched down behind the gravestones up on the hill, getting ready to pour it on them Eversoles,* Breck thought. He could remember the fierce old man's voice as he cried, "It was like a turkey shoot — like a God-almighty turkey shoot!" *Have to remember to aim low, being up on the hill here. That'll put the lead right through their gizzards, like Gray-gramp said.*

"Hey, Hord, how you feel?" called Troutman softly. He was behind a walnut tree ten feet to the left. He had lowered his shotgun to the ground, and was grinning nervously at Breck.

"I feel all right. How about you?"

"I just wish they'd get here, is all. Feel like we've been waiting for hours."

"Don't reckon it's been more than forty-five minutes since we was in the movie theater."

"Well, it sure as hell feels longer." He was silent a moment, then went on plaintively: "Besides, I got to pee."

"Well, pee," said Breck. "Only just keep behind that tree while you do."

Troutman got to his feet and opened his fly. At that moment a voice from below shouted, "They're coming! There's three cars full!"

*

In Evarts, Aunt Cloa Burkett heard the first shot as she was crossing the street in front of the Holiness Church. She straightened her back and said aloud to herself, "Matthew ten, thirty-four: 'Think not that I am come to send peace on earth: I came not to send peace, but a sword.' "

*

Jim Darling's car slewed wildly and came to a stop, blocking the road. Darling flung the back door open and leaped out. The echo of the single shot still trembled in the air. For a moment nothing moved, nothing breathed. Then five or six shots cracked together from the hill, and simultaneously Darling raised the Thompson to his shoulder and fired a short burst. The submachine gun's yammering was shockingly loud. Its recoil pushed the muzzle upward and to the right, and Darling brought it back down to bear on the hillside and fired a second burst, then a third and fourth.

Behind him the two cars carrying the remaining deputies pulled up side by side and a yard apart, their radiators only a few inches from the lead car, which was crosswise in the road. Together, the three cars formed a U, with the sides of the letter parallel to the road and the bottom facing toward Harlan Town. In the center of the U, the deputies quickly unloaded their guns and ammunition, took what protection they could find, and began to return the strikers' fire. In seconds, the firing from both sides was a continuous drum roll, intensified by raucous spasms of machine-gun fire.

Darling paused to change ammunition drums. His slitted

eyes flickered across the hillside facing him, searching for targets. It was hard to see much to shoot at — a flash, a smoking muzzle, an inch or two of flesh or cloth, glimpsed for a second. He swore in a casual tone that was belied by his concentrated expression. "God damned smoke makes my eyes water," he said Just then he saw something that made him grin like a wolf. "Well, now — you just stay right there. Don't you move, you hear? Stay right like you are, honey. Stay right there, for old Jim." He kept talking to himself, crooning softly as if to a baby, as he carefully moved a few feet to the left. "That's better — that's the way. Now!" He straightened up and raised the Thompson to his shoulder, pressing the trigger before the gun bore on the target and allowing its recoil to bring the sights into alignment. He hammered out ten shots, relaxing his finger only when the gun pointed at the sky. Anxious to see the results of his marksmanship, he stood peering across the hood of the Buick, exposed from the chest up.

A .30 caliber slug with a hollow point entered his forehead, passed through his brain, flattening out in the process, and carried away a large part of the back of his head. Blood and tissue splattered the other deputies crouched among the cars. Emory, standing only a foot away, screamed as a clot of bloody hair slapped him in the face. Darling was killed instantly, but as he lurched backward his finger tightened convulsively on the trigger, and the Thompson sprayed the air.

*

Breck had no way of knowing if it was his bullet that had killed Darling. At the moment he had fired, other guns had fired all around him. But as he glanced at Sam Troutman, he hoped it had been his bullet.

Darling's burst had caught Troutman in the neck and the right shoulder. The bullets had entered his body from the top, and passed downward into the chest cavity, some traveling on as far as his pelvis. The shoulder was splintered; white fragments of bone glittered in a blood pudding of meat and sodden cloth. The force of the bullets had knocked Troutman away from the tree, and he had rolled a foot or two farther. He was lying in the open, still alive.

He tried to pull his knees under him, and pushed against the ground with his left hand, struggling to rise. He didn't understand why he couldn't. He strained like a fat boy trying to do a push-up, his eyes distended, his mouth open. "Breck —" he called weakly, and suddenly vomited blood. "I can't — I can't," he groaned. His muscles relaxed, and he died.

Breck lay looking at Troutman. The deer rifle rested easily and comfortably in his hands. *You surely are dead, Sam,* he thought. *There ain't no point in worrying about you any more. Only way a man can do anything for you now is to pay them fellers back for what they've done.* And, supported by the feudist's memory, which only remembers the outrages of the other side, he settled his cheek against the rifle stock, and moved slightly to one side until he could see around the trunk of the maple tree and superimpose his sights over the cars in the road below.

*

Francis Duffy, neat as a pin, crouched behind the highway maintenance truck. He was holding an old Remington .22 bolt-action single-shot rifle, the only weapon he had been able to find. When Jim Darling suddenly came into view, he fired a quick but inaccurate shot, and simultaneously saw

Darling's head disintegrate. For a thrilling instant he believed it was his shot that had done the damage. "Mary, mother of God, I've killed the bugger!" he cried, the joy in his heart as sharp as any pain he had ever felt.

*

Claiborne had also fired at Darling, from his position behind the pile of railroad ties, and had also missed. He gasped in awe as he saw the deputy die, then levered another cartridge into the breech of his carbine.

Since he had taken control of the meeting in the movie theater, Claiborne had been possessed by euphoria. Never before in his life had he felt so confident, so competent, so important. It had been his decision and his actions that had armed the miners and brought them to their ambush; he was more responsible for the death of Darling than the man who had fired the shot.

He felt physically bigger than he had been — felt that his chest had deepened and held more air than before, that his hands were larger and steadier, his eyes sharper, his muscles tighter. His voice sounded lower to his own ears, and he spoke with a new decisiveness.

He moved from one man to the next, talking to each of the men behind the ties, patting shoulders, joking, and swearing. "You just keep on slipping them bullets in there, buddy. You just keep that good eye of yours peeled, hear? One of them gun-thugs shows his face, you just punch yourself a hole in it. God dog, this is more fun than a cock fight, damned if it ain't! Ain't that right, boy?" Every few moments he interrupted his exhortations to fire a shot or two at the cars in the road.

*

Minutes passed, and the firing continued, unabated. A deputy named George Dawn took possession of Darling's Thompson and dropped a striker with it. Emory believed he had hit at least one man, more probably two, but there were no bodies to confirm his marksmanship. Hondell was blasting away with a double-barreled shotgun, Gill with his pistol, the other deputies with whichever weapons suited them best. The smoke hanging over the road was so thick it sometimes obscured their vision.

Pausing to reload his Smith & Wesson, Emory shouted to Hondell beside him, "How the hell you figure we can get out of this mess?"

"Have to wait till somebody comes down from Black Mountain to help us. Or up from Harlan. We ain't going to shout our way out, that's for sure." Hondell fired both barrels in rapid succession, then broke the piece to reload. He reached for an open box of shotgun shells, moving his body a few inches to one side — then suddenly spun around and sprawled backward as if he had been hit with a club. An expression of startled disbelief crossed his face. The shirt cloth around his deputy's badge darkened. "I — they — " he gasped.

"Hondell! Hey, buddy!" Emory bent over the wounded man. Hondell looked up at him imploringly. His mouth opened as he tried to speak, but only a brief, guttural rasp came out before awareness faded from his eyes. He died less than ten seconds after he was hit.

Emory wasn't a man with an affectionate nature, but in his own way he had been fond of Hondell. The man's death infuriated him. His thick, Cupid's-bow lips thinned and whitened, and his eyes slitted. "All right, you yellow-belly bushwhacking sons of bitches, I'm going to kill your ass! This is the sorriest day's work you ever done, and you're going to wish you never started it before I'm through with you!" Deliberately he emptied his pistol, reloaded it, emptied it again. He moved around the U formed by the three cars, taking advantage of the cover and firing at every possible target. Twice he hit someone. The second time it was a man who had been located behind the piled railroad ties. The man fell to the ground and lay exposed briefly, until another man leaned out and pulled him back to safety.

The other man was Claiborne Hord, and Emory recognized him.

*

The Battle of Evarts had been going on for twenty minutes, and Breck's rifle barrel was hot. Of the ten deputies who had begun the fight, four were dead. Of the sixty or seventy-odd strikers, the only fatality Breck could be sure of was Sam Troutman, whose body contained a number of other bullets in addition to those from Darling's submachine gun.

He was sure of it now: the volume of firing was diminishing — both from the hill around and behind him, and from the road below. *Some of our boys have pulled out,* he thought. *Must be help coming for the gun-thugs. Reckon it's time for a man to leave.*

He looked at Troutman's body pensively. *Poor Sam. How come him to be the one that got killed, instead of me? Because he happened to move at the wrong time, is all. Just as easy could have been my body there. And then, what would I have died for? What in the world would I have died for? To kill me some damn gun-thugs.*

Carefully he squirmed backward, keeping the protecting tree trunk between himself and the cars below, until he was able to substitute another for it. He proceeded in this manner until he was far enough up the hill to be invisible from the road. The shooting was all but over. He got to his feet and began trotting through the trees and thickets, in a direction that would allow him to skirt Evarts to the north.

A man goes out killing people, he ought to have some more reason for it than just not liking them. If he's sober, he should. Killing is an important thing in a man's life. It ought to mean something. He pushed underbrush aside with the stock of Troutman's deer rifle. *I reckon it means something important to Claiborne, the way he took on at the meeting. I ain't never heard him like that before. He stood up and talked as good as any preacher. Maybe none of this would have happened, without Claiborne made that speech.*

He moved through the woods for a half hour, until he could look between the tree trunks and see the tarpaper shantytown where his family lived. He hid the deer rifle under a log, planning to return later to wrap it and bury it. Then he left the protection of the trees and walked quickly across the pasture.

It's going to be a hell of a mess. I just wish it was more important to me, what we done it for.

*

Five carloads of deputies from Harlan Town arrived at the scene, and were joined two minutes later by another four carloads from Black Mountain. By the time they had piled out of their cars and reconnoitered the maintenance truck, the stacked railroad ties, the warehouse across the creek, and the wooded area immediately beside the road, there wasn't an armed miner within a half mile of them.

A deputy named Elzie was in charge of the Harlan Town reinforcements. He was a short man with a bald head, a beer belly, and one blind eye that was milky white. He spoke to Nugent Emory, whom he knew. "You got yourselves bushwhacked. How come Darling didn't haul ass out when the shooting started?"

"Damned if I know," Emory answered. "He told Gill to stop the car, and then jumped out with his chopper. Started spraying the damn hillside. Guess he figured there was only one or two of them up there."

"He found out different soon enough," said Elzie dryly.

"By then it was too late to get out. Them cars was all shot to shit. Look at them." Both men gazed at the three cars that formed the U in the middle of the road. Their tires were flat, their tops shredded and open, their hoods and side panels perforated with hundreds of bullet holes. Broken glass, gasoline, and blood surrounded them. "Wasn't nobody going to drive one of them cars away."

"I reckon not," Elzie agreed. "There must have been a hundred of them redneck bastards shooting at you." He paused and stepped back to let two deputies pass, carrying the body of Jim Darling. When they had maneuvered it onto the back seat of one of the Black Mountain cars, covered it with an army blanket, and gone back for another body, he resumed: "How many can you identify for sure?"

"There was four or five I've seen around, that I could pick out from a line-up. But there's one I know the name of. Hondell and I kicked his ass out of a cabin over in Aleck's Hollow, two months ago. Claiborne Hord, his name is."

"Well, ask the other boys if there's any names they know for sure, will you?"

*

J. C. Stackpool was in Verda, two miles from Evarts, all during the battle. He had been riding in the cab of the truck with one of the deputies, and his wife and small daughter were following in a car with the other deputy, when the sounds of firing had reached them. They had immediately pulled over and stopped.

"There's a hell of a lot of shooting going on up there," said J.C. unnecessarily. "You ain't planning on driving into it, are you?"

"Not so as you would notice it," the deputy replied. "I got to call in and tell them about it in Harlan, though. You wait here." He left the cab in search of a telephone. J.C. sat and listened to the firing, rubbing his chin with his hand. *Somebody's got a machine gun. Sweet Jesus, that's more than a man ought to have to face up to. But I reckon it's the guards is using it. It better be.*

The deputy returned. "I told them down in Harlan. They're sending up a bunch of boys from there, and bringing some more down from Black Mountain. The Harlan boys will be coming through here in ten minutes."

"Ten minutes is a long time being shot at."

The guard shrugged. "There ain't nothing I can do about that. I'm going to get me a cup of coffee." He turned away from the truck, waved to the other deputy in the car behind them, and the two men crossed the street and entered a café.

J.C. remained in the truck a few moments, listening to the distant gunfire. He couldn't sit still. He climbed down and walked back to the car where his wife and child sat waiting. "Listen — them guards want me to get together with them across the street there. You just wait in the car, you hear? We'll be back directly."

"We ain't going up to where the fighting is, are we?" his wife asked, a frightened expression on her round face.

J.C. glared at her. "Just never you mind what we're going to do! Goddamn! I got enough to worry about without you jawing at me all the time — fatty!" He followed the deputies across the street and into the café.

The five police cars from Harlan Town roared through Verda without shifting gears. The sound of firing ceased. The two deputies decided to give it five more minutes, just to be on the safe side, and had another cup of coffee apiece. By then it was getting on toward eleven o'clock.

When they approached Evarts, the three damaged cars had been pushed over to the shoulder of the road, and the dead men were gone. Still, in the presence of fifty edgy guards with guns in their hands, broken glass, spilled gasoline, cordite stink, and tree branches littering the road and hillside, the battle was implicit.

"Who-eee," breathed J.C., as the truck carrying him and his belongings inched past the pile of railroad ties, each tie bristling with the splinters caused by deputies' bullets. "What in the world do you think started this?"

The guard at the wheel answered with a grunt.

When they drove into Evarts, it was as if the town had been deserted for days. Not a person could be seen. They had been wary of possible snipers, but their fears were groundless. The remainder of the trip to Black Mountain was uneventful.

*

Sizemore was at the wheel of a two-year-old Chevrolet coupé, approaching the town of Pineville, Kentucky. His Gladstone bag was on the seat beside him.

His hurried telephone call to District 19 headquarters had resulted in orders to leave Harlan County immediately. A wildcat strike was bad enough, but the UMW had no intention of being in the same county with an ambush of mine guards. Sizemore had been able to collect his belongings, pay his bill at the boarding house, and get his car past the Evarts bridge before Darling's flying squad arrived there.

As yet, he didn't know what had happened in Evarts after he had left — although he would have been willing to make a bet against odds.

What will they think of me, when they find I've pulled up stakes on them? he said to himself, as he had said ten times before in the past few minutes. *What will they think of the union? That's more important. They got to understand — we can't get messed up in something like this. The union is more than just Harlan County. The union is —*

"What?" he cried aloud. He hit the steering wheel with his fist. "What? What? What?"

LATER

Nobody ever knew how many miners were wounded at the Battle of Evarts. Everybody realized that a bullet wound that day would be considered prima-facie evidence of participation in the ambush, so all doctoring was done by the women in the tarpaper shacks. Aunt Cloa Burkett was busy all afternoon. It was five o'clock before she was able to stop by the Hord cabin for a cup of coffee. She sat on the front porch, only the toes of her tiny feet touching the rough floorboards, and stirred the sweetening into her coffee aggressively.

"A fine day's work, I must say," she said. "The Lord only knows how many boys got their selves shot up — I took care of seven myself this afternoon! All told, I wouldn't be surprised if they was twenty or thirty wounded, and eight or ten of them will surely die. Plus poor Sam Troutman. And all to kill four gun-thugs! Why, it's just not worth it!"

Claiborne was sitting on the steps, his back against the four-by-four that supported the roof. "It was that damn machine gun, Aunt Cloa," he said moodily. "A man with a rifle don't have no chance against one of them."

"I'd have thought you'd have knowed that before you started the fool mess," the old woman said tartly.

"Well, we didn't. Last time I seen a machine gun was in nineteen eighteen, and it was a different kind besides. Who'd expect Jim Darling to start shooting one right here in Harlan County?" The excitement that had buoyed Claiborne that morning had drained away, leaving him nervous and depressed.

"You can't blame Claiborne, Aunt Cloa," agreed Joicy. "He did the best he knew how. Everybody did. It was just bad luck about the machine gun."

"In this world there's times when people make their own luck," said the old midwife, taking a sip of her coffee.

"That's a fact," said Jubal Early, sitting on a cane-bottomed chair and massaging his thigh muscles with his bony fingers. "That's a fact. But on the other hand, there's times a man can't win for losing. Days when it ain't hardly worthwhile getting out of bed, there's so much trouble waiting on you. And that's a fact, too."

Breck, standing with his back to the others, looking towards Evarts, spoke for the first time. "That Sizemore, that union man, he up and left — pulled out this morning before the fight. What's that mean, Claiborne?"

"Appears to me it means your brother's the feller holding the bag in the snipe hunt," said Aunt Cloa. "Everybody saw him up there at the movie theater, stirring folks up. Only then, it was that Sizemore who was in charge. But once the shooting started, Sizemore was long gone, and it was Claiborne Hord who was in charge. Which makes a considerable difference."

Claiborne shifted his position, scratching his back against

the timber behind him. "The only way the gun-thugs would know that is if one of our boys was to tell them. I don't reckon that's very likely."

"What if they seen you themselves, during the fighting?"

"Don't see how they could. I was behind a pile of ties the whole time."

"Well, I hope you're right. But it's my experience that the only time folks ever see anything is when it's the thing you don't want them to do." She stirred her coffee, sipped, and added some more sweetening.

"About that union man pulling out," Breck said. "You didn't say what you thought it meant."

"Why, God dog, it means the UMW of A don't care no more about us than a pinch of possum sh——" He stopped himself guiltily, and revised his simile. "Don't care no more than if we was all living in China!"

"You don't reckon Sizemore plans on coming back?"

"Why, no. But that don't mean we got no union. We got our own union, with our own officers — and we got our own strike, whether John L. wants to help or not!"

"You reckon our local could go it alone? Just us here in Harlan County?"

"Don't see as we got any choice. Either we close all the mines down, or we starve to death. You know that. Sizemore said it often enough."

"Sizemore's gone."

"That don't alter cases none. It's still the same as it was. As long as there's coal going north, and five miners for every one job digging it, them operators will pay what they want, and not a penny more. The only way in the world to raise the price of coal is to shut down the whole kit and b'iling!" As he talked, Claiborne's confidence began to return. He rose to his feet and walked briskly to his brother's side.

"And we're going to do it! Ain't no gun-thugs can stop us, little brother! We showed them that this morning!" He hit Breck affectionately on the bicep. "Didn't we? Didn't we show them?"

Breck didn't reply, but Aunt Cloa did. "And you think they're going to let it go at that?" she snapped. "Folks who sow the wind are bound to reap the whirlwind — not that I blame you one tiny bit, you understand!"

*

Wellington's Victory, by Waterloo out of Saucy Lady, looked down from the wall with sad hound's eyes. W. F. Tasker returned the bitch's somber gaze. "You're not the only one feels that way, Vicky," he said aloud. He had a throbbing headache, a nervous tickle in his groin that made him think he had strained himself, and a deep uneasiness caused by the news of the Battle of Evarts. Outside, an armed guard leaned back in his chair, turning the pages of a dog-eared copy of *Film Fun*. The mine was in operation; under the hill twenty-five men were working their five-hour day.

Crazy mad dogs, he thought, unconsciously transferring the canine characteristics of his coon hounds to the striking miners. *Crazy mad dogs, you got to shoot them down before they can bite you, or you're a goner. If they get away with this, there's no telling what they'll do next. Try to take over the whole damn minefield, most likely. Well, this is the time to stop them. There'll never be a better.*

In his mind he reviewed his position in the Fairleigh empire, hoping to foresee the effect of the day's events on his future. *So far, so good.* He had kept the mine open and producing. He had supplied Detroit with the coal they needed. And the economics of the Excelsior mines being what they were, his coal cost the company as little as any coal produced anywhere in the United States. *They just can't ask for anything better than that.* If he could keep the coal flowing north on schedule, he was confident he would have the managership of one of the vast Wallins Creek mines within six months. *If* he could keep the coal flowing north — that was the catch.

But what if they strike me — what if they close me down? What if I can't keep the coal moving to Detroit? He knew enough about the white-haired old tyrant who owned the Fairleigh corporation and the hand-picked staff that exercised his instructions to guess the answer to that: *If I can't, they'll get somebody who can.*

It'll keep moving. By God, it'll keep moving! If I have to hire an armed guard for every drag-ass coal digger in Dead Dog, it'll keep moving!

It was impossible for him to remain seated at his desk for more than a few minutes at a time, because of the irritating tickle that seemed to be seated just above the base of his penis. It felt as if a tiny trembling feather was lodged in his seminal duct. He rose and walked around the room, stamping his feet hard on the floor.

That Goddamned Amy — she can't even get it up for me anymore! Old bag! Makes me work so hard I strain myself! Thinking over the previous night's adultery, he decided he deserved better.

Have to get me some fresh young stuff. I've got too much important work to do to keep knocking myself out this way.

*

In Harlan Town, high sheriff John Henry Blair conferred with Judge D. C. "Baby" Jones. They agreed to send a message to the governor of the state requesting him to order the National Guard into Harlan County, and shortly afterward Blair left the city with more than fifty deputies, to arrest those strikers responsible for the ambush at Evarts.

*

Six deputies came for Claiborne. Each was armed with a pistol, and in addition Nugent Emory carried a riot gun and one of the other men had a shotgun. Emory had chosen the riot gun in hope that he might have the opportunity of using it on Claiborne. He had heard that it made an unbelievable mess of a man at close range.

Blair intended to arrest forty strikers. Six of them had been identified, like Claiborne, by one or another of the deputies who had survived the day's battle. The other thirty-four were known to be "troublemakers."

The plan was to seize the six identified strikers first, and then sweep up the others in a rapid dragnet. The deputies entered the Evarts shantytown simultaneously — six cars roaring up to six specified shacks, the others blocking roads in and out of the area. It was a well-executed operation.

When Emory's car screeched to a halt outside the Hord cabin, Claiborne was sitting at the kitchen table, talking to Joicy, Jubal Early, and Hannah. Bonnie Brae and Phoebe and the children were in the next room; Breck was out trying to exchange Fairleigh scrip for coal oil.

Emory kicked the door open, splintering the door frame. "Just hold it like that," he shouted, his handsome, heavy face twisted with anger and joy. He stepped into the room, and the other deputies pushed in behind him. His riot gun stared at Claiborne with its cold, round eye. "Just hold it there, or I'll splatter you over the wall!"

Claiborne rose slowly from the table, with his hands held open in front of him. His mother, his father, and his wife also rose. "Why, what in the world have you done to that door?" asked Jubal Early. Nobody took any notice of the question. Claiborne looked unwinkingly at Emory, his thin face as edged as an ax head.

"I seen you before," Claiborne said. "At Aleck's Hollow. Before our cabin burnt down."

"You seen me since then. You seen me this morning, you bushwhacking bastard." He pushed the muzzle of the riot gun at Claiborne's face. Claiborne jerked his head aside, and the metal scraped his cheek. "You shot my buddy, and you're going to hang for it, you hear?"

"I don't know what you're talking about."

"Hell you don't. I seen you there. I seen you behind them ties, and that's going to put a rope around your neck, and stretch it like a damn chicken."

Claiborne didn't answer, but Joicy did. "Mister, you're wrong about that. He wasn't out nowhere this morning. He was right here with us — he's been here all day."

Emory flicked his glance at her and grinned mockingly. "That's all right, Big Tits — you can tell the judge all about it in court. Give Baby Jones a feel, maybe he'll even believe you."

"Come on, Emory, let's get a move on," said one of the other deputies nervously. "Let's get him in the car and get out of here."

"Now, just hold your horses a minute," Jubal Early said. "Joicy told you the God's truth. Claiborne was here all morning long. Why, hell, I seen him here myself. My wife seen him. The children seen him — didn't you, honey?" He shot a questioning glance at the five children crowded behind Bonnie Brae in the bedroom doorway, and they all nodded in grave agreement. "See? They all seen him too. So I reckon you all are mistook. You got no call to take my boy away."

Emory didn't look at Jubal Early as he was speaking, and didn't answer him when he was through. "Come on, Hord," he said flatly. "Let's go."

Claiborne looked at Joicy. "Take care, hon. And don't fret yourself. I'll be out before you know it." He added a farewell word to his mother and father, and gave a crooked smile to his sister and sister-in-law. The deputies opened a path for him, and he passed between them and out to the waiting car, with Emory behind him pointing the riot gun at his head.

It was full dark before Breck got back. He had been unsuccessful in his search for coal oil. Bonnie Brae met him on the porch and told him of Claiborne's arrest, while the children watched, big-eyed and silent, from the doorway. "I reckon it'll go hard on him, him being an officer in the union, and all," she concluded.

"I reckon," Breck agreed soberly. "And being recognized by a gun-thug on top of it — it could turn out real bad for him. Did they say anything about me, Bonnie Brae?"

"No, not a word. I guess because you never messed yourself up too much in the union." She peered at his face in the darkness. "Thank the Lord for that. When I seen them take Claiborne away, all I could think of was, thank the Lord Breck ain't never messed himself up in the union. There but for the grace of God is what I thought."

Breck cleared his throat as though he were going to say something, and then thought better of it. From the door Claiborne's eldest son, Jewett, spoke: "Uncle Breck, how come they took papa away?"

"Well, I'll tell you, Jewett — I think there was two reasons for it," answered Breck. "First off, it's because of the union. Your daddy was a big man in the union, and them gun-thugs, they hate and despise union men. They just can't wait to put them in jail." He was silent for a few moments, and Jewett grew impatient.

"What's the other reason?"

"Why, because of his blood, son. He's got Hord blood, and no Hord's going to let thieves and gunmen and bloodsuckers push him around like he didn't amount to nothing. Here's something for you young'uns to remember" — Breck's voice grated harshly in the darkness — "Hords don't take to pushing around. They'd as lief die."

Bonnie Brae said, in a carefully neutral voice, "I declare, it's gotten downright cold since the sun went down. I'm going inside — you coming, Breck?"

*

In the Black Mountain camp, J. C. Stackpool and his wife prepared to retire for their first night in their new home. J.C. was too keyed up to sleep, even though he knew he had a trying day ahead of him in an unfamiliar job.

"Goddamn, that sure must have been some fight in Evarts today," he said, sitting on the edge of the bed. "Wished I could have been there. I'd have killed me some of them rednecks, you can bet on that!" His wife mumbled something. "Silly bastards let themselves get bushwhacked," he went on. "Can you imagine them being so damnfool stupid as that? I'd never have got myself into a spot like that. What's a man got eyes for if he don't use them? You ever hear of anything as stupid?" When his wife didn't answer, he poked her, and she mumbled again. "Well, this is a right nice house, I must say," he said chattily. "Sure beats hell out of anything in Dead Yellow Dog, you got to admit that. Except Tasker's house, that is. Bet you never expected to end up in a house as good as this, did you? Six rooms, and a bathroom upstairs, and all the hot water you can use? And a garage out back? That old bitch of a mother of yours, she'd drop her teeth out if she could see this place, you know that? Wouldn't she?" He waited for an answer, but none was forthcoming. "You bet she would. She'd have to admit that J. C. Stackpool wasn't just something the cat drug in." He sat silent a moment, casting around in his mind for another topic of conversation. Then, remembering the day in store for him, he sighed and climbed under the covers. His wife was snoring gently, sleeping on her side with her back toward him. He slipped an arm around her, cupping his palm over her swollen breast. *Too damn nervous to go to sleep,* he thought. *Maybe I can get my rocks off without waking her up.*

And as he pulled up her nightdress and maneuvered himself against her buttocks, he thought incongruously, *That Breck Hord — I wonder if he was out there in Evarts today? That was some old boy.*

Chapter 8

Rogoff

MIKE ROGOFF awoke in darkness. It was a little after 3:00 A.M. Outside, the night sounds of the Near North Side were subdued — the distant screech of an all-night street car, the rumble of a truck crossing a bridge over the river, the footsteps of an after-hours reveler tapping an unsteady tattoo. Rogoff lay in his bed, eyes open and staring at the invisible ceiling, wondering what had awakened him. Two or three minutes passed before he realized the answer.

It was the fear of death.

Rogoff had always thought he was famliar with the idea of death — familiar enough to be, if not comfortable with it, at least unfrightened by it. He had attended several funerals, and was aware of the deaths of a fair number of his friends and acquaintances. He had seen movies about death, and read books about death, and, as a younger man, participated in long philosophical conversations about death. But until this hour, he hadn't actually faced the idea of death at all.

What does it feel like not to exist? For me — Mike Rogoff — not to exist? While other people are going on with their lives like everything is normal? An adrenalin chill tingled through his body, and he was aware of the weightiness of his arms and legs on the mattress. *No — that's foolish; nobody can feel anything if he doesn't exist.*

Then how does it feel not to feel?

He squirmed; his skin felt as if something that had no physical substance were crawling over his body. *How does it feel not to feel?* His mind articulated the nonsense line word by word, and over and over: *How does it feel not to feel?*

He got out of bed and fumbled in the darkness for the lamp, found it, turned it on. The forty-watt bulb flushed the room with weak yellow light that was still bright enough to make him squint his eyes against it. *What is this? What's happening to me? Am I afraid of the dark?* he asked himself. He rolled himself a Bull Durham cigarette and lit it, then raised the window shade and stood by the window, looking out into the air shaft. There was absolutely nothing to see.

Think about something else. Think about the Party. Think about what you believe in, about what you've lived for. Think about dialectical materialism. Think about the dictatorship of the proletariat.

How does it feel not to feel?

Rogoff swore and crushed out his cigarette. "Might as well read something," he said aloud. He picked up Veblen and flipped through the pages until he found his place, then sat down in the frayed armchair and crossed his legs. It was no good, he couldn't follow the argument for a paragraph at a time. He put the book aside and stood up again. "Hell, if I can't sleep and can't read, I might as well go out for a walk," he said. He reached for his shirt, then stopped, staring out the window into the air shaft again.

I can't go out there! I'm afraid! I'm afraid to go out into the night, God help me! Incredulously, he faced a fear he had never known existed. *I'm afraid to go out, because I'm afraid of death! I'm afraid of finding out how it feels not to feel!*

In an agony of terror and self-disgust, Mike Rogoff sat in

his room until the darkness in the air shaft turned gray. Only then did he lie back down on his bed and go to sleep.

*

Mike Rogoff was twenty-eight years old, short and stocky, with bandy legs and a long Semitic face. His body was very hairy, and his pores were large. His eyes were a chocolate brown, soft and liquid, with slightly dingy whites. They were his most attractive feature; when people looked into them, they tended to believe what he said. He had a lively intelligence, with a particular flair for analytical problem-solving. If his father hadn't worked in a sweatshop all his life for ten dollars a week, Mike Rogoff might have become a mathematician. As it was, he was an organizer for the Communist Party.

It was nearly ten o'clock when he awoke and dressed. He was due at Party headquarters sometime before noon, so he had plenty of time for breakfast and a stroll around the Loop. He left the rooming house and walked briskly toward Clark Street, where there was a Thompson's Restaurant. The sky was overcast, and there was a biting wind off the lake. It was a cold day for May, and he was thankful for his heavy suit. Shabby though it was, there were plenty of men along Clark Street who would have traded him for it.

He turned into Thompson's and hesitated a moment just inside the door. He liked to try to sort out the various smells that combined to create the unique olfactory experience of a skid-row cafeteria. Sniffing deeply and smiling, he identified: coffee, onions, bacon, steam heat, dirty socks, tobacco, whiskey, male sweat, stale grease, cabbage, and spiced fruit—and, underlying them all, the smell of a musty old building with inadequate plumbing. It was strangely comforting, considering some of its ingredients.

He took a tray, knife, fork, spoon, and a paper napkin, and waited in line until it was his turn to order. Then he asked for a hamburger steak, fried potatoes, string beans, and bread and butter. "And gravy on the meat and potatoes both, O.K.?" When the counterman handed him his plate, he put it on his tray and moved along toward the cash register, pausing to pick up a small dish of Jell-O and a thick-bottomed mug of creamed coffee. His total check came to fifty-two cents. Walking past occupied tables, looking for an empty one he wouldn't have to share, he was conscious of the eyes of hungry men on his food. *I suppose I shouldn't have bought so much — but, goddamnit, I had an awful night last night. Besides, wherever I'll be headed tomorrow, the odds are I won't be eating too good.*

He stopped at an unoccupied table for two, pushed some dirty dishes to one side, unloaded his food, and sat down. Almost immediately a busboy appeared beside him and began to pile the dirty dishes into a cart. Actually, "busboy" was a misnomer; he was a seventy-five-year-old man with bleary eyes, and the smell of him hit Rogoff like a clenched fist. He leaned away and held his breath until the old man finished wiping the tabletop with a filthy washcloth and shuffled away. Then he began to eat — but the edge was off his appetite.

*

Rogoff walked down Clark Street and crossed the Chicago River, then cut over to State Street. He paused outside each of the ornate motion-picture palaces to look at still photos of the actors and actresses, then crossed the street to window-shop at Marshall Field and Carson, Pirie, Scott. It was pleasant walking; the sun broke through the overcast, and the Loop skyscrapers baffled the onshore wind.

The stores cheapened as he went south. By the time he reached Van Buren, where State Street left the noisy embrace of the Elevated tracks and proceeded in relative quiet toward the Black Belt, the smart store windows had given way to tattoo parlors, penny arcades, hock shops, and small, dark, unhealthy cafés.

He turned west and walked along Van Buren, along a sidewalk crowded with whores, thieves, and derelicts. The iron wheels of the El shrieked above his head, and the sunlight filtering through the tracks cast bars of light and shadow on the street beneath. Every pair of eyes that met his were predatory; nobody who wasn't on the make bothered to look at anybody else.

We'll get rid of this, he thought. *This greed, this squalor, this abortion of hope — we'll splash it out on the ground like a dishpanful of dirty water! This* lumpenproletariat! *There's no place for it in the future of the human race!*

Like a tree surgeon, he accepted the need of pruning a sick tree to strengthen its grip on life.

At Wells Street the Elevated tracks turned north, and so did he. This was the street of sweatshops. His father had worked here, on the second floor of a building on Wells near Madison — twelve hours a day in front of a machine, in a vast, ill-lit room with two hundred other Jews, with the trains roaring by outside the soot-filmed windows. As a boy, Mike had sometimes ridden past the building in an El car, peering at the opaque glass, hoping for a glimpse of his father at work. But he never saw him — the windows were never clean enough.

Party headquarters was only a few doors from that sweatshop. Rogoff turned into a dark, dirty lobby, walked past an open cage elevator with an out-of-order sign on it and up two flights of stairs with red rubber treads. On the third floor, he passed four office doors and stopped at the fifth, which bore a number but no name. He opened the door and entered a tiny anteroom with a single wooden armchair. Another door on the far wall was ajar, and beyond it he could hear the sound of unprofessional typing. Closing the hall door behind him, he rapped his knuckles on the inner door.

"Mike Rogoff," he said. "Can I come in?"

"Come," said a man's voice, and Rogoff pushed the door open.

A man in shirtsleeves sat before an upright typewriter in an office hardly larger than the anteroom. He wore a blue denim work shirt, open at the neck, and dress trousers; his suit coat hung on a hanger on the door. His face was unmemorable; a pale complexion, thin colorless hair carelessly brushed, small hazel eyes, bad teeth kept hidden behind pursed lips. Deep creases ran down both sides of his mouth, and the skin on his neck was crepy. He gestured to a second chair and said, "Come in. Sit down." Rogoff sat down, the other man pushed the door closed, resumed his seat, and for a few moments they inspected each other frankly.

"Comrade, exactly how much mining experience have you had?" asked the man at the desk, known as Brown.

"You mean organizing, or working in the mines?"

"Organizing."

Rogoff paused to think. "I spent six months in Pennsylvania for the NMU in twenty-nine — four months in the anthracite fields, two months in Pittsburgh doing paperwork. Then when Foster decided to open up the Kanawha Valley, I went down to West Virginia for three months. But that didn't pan out. Say nine months, all told."

Brown looked at him expressionlessly. "In the valley, how'd you get along with the hill people?"

"All right — I get along with most people all right."

"No prejudice — no anti-Semitism?"

"Not to speak of. I've never found hillbillies anti-Semitic." He noticed Brown's mouth twist in irritation at the word "hillbillies," and once again was surprised at the emotional reaction many of the comrades had to minority epithets. In the West Side ghetto where he had grown up, boys were often in their teens before they discovered that "Italian" was a two-bit word for "Dago." Words used so commonly can't keep from cooling off after a while. It was strange that many Party intellectuals couldn't see that. "It's rare to find much race or religious prejudice among Appalachian whites," he said carefully.

Brown gave a curt nod. "All right. Now, tell me this. Have you ever been to Harlan?"

"Harlem?"

"No, not Harlem — *Harlan,* H-A-R-L-A-N."

"Not only have I never been there, I've never even heard of it."

"It's the name of a town and a county in southeastern Kentucky, right on the Virginia line. The only industry is coal mining — bituminous coal — and there are ten thousand miners in the county. Eight thousand of them are on strike, and, at this point, they have no union to represent them."

"What about the United Mine Workers? I thought they had the mountains wrapped up."

"Not so," said Brown pedantically. "They gave out a local charter a few years ago, but never really built the local up. When the Harlan miners voted to call a strike in March, the UMW wouldn't authorize it. The men went ahead anyway, so the national organization declared it a wildcat. Since then, it's been an uphill fight, with no help at all from the UMW.

Now, after what happened in Evarts, they've pulled completely out of the county."

"Evarts?" asked Rogoff.

"We'll get to that in a minute. First I want you to understand a little background. Now, as you may remember, the National Miners' Union was founded by Bill Foster in the late twenties. It was part of the Trade Union Unity League, which means it was ideologically sound, but except for a little strength in Pennsylvania, where you worked, it never got started. The UMW had its nose too deep in the trough. The rank-and-file miner was slow to develop his social consciousness — in rural districts, the tradition of individualism has deep roots."

"It does seem to hang on," said Rogoff.

"Yes — well, three things have happened that could change that. First, John L. Lewis has an internal fight on his hands with the Farrington people in Illinois. Last year they had two different conventions — District Twelve boycotted the regular convention, and held their own in Springfield. From where we sit, it looks like the UMW is shaking itself to pieces." Brown picked up a rubber band from his desk and began to loop it around his thin white fingers. "That's the first thing. The second is this: A few weeks ago a man named Duncan, a former UMW organizer in Harlan County, wrote a letter to the *Daily Worker,* requesting an NMU organizer for the Harlan coalfields."

"I don't believe it," said Rogoff incautiously.

Brown looked at him speculatively, as if he were weighing new evidence about him. "I can't help what you believe, Comrade," he said evenly, "the letter appeared in the *Worker.* I read it. So would you, if you were conscientious about keeping up with the news of the class struggle." He hesitated, to allow Rogoff to offer an excuse. *I'll be damned if I will,* Rogoff thought, and continued to look expectantly at Brown.

Brown's eyes narrowed, and after a moment he continued. "At any rate, whether it seems incredible to you or not, this Duncan wrote asking for help. According to him — and other evidence confirms it — the majority of striking miners in Harlan County feel they've been deserted by the UMW, and would welcome the NMU and what it stands for. The Party leadership feels this is an important fact. It's something to build on."

"I agree," said Rogoff. *If true, I agree,* he amplified to himself.

"All right. That brings us to the third thing. Yesterday there was a violent gun battle in Harlan County, at a little town called Evarts. There's been very little about it in the labor press, and the AP and UP stories are typically unreliable, but apparently ten or so armed mine guards were ambushed by a much larger number of striking miners, and at least four of the guards were killed. There are no figures on the losses to the miners, but obviously there must be a good number. Since then, the mine guards — who are mostly deputy sheriffs, incidentally — have been making mass arrests, and the governor has ordered the National Guard in."

"It sounds like the whole county's ready to go up for grabs," said Rogoff, leaning forward in his chair.

"The leadership feels the situation has great potential, yes. For the time being, the UMW has ceased to be a factor. The bourgeois labor-fakers are out of the picture, and the conflict has polarized. But it won't stay this way forever. We've got to move in fast."

"How many of our people are going in?"

Brown looked at Rogoff speculatively, as if debating with

himself whether or not the other could be trusted with this information. After a moment he said carefully, "You, Rasmusson, and, I think, Coy, for the NMU. Jennie Markwell for ILD. Ike Silver for the Labor Syndicate. Liz Craig for Family Relief. There'll be others, but that's the core group."

"Fine. How about contacts down there?"

Brown pulled out the center drawer of the scarred pine desk and produced a sheet of yellow paper. "Here's a list of the officers of the local, plus some others who have showed leadership ability. The ones that are starred are the ones we think may be politically aware." Rogoff glanced at the list and then tucked it into his breast pocket. "I don't have to tell you that list is to be used with discretion," Brown said. Rogoff nodded. He frowned in concentration, taking the tip of his long nose between his thumb and forefinger, and bending it from side to side.

"All right," he said after a moment. "How about money?"

"I can let you have two hundred dollars. Next month I can wire you more, but right now we don't have it to spare. You'll just have to make do."

Rogoff grimaced. "Great. Just like always. Next, what about reporting? Do I report back to NMU in Pittsburgh?"

"You do not. You report to this office."

"Isn't that a little unusual?"

Brown shrugged his shoulders. "It's an administrative thing. The Pittsburgh people report to Pittsburgh, Liz Craig and Ike Silver report to New York, you report here. No problem."

No problem, hell, Rogoff thought. *We could get screwed up six ways from Sunday, is how much of a problem it isn't. Just because you want to keep your nose in, Comrade Schmuck!* "All right. Last thing. When do I leave?"

Brown flipped the rubber band off his fingers and put it carefully back into a glass dish on his desk. "Now," he said.

*

Rogoff was able to arrange a ride with a sympathetic truck driver as far as Louisville. From there he hitchhiked to Lexington, covering the eighty miles in three different cars. He had never been in the Bluegrass before and viewed the lush, rolling pastures, the immaculate white fences, and brightly painted barns with wry disbelief. *Land like this, and it's for horses?* he thought. *People should have it as good.*

From Lexington he traveled southeast toward the mountains — first to Richmond and Berea, then past a series of crossroad villages named McKee and Tyner and Egypt and Burning Spring, to Hyden. Hyden was in Leslie County, just across Pine Mountain from Harlan. There weren't many cars in Leslie County — at least not many running — so Rogoff walked most of the last fifteen miles. It was evening when he got to Harlan, and he was bone-tired and hungry as a wolf. He decided to put himself up for one night at the Lewallen Hotel.

Chapter 9

Red Is the Color of Hope

WITHIN THREE DAYS of the Battle of Evarts all the members of the core group had arrived in Harlan County. They held their first meeting in the cinderblock meeting hall of a veterans' organization local in Evarts. Present, in addition to Michael Rogoff, were:

Charlie Rasmusson, organizer for the National Miners' Union. Rasmusson, a big, rock-hard man with the face of a boxer who had fought too often, was a product of the Western Federation of Miners and the IWW. He was a rarity — a homegrown radical, educated in the Wobblies' free speech fights on the West Coast, jailed in 1918 for resisting the draft, a friend of Big Bill Haywood and Frank Little, who nevertheless moved to the American Communist Party in the late twenties. The change had cost him most of his old friendships, and he hadn't made many new ones.

Beside him sat Wayne Coy, also of the National Miners' Union. Coy was just thirty, almost ten years younger than Rasmusson, and two years older than Rogoff. He was slight and wiry, with the narrow face, high cheekbones, and long upper lip of the mountaineer. He had joined the Party while he was a miner in the Kanawha Valley, and since then had worked exclusively in the coalfields. Behind a countrified manner, Coy concealed an alert intelligence and a committed will.

Ike Silver, correspondent for the International Labor News Syndicate, sat beside Coy and drew geometrical shapes on a pad of paper. Silver was a graduate of the College of the City of New York, a failed poet and Greenwich Village intellectual who had reached such a depth of disgust with his own individuality that he had repudiated the whole concept of individualism by becoming a Communist. More than anything else about the Party, he valued the discipline. A slight, nervous man with rebellious black hair and a bad skin, he resembled the typical cartoonist stereotype of the radical more than any of the others in the room.

The other two members of the core group were women. Jennie Markwell of International Legal Defense was the best-known person present. Her square, stubborn face was familiar to every reader of the *Daily Worker,* and to many *Time* and *Literary Digest* subscribers as well. She had represented ILD at most of the important strikes since 1925, serving as legal catalyst, recruiting local lawyers to represent jailed strikers, and publicizing their efforts. Her sharp tongue, combined with a brilliant eye for propaganda opportunities, had resulted in the nom de guerre bestowed on her by some unremembered prosecutor, Pinkerton agent, or reporter: "The Mouth."

Elizabeth Maitland Craig of Labor Family Relief closed the circle around the table. Liz Craig had been a rebel since she seduced her high-school French teacher at the age of fifteen, but she had only channeled her rebelliousness into the class struggle when Sacco and Vanzetti were executed. Since joining the Party, she had worked with unquestioning obedience at any task assigned her, but her Bohemian morality was held against her by some of the more puritanical among the leadership. She owed her presence at the table not so much to her revolutionary zeal as to the two million dollars her grandfather had left in trust for her, against the advice of everyone else in the family.

Rogoff had been Liz's lover for a week in 1930, but he was much closer to her than that: he was her friend. He was delighted to see her sharp-chinned, large-eyed, and slightly worn-looking face across the table. Catching her eye, he gave her a wink, and she grinned back raffishly.

Charlie Rasmusson was speaking. "It breaks down to the same three things, just like it always does — organization, legal defense, and publicity. The NMU will handle organization —"

"Haven't you forgotten something, Charlie?" Liz interrupted brightly. "There's the little question of family relief, too."

Rasmusson looked embarrassed. "Yes, that's right, Liz — there's family relief, too. Of course. That'll be your problem. Publicity is Ike — is there anything you'll want from us, Ike?"

"Just don't talk to those scissorbills from the kept press," Silver answered. He spoke in a high-pitched voice, but so softly the others automatically leaned toward him. "Any information they print on the NMU, I want them to get it from the Syndicate. We're news down here right now, don't forget. The Evarts thing made every big paper in the country, and the governor ordering in the Guard helped it along. Harlan's full of reporters — AP, UP, INS, the *Courier-Journal,* the Lexington and Chattanooga papers, God knows what else. When they spot you — particularly you, Jennie, and you too, Liz — they'll be after you with their tongues out. But don't give them the time of day. I'll handle whatever press handouts there are."

"I expect we'll have some stuff for you on NMU recruiting in a week, Ike," said Rasmusson. "We want a kickoff meeting as soon as possible, but we've got to lay some ground work first."

"About that first meeting, Charlie," Liz said. "Why couldn't we make it for miners *and* their wives? Get the women in right at the beginning, get some of them up on the platform, form a wives' committee, give out statements about the wives' grievances, really milk them. You know how the women can screw you if they're not behind you all the way. Why not get them tied in right at the start?"

"Hey, you know that's a right good idea," said Wayne Coy. "I've seen some of these little old gals down here twist a jack rabbit's tail and make him think he was a bobcat."

"Make a good story," agreed Ike Silver. "Don't mention it to anybody."

"Jennie, how about it?" asked Charlie with a touch of deference.

In private, Jennie Markwell was as laconic as she was verbose in public. "Good," she said.

Rasmusson glanced at Rogoff. "I like it," Rogoff said, smiling.

"Okay, that's what we'll do." Rasmusson made a note. "What else?"

"What about literature?" Silver asked. "With this *lumpenproletariat* here, the social consciousness is about zero minus. We need pamphlets, songbooks, posters, the whole schmeer. You want me to ask the Syndicate to send us a shipment?"

"Might as well — it doesn't make any difference who sends it, as long as somebody does," Rasmusson said. "Only don't have it sent to Harlan County. Make it Manchester or Corbin, and we'll have it picked up there."

Rogoff was frowning. He pulled at an ear lobe, started to speak, stopped, then started again. "About the literature — I think you better remind them in New York that the people who'll be reading it are Kentucky mountaineers."

"What's your point, Mike?" asked Rasmusson.

"Well, these people are different. They may not be socially conscious, but I wouldn't call them a *lumpenproletariat,* either. I think somebody should be pretty careful about screening the literature that goes out to them."

"What particularly is it you want to protect them from?" Ike Silver asked in an edged voice.

"Well, you know that all our stuff is written for workers who can accept the idea that class interests are more important than their own individualism. These people here aren't ready for that, and I don't think we can change their attitude overnight. Hell, they're all feudists at heart! They'd rather shoot their next-door neighbor than the employer who's screwing them blind!"

"And your point is that we should leave them that way, is that right? They're rugged individualists, so we should throw Marx and Engels into the trashbasket, and give them Hatfield and McCoy instead? It's too bad the Party leaders are so stupid they didn't realize that!" Silver was sitting up straight for the first time that afternoon, and his lips were white with anger.

"Oh, hell, I didn't say anybody was stupid, Ike. Some groups have more revolutionary potential than others, that's all I meant." Rogoff moved his left hand in a circle, as if trying to change the axis of his argument.

"Silver's right, Mike," Rasmusson said evenly. "Because people haven't got a class consciousness is no reason they shouldn't be educated to develop one. It's the other way around. There's *more* reason why they should get the same treatment as other workers who are more sophisticated. Obviously." He wrinkled his brow questioningly. "I still don't get your point."

"What makes you think he's got a point?" asked Silver.

"All right, what I guess I mean is the antireligious stuff. The wanted poster for Jesus, and all that. I don't think it's right for down here." Rogoff looked around the room for a face that showed sympathy for his position, but found none: Jennie Markwell's expression registered disapproval, Wayne Coy's an amused lack of interest, Liz Craig's perplexity, Ike Silver's rage, Rasmusson's judicious disagreement. Rogoff went on doggedly, with the foreknowledge of defeat: "Atheism is always a tricky issue — sometimes it can backfire, you know that. With Catholics, for instance —"

"These people aren't Catholics."

"I know that, Charlie, but in a way I think they're worse. They're Fundamentalists; they believe every single word in the Bible is straight out of God's mouth. When you're dealing with people like that, you damn well better walk carefully on their prejudices."

" 'Religion is the opiate of the people' — or did I just imagine I head that somewhere?" Silver said excitedly. "Is this the new Party line? Religion is reactionary, except religion in hillbilly Kentucky? If we're making exceptions, why not Chicago, too? You want to go back to Hebrew school, *boychik?* Read the Torah instead of the *Worker?* Let your curls grow? Marry a Rebecca who keeps a kosher kitchen? Go into business with your father-in-law —"

"Ike, shut up!" Rasmusson commanded. Silver stopped in midsentence, cutting off the exhilaration of his rage for the calming satisfaction of obedience to authority. The old Wobbly sat in silence a moment, rubbing the back of one knobby hand with the harsh palm of the other. "Look, Mike," he said almost diffidently, "you know the Party's position on religion. It's part of what we're fighting against. We have to show the workers that the church is their enemy, just as much as the bourgeoisie is. It's a crutch for capitalism, and we have to kick it out from under the bastards — you know that."

Rogoff looked at the tabletop in front of him. "I know, I know," he said. "But sometimes —" He raised his head and looked at Wayne Coy. "Do you see what I mean, Wayne? You're mountain-born — do you think we ought to use this antichurch stuff?"

Coy smiled reflectively. His voice was as relaxed as if he were exchanging pleasantries with a friend, but his eyes were hard. "Why, Lordy, I've knowed churchy people since I was yeah-high to a tad. I got nothing against them — except somehow or other, whatever the bosses want always seems to work out to be what they want, too! 'Long-haired preachers come out every night, try to tell you what's wrong and what's right.' There was plenty of them in the Kanawha Valley, but when we needed them, it was like what Joe Hill said — all they had to tell you was, you'll get pie in the sky when you die!" He looked from one to another of the men and women in the room. "Hell, I hate the goddamned church like a snake! If it was me, I'd hand out our booklets to every man, woman and child in Harlan County!"

With the only native mountain man in the group against him, Rogoff knew it was futile to argue any longer. He raised his shoulders and turned his palms upward. "All right, already — so take yes for an answer!" he said in an exaggerated Maxwell Street accent. "Forgive me for living! Now can we please get on with the meeting?"

Rasmusson cleared his throat and moved his notes around, and the tension in the room eased. The discussion moved to legal action and family relief, with Jennie and Liz taking suggestions and criticism from the others. After twenty minutes of this, the beginnings of a systematic plan had emerged.

"I guess that's all we can get decided for now," Rasmusson said. "But before we leave, there's one more thing I want to say: Be careful." He looked at each of the group in turn, his lopsided face grave. "I mean that. Be careful. These people down here don't think any more of killing you than a Chicago cop would think about poking you with a nightstick. There'll be martyrs enough without any of us getting shot before we even get things organized."

"You think they'll try to get us while the Guard is still here?" asked Rogoff.

"They might – though I'd guess not. But the Guard won't stay here forever. And once they pull out, it's Katie bar the door. Jesus, this county is the nearest thing to a police state in America. The operators own it, and Blair and Judge Jones run it for them, with the help of two hundred or so licensed killers. Now they're mad, and they're scared, and they know nobody's going to hold them accountable for anything they do to us, once the troops are gone."

"The world will hold them accountable," Ike Silver said. "When the world hears the truth, the world will judge them. The people will judge them."

"What I'm telling you is that the world may not hear the truth for a while, if you get yourself shot," Rasmusson said with irritation. "Listen, I'm not kidding. We've got until the troops leave to surround ourselves with rank-and-file militants. We've got to work behind a human wall – make sure we're never alone, never outside of calling distance from plenty of comrades we can trust — or Blair's gun-thugs will get us within the first twenty-four hours after the Guard goes!"

"And once them boys get you alone, there's just three things can happen," said Wayne Coy, with the wisdom he had gained in the Kanawha Valley. "They work you over and put you in jail, or they work you over and put you across the state line, or — they kill you."

"That's right," said Rasmusson. "And one slip-up is all it takes."

"How long till the Guard leaves? Do we have any word on that?" asked Jennie Markwell.

"No word. It depends on too many things. It could be any time between two weeks and two months. So we have time — if we use it."

After the others left, Rasmusson, Coy, and Rogoff divided the county into three districts, for organizational purposes. Rasmusson took the camps along Martin's Fork and Crummies Creek, south of the town of Harlan; Coy took Wallins Creek, and everything west of the town; Rogoff took what was left: the large mines along Clover Fork and the small ones on Poor Fork. "That means basically I'll be operating out of Cawood; Wayne will be in Wallins Creek; Rogoff will work from here in Evarts. Is that all right with you guys?"

Coy nodded. "Why not?" Rogoff said cheerfully. "I can't tell one coal mine from another without a program, anyway."

*

One of the names Rogoff had been given in Chicago was Claiborne Hord. Brown had starred it, so Rogoff started looking for Claiborne right away. When he found the Hords' shack, Jubal Early was sitting on the front porch, leaning his chair back against the side of the house at such an angle that Rogoff could see the worn blue cloth of his overalls through the broken seat.

"Hi, there," Rogoff called. "Could you tell me where I can find Claiborne Hord?"

Jubal Early looked at him with alert, wary eyes. "I reckon I could — but who might you be, mister?"

"My name's Rogoff. I'm from Chicago. Some people there gave me Mr. Hord's name. I have to see him about business."

"Union business? From Chicago?" Jubal Early was so interested he leaned forward in his chair, causing its two front legs to descend to the floor with a bang. "Are you saying that people in Chicago know who Claiborne Hord is?"

"I'm not saying anything. Look, I don't want to be rude, but the only person I want to talk to is Mr. Hord. Can you tell me where he is, or how I can find him?"

"Best way to find him is get yourself arrested by John Henry Blair. Claiborne's in the Harlan County jail."

The door opened and Breck stepped out onto the porch. Phoebe and Bonnie Brae stood behind him in the doorway.

"Was he one of the men Blair arrested right after the Evarts fight?" Rogoff asked.

"They come for him the same day. There was six of them — they knowed it don't pay to go up against a Hord unless you got him outnumbered to Hell and gone," Jubal Early said proudly.

"Pa," Breck said in a quiet but commanding voice. "You going to tell this feller our whole family history?"

"Why, no — but there ain't no law says you can't be civil to a man when he asks you a question!" Jubal Early looked at his son with an aggrieved expression. Rogoff looked at him too, and Breck returned the organizer's look. Rogoff noticed the broad brow under its shock of dark hair and the direct gaze, neither aggressive nor overcautious. Breck noticed dark eyes that appeared to shine with sincerity and belief, and a long, thin mouth that twisted down slightly at both ends, as if to mock the intensity of the eyes. Both men liked what they saw.

"My name's Breck Hord. Claiborne Hord's my brother. This here is our pa."

"Pleased to meet you. I'm Mike Rogoff." He shook hands with Breck, and then with Jubal Early, and nodded courteously to the two women in the doorway. "I'm sorry your brother's in jail. In a way, that's why I'm down here. And you're right, Mr. Hord," he said with a glance at Jubal Early, "it is about union business. Is there a place where we can talk for a few minutes?"

"Come on into the kitchen," Breck said, stepping to one side of the door so Rogoff could precede him into the house. The organizer entered, passing close to the two women. He smiled at Bonnie Brae, registering and immediately dismissing her worn, blond prettiness. His eyes moved to Phoebe's face. She looked back at him with a kind of timid defiance, as though she knew he brought mortal trouble with him yet would rather chance it than show her fear. Her pretty mouth was slightly open, and the thinness of her face made her dark eyes seem even larger than they were.

Hey, this is somebody! Rogoff thought. He sat down at the rickety kitchen table and then turned to look at her again, just as she walked across the room to the stove. Rogoff felt a pang of sorrow as he noticed her limp, and the withered leg that caused it. *Jesus, tough,* he thought, and then moved her to the back of his mind.

Breck and Jubal Early sat down, and Breck said abruptly,

"What is this here union business you want to talk about? Is the UMW figuring to come back to Harlan County?"

"The union business I want to talk about doesn't have anything to do with the UMW. What I want to talk about is the NMU."

"The what?" asked Breck, wrinkling his forehead in puzzlement.

"The NMU — the National Miners' Union. It's a new union in Kentucky, but it's powerful in Pennsylvania," said Rogoff untruthfully. "It's a real rank-and-file outfit, run for the miners, not the potbellies in the front offices. Now that the UMW has shown its true colors, we're going to move in to Harlan and give you fellows some real support. We're going to stand behind you all the way, until you get everything you're striking for — and we're going to organize every mine in the county."

"I never heard of the National Miners' Union," said Breck. "Did you, Pa?"

Jubal Early scratched his chin reflectively. "Seems to me like once I heard of something that sounded like that — feller from West Virginia mentioned it, seems like. Said there was this Rooshan Red union stirring up a stink in the valley, causing all kinds of trouble." He smiled politely at Rogoff. "That wouldn't be the same bunch you're talking about, would it?"

Rogoff's mouth twisted downward at the corners, humorously. "I wouldn't be surprised. We were there. I was there myself, as a matter of fact."

"And are you a Rooshan Red?" asked Breck, frowning.

"Well, my daddy came over from Russia before the turn of the century — and if being a Red means fighting for the working stiff against the banks and mine operators and Pinkertons and scabs who are picking his bones like buzzards, then I guess you could call me a Red. If you like calling people by names, I mean." He smiled disarmingly. "As far as I'm concerned, I go by what a person *is,* not what he's called."

"And this NMU, this National Miners' Union — is it all Rooshan Red?"

"Of course not. I just happen to be Russian. I don't know anybody else in the whole union who is. Most of them are English and Scotch-Irish, like you people here in the mountains. But that's not the point. The point is, they're working people — people who've been ground down and exploited until they decided to fight back because they didn't have anything else to lose! They've seen how the system works to make the rich richer and the poor poorer, and they're going to do something about it — not like the fatcats in the UMW who sell out their own membership for a dollar cigar!"

"I ain't never had nothing to do with Reds," Breck said.

"I ain't neither," agreed Jubal Early, "which means I ain't never been cheated by one at the commissary, nor been given false weight by one, nor been beat up by one for talking about a union. There's others I wish I could say the same for."

Breck appeared to ignore his father. "Anyway, Claiborne's the union man in this family," he went on. "They got him in jail over to Harlan, and it don't look like he'll be out for quite a spell."

"That's right." Rogoff looked into Breck's eyes with an intense, brown-eyed sincerity. "But I'd like to talk to *you* a while. Breck — do you mind if I call you Breck? Breck, I think there are things we can do together."

"What kind of things?"

"Things for the miners. Things for your family. Things for Harlan County."

Breck gave a short laugh. "I ain't been able to do none of those things by myself, that's for sure."

"Well, you're not by yourself anymore. That's what I'm trying to tell you. From now on, you'll never have to be by yourself again!" He leaned forward in his chair and rested both elbows on the table. "Now, let me ask you a couple of questions."

*

The "groundwork" Charlie Rasmusson had mentioned took longer than it should have, and it was early June before the NMU was ready to call its first conference of Harlan miners and their wives.

The Hords, together with Aunt Cloa Burkett, walked to the high-school gymnasium where the meeting was to be held. Aunt Cloa had written a new song which would be sung during the program, so she sat in the exact center of a row of reserved seats. Bonnie Brae and Phoebe were in the mixed chorus that would sing the song, so they also sat in the reserved section. Hannah, Joicy, Jubal Early, and Breck sat toward the rear of the general seats.

The gym was crowded, and there was electricity in the air. Everyone was curious about the new union; some mixed their curiosity with glowing hopes, and a few with queasy apprehension, but they all wanted to know more. As they waited for the program to begin, they studied the men and women on the improvised platform for clues to their intentions and abilities.

Only three members of the core group sat on the platform. Rasmusson was to chair the meeting, and Jennie Markwell and Liz Craig were to speak. The other eight people crowded together in lonely prominence were all Harlan

County natives. Ike Silver, Wayne Coy, and Mike Rogoff sat in widely separated seats in the audience.

Rasmusson handled meetings well. Before the eager impatience of the crowd could sour into irritability, he rose from his folding chair, gestured for quiet, and, with a glance at the mixed chorus, called out, "Ladies and gentlemen, our National Anthem!" There was a moment of silence, then the chorus launched itself hopefully into "The Star-Spangled Banner." They gained confidence and volume as the audience joined them, and everyone ended the song flushed and pleased.

Rasmusson introduced himself and said a few words about the NMU. He was very brief, for two reasons: first, because there wasn't much that he *could* say about the NMU, and, second, because he knew the miners would rather hear about themselves anyway.

Then he called on the Harlan County natives on the platform, one after another. Each was introduced as the representative of a committee — the Workers' Organizational Committee, the Mine Safety Committee, the Legal Defense Committee, the Family Relief Committee — and each had a statement to read. The statements were dramatic indictments of mining practices and living conditions in Harlan County, and the facts were bitterly familiar to everyone who heard them. Angry murmurs spread through the hall.

To sum up the miners' grievances, Rasmusson called on Aunt Cloa. "Here's someone you know who's set the whole thing to music for you! Let's give a welcome to Aunt Cloa Burkett!" The old woman stood up and glared at the applauding audience as though they were making irresponsible demands on her, then folded her plump little hands together and waited for silence. When she got it, she began, in her high, raspy voice:

A miner's life is like a sailor's
Threatened by that sea of blue.
Every day his life's in danger
Till he joins the NMU.

Watch the scabs, they'll rob your children,
Take from you your family's bread —
When a man deserts his comrades,
Surely he'd be better dead.

She turned her head to look at the chorus, and her hard little eyes commanded them to join her in the refrain:

Union miners, stand together!
NMU will never fail!
Keep your hand upon the dollar,
And your eye upon the scale!

There were three more verses, each followed by the same refrain, and, by the time the song was finished, Aunt Cloa's revised version of "The Miner's Lifeline" was etched in every brain. She sat down to enthusiastic applause.

Rasmusson harnessed the thrust of her words. "Aunt Cloa said it, friends. Union miners, stand together, and the NMU will never fail! That's right — all we got to do is stand like men, all linked together, and be sure that we'll prevail — with our hand upon the dollar, and our eye upon the scale! Isn't that right? And that's what we aim to do! Here's Dewey Jarboe of the Miners' Rights Committee, to read you the NMU demands — *our* demands — for what you got coming to you! Come on up here, Dewey!"

A small man in bleached overalls and a clean white shirt buttoned at the neck stood up and walked to the front of the platform. He began to read from a sheet of paper in a voice so weakened by stage fright it was inaudible past the third row. At cries of "Louder! Can't hear you, Dewey!" he started over again, and this time his voice trembled feebly but audibly throughout the gymnasium.

The NMU demands went beyond anything ever imagined by most of the listeners, not because any particular demand was excessive, but because no past inequity had been overlooked. Living conditions, as well as wages and working conditions, were covered. Each demand was realistic, but the sum total seemed breathtakingly utopian: Union checkweighmen at every mine, and regular testing of scales at each driftmouth; an end to wage cuts for funeral expenses, teachers' and ministers' salaries; abolition of company scrip and the freedom to trade in private stores; disability insurance in cash; and a maximum rent in company housing of $1.50 per room per month. Cash wages were to start at $5.55 a day, with a tonnage rate of 66 cents, plus a 2-cent-per-ton bonus for coal mined under hazardous or time-consuming conditions; and wages for laborers outside the pits were to begin at $4.75 a day.

When Dewey Jarboe's nervous voice stopped, there was a moment of expectant silence, and then the applause broke like a wave over the platform. Men stamped on the floor and whistled; women cried "Hallelujah!" and "Amen!"; children shrieked in hilarity or fright. Rasmusson wrapped one arm around the startled Jarboe, and raised his other hand in a fist above his head, his battered features radiant.

"You heard it, friends! You heard the demands — *your* demands — the demands the NMU will make with *your* voice, in *your* name! Well, you're not the only ones going to hear those demands! No, sir! The operators are going to hear them — and the scabs are going to hear them — and the gun-thugs and J. H. Blair are going to hear them — and before we're finished, the President of the United States is going to hear them! And you know something? They're going to give us what we want, and what we need, and what we deserve — because they won't have any choice! They're going to give it — or we're going to take it! Am I right?" The audience roared their approval at him.

After that there were two more short speeches: Liz Craig told about the union's plan to establish a chain of soup kitchens in the county, with the first to be opened in Evarts the following week; and Jennie Markwell, with the bitter eloquence she was known for, discussed the legal problems facing the strikers arrested after the Battle of Evarts, and held ever since in the Harlan County jail, without benefit of counsel.

Then Charlie Rasmusson wrapped it up: "Well, you've heard it, folks — that's the way it is with the National Miners' Union! That's the kind of help and support you can expect from the NMU, when you stand together in solidarity with workers all over America! The NMU cares about you, wants to know your problems, your hopes, your dreams! What? You say you don't believe it?" He cocked his head to one side and cupped one hand behind his ear, exaggerating the gesture of an old man with poor hearing. "You say there used to be a union here, and it didn't give a damn whether you lived or died? You say all it cared about was getting in the dues and staying out of trouble? Well, you're right! But this is the NMU we're talking about now, not the UMW! In the old days, it was *you* that belonged to the UMW — but now it's the NMU that belongs to *you!*

"Maybe this will prove it to you: we're sending a delegation of miners and miners' wives from right here in Harlan

County up to the NMU National Convention in Pittsburgh next month! There'll be twenty-five or thirty people going — maybe you'll be one of them — and they'll be guests of the national headquarters while they tell the world about what's happening here in Kentucky! Does that sound like the NMU cares, or doesn't it?" He waited a moment for the applause to peak, and then shouted above it, "But there's one thing you got to do, folks, or none of this is going to happen. You got to join the NMU! You got to put your John Hancock on the dotted line, you got to link your arms with ours and join your heart to our heart in the struggle! Come in with us, friends! Join your brothers and sisters in the fight for a decent life on this earth! Join the NMU! You can sign up with one of the ladies at the doors as you pass out of the hall. Don't worry about dues — all we're asking you for is your name on a piece of paper — just your name, to show that you're with us, that you believe in what we're doing here!" He raised both hands above his head. "So good-bye for now, folks — see you soon. And sign up as you leave!" He nodded to the chorus, and they immediately rose and began to sing:

Oh, the NMU's behind us, we shall not be moved
Oh, the NMU's behind us, we shall not be moved —
Just like a tree that's standing by the water,
We shall not be moved!

Breck and Jubal Early walked toward one of the exits, followed by Joicy and Hannah. Jubal Early was talking. "I'll be dogged — those folks sure know how to rile a man up, don't they? I wish Claiborne could have heard it. Would have done his heart good." They neared a cluster of men and women who were waiting to sign up with the union, or the ladies' auxiliary. "I do believe I'll put my name down on that list." He glanced at his son. "You figuring on signing up too, son?"

"Nope," said Breck.

"Oh, how come is that? You reckon it would make you out a Rooshan Red?"

"Nope. I signed up two weeks ago."

Breck waited while his father, mother, and sister-in-law added their names to the membership rolls.

Outside, a squad of National Guardsmen stood near the high-school entrance. They were at parade rest, with the butts of their Springfields between their shiny shoes. Beyond them, dimly visible in the darkness, were two carloads of deputy sheriffs. Their cars were parked along the shoulder of the road, with the lights off. They were watching the miners pour out of the school building behind the screen of soldiers.

Breck noticed them as soon as he stepped out of the door. "Gun-thugs, Pa, two cars full."

Jubal Early squinted toward the road. "Ain't doing nothing — just setting there. 'Cause of the soldiers, most likely."

Breck nodded. "One day them soldiers got to leave," he said.

When Rogoff came out with Liz Craig a few minutes later, he said nearly the same thing. "See the two parked cars there, Liz? They're just looking us over tonight — but wait till the soldier boys pull out. *Oi gevalt!*"

"We'll just have to be ready for them, Mike. We'll just have to be strong enough to take whatever they dish out." She spoke in a brisk, confident tone. "Now where'd you leave your car?" she asked.

"Up the road, there — about thirty cars up." He had the use of a Model A Ford, and had offered to drive her to her rooming house in Harlan Town. He took her arm as they walked over the uneven ground beside the miners' cars that lined the road. "Watch your step here," he cautioned her. When they reached his car, he helped her in.

They sat waiting for an opening in the procession of cars that passed them, taking miners and their families home. The moving headlights illuminated their faces with a flickering alternation of light and shadow, like some skid-row tavern's neon sign. "Jeez, there are enough of them," said Rogoff wryly. "I don't think we're ever going to find a hole."

"It was a fine turnout," Liz answered. "If even half of them signed up, we're in good shape."

"Um-hum." He saw an opening approaching, and raced the motor in anticipation.

"Well, wouldn't we be? In good shape?" She looked at him. He was watching the traffic. When the car in front of the opening was almost past the Model A, he jerked out into the procession. The car behind honked angrily. "I hope that's not a new comrade," he said. "Or, if it is, I hope he didn't recognize me."

Liz repeated her question. "Wouldn't we be in good shape?"

"Compared to what?"

"Wouldn't we be in good shape to win the strike?"

"Well, better than if nobody signed up."

"No, I mean it, Mike. Don't you think the odds would be pretty good?" For the first time, there was a hint of uncertainty in her voice.

"Hell, Liz, you're family — when have odds had anything to do with anything?"

"You could say, when has winning had anything to do with anything?" She stared at his long-nosed profile, edged in yellow from the reflected light of the headlights.

"All right, you could say that," he agreed.

They rode in silence for five minutes. Cars peeled off at each intersection, until the procession became only a small number of cars going home. Abruptly Liz said, "Find some place to pull off, will you, Mike? I want to talk."

"Sure."

A few moments later the headlights showed a rutted dirt road running off to the left, and Rogoff turned into it. They bumped along for fifty yards, climbing a rise and descending behind it. Then Rogoff turned off the lights and switched off the ignition. The sudden darkness was startling.

"It's your nickel, Liz," he said quietly.

"Do you still smoke that Bull Durham?" He grunted affirmatively. "Then roll a butt for me, would you?" She waited while he found his papers and bag of tobacco, rolled her a cigarette, and lit it for her. She took a deep drag, and a tiny flame flared brightly in the draft. "Mike, if there's anything in the world I'm afraid of, it's being played for a sucker," she said. "I'll go by the rules — if I have to take some lumps, then I'll take some lumps. That's all right. But I want to know the rules first."

"Everybody does."

"No, but you said yourself, I'm family. I've got a right to know. Don't I?"

Rogoff sighed. "I don't know if you do or not. That's not my department. I don't make policy, I just work here."

"Mike. Just what you think, that's all. Not policy — just Mike Rogoff, one man. One man, talking to one woman. We've talked that way before."

He hesitated a moment, then said, "All right, let's talk that way again."

"What's really going to happen with the strike? Is there any chance at all of winning it?"

"Sure there's a chance. Actually a pretty fair chance.

Obviously, the odds are against it — anybody with half an eye can see that. There just aren't enough jobs here for miners anymore. There's not enough demand for coal up north to keep ten thousand men busy down here digging it. That's plain arithmetic. But *maybe* there's enough demand to keep five thousand men busy. And *maybe* we can make sure those five thousand are represented by the NMU. At least, that's what we're here to find out."

"There's nothing in the rules that says we want to lose this one?"

"Liz, look — as far as I know, the Party wants to *win*. Everything I've seen makes me think so. If we can shut down the whole county, I think we've got a chance to pull it off."

"Of course, whether we win or not, the Party stands to gain, doesn't it?" said Liz, with the slightest trace of an edge to her voice. "If we win, the Party gets new members for the NMU and new power in the coalfields — if we lose, the Party gets publicity, anger, bitterness, martyrs —"

Rogoff's voice was a shade blander than before, as if to balance the increased sharpness of Liz's tone. "That's the way it works out. Isn't it lucky? Marx had a phrase for it — historical inevitability. That's why we're down here, isn't it? To be on the side of history — to be on the inevitably winning side?"

"I've never given a damn about winning anything in my life," said Liz scornfully.

"You could afford not to. But that was your bourgeois individualism. You're through with that crap now — or if you're not, you should be. Liz —" His voice became more intense, and he put his hand on her shoulder and tightened his fingers against her flesh. "Liz, you're here to do a job. It's a job you believe in. It's not easy, and, for all we know, it may be a failure. But that's not important. What's important is you do it. You shut up, you don't worry — you do it. Understand?"

She sat with her eyes closed and her head resting on the back of the seat. She could feel his closeness. "The people here — they're so strange. Not like working people in the North. I've never met anybody like them. They have a capacity for violence that frightens me."

"You're damn right they do. And don't forget it."

"Sometimes I feel so — so *isolated*. So foreign, so New York, so poor-little-rich-girl." She opened her eyes and looked at the shadowy mass of the man beside her. "Was this what I got myself booted out of Bryn Mawr for?" she said with a smile.

"You know what you got yourself booted out of Bryn Mawr for," he said gruffly.

"Sometimes I can hardly remember." They sat in silence in the darkness. Outside there were night sounds — something small moving in the grass, an owl, water splashing over rocks. Far away the muted whine of a truck laboring up a grade.

"All right, Mike — so much for that foolishness. I apologize."

"Don't be stupid, Liz."

"You know, you always could make me feel better."

"Could I?"

"You know you could." Through half-closed eyes she could see the bulk of him moving closer, and she put an arm around his shoulder. "Ah, Mike — make me feel better now," she whispered, pulling him to her.

*

Through the rest of June and the beginning of July the National Guard stayed in Harlan County. Little violence occurred, on the part of either miners or deputies. The Coal Operators' Association contented itself with hiring an additional twenty-five gunmen, increasing the high sheriff's arsenal with a number of machine guns, and placing a series of advertisements in most of the newspapers of southeastern Kentucky branding the NMU a subversive, atheistic, Communistic, and terroristic organization preying on the gullibility of the miners.

The core group took advantage of the time they had. During the month of June Rasmusson, Coy, and Rogoff were able to sign up nearly three thousand miners. They sent twenty-eight delegates to the NMU convention in Pittsburgh. Ike Silver cranked out a steady stream of stories for the *Daily Worker,* and managed to place articles in a number of progressive northern magazines. Liz Craig opened the first NMU soup kitchen in Evarts, and was well on the way to following it with others in Wallins, Panzy, Elcomb, and Clovertown. Jennie Markwell was unable to help the imprisoned men packed into the sweltering cells of the Harlan County jail, but she was able to generate considerable publicity from their plight.

On the nineteenth of July, time ran out for the NMU. The National Guard left the county.

Chapter 10

A Mite Late to Go Home

THE EVARTS SOUP KITCHEN didn't last long, but during the time it was operating, Phoebe Hord put in more hours working there than anybody — even Liz Craig.

When Liz began looking for volunteers among the Evarts women, Rogoff recommended Phoebe to her. "She's not married, not tied down to taking care of a house or kids, so she ought to be free to put in some hours for you. She's a gimp, which probably cuts down on her tap-dancing but shouldn't interfere with her dishwashing any. Why don't you look her over?" Liz paid a call on Phoebe, and worked patiently to overcome the girl's initial suspiciousness. By the time she left the Hords' shack that afternoon, Liz had recruited a dedicated partisan.

It was a lot of work getting the soup kitchen ready to open, and a lot more keeping it running. There was the preparation of the building itself, a ramshackle two-room cabin whose only advantages were its emptiness and its central location. There was food to get — by donation if possible, by purchase if necessary. There were the cooking and the cleaning-up to do, and no sooner was one meal out of the way than the fire was kindled to begin the next one. There were workers to find to replace the inevitable two or three who failed to appear as promised each day. And with four other soup kitchens in varying stages of unreadiness, Liz Craig could give only a few hours a week to the Evarts operation. Phoebe took up the slack.

Mike Rogoff came by about ten o'clock one morning. He stuck his head through a window and called, "Hi — is Liz Craig around?"

Phoebe looked up from the onions she was chopping for the day's pinto bean soup. She was temporarily alone in the kitchen. "Nope. She was in a while back, but she left. Said she was going over to Panzy. Something I can do?"

"Oh, I guess not. I'll catch up to her sooner or later." He gave her a friendly smile to show he recognized her. "I haven't seen you since you opened up here. But I've heard you've been working harder than everybody else put together. Is that right?"

Phoebe pushed back a loose strand of hair from her cheek, wrinkling her nose at the smell of onion juice on her hand. "Oh, pshaw, everybody's done some working. I don't reckon I've done more than some others."

"That's not what they told me. Anyway, keep up the good work — there's plenty of hungry kids that are obliged to you." He hesitated a moment for her response, but she sat with her eyes lowered to the table in front of her, without speaking. "Well, tell Liz I'm looking for her, in case she comes back," he said. "And take care of yourself." He leaned back from the window, preparing to leave.

Phoebe raised her head. "Wait. Would you like some coffee? I got some fresh made."

"Hey, that would be fine. I don't think anybody would mind if I took ten minutes off for some java." He disappeared from the window, and a moment later pushed open the kitchen door. "Hello again," he said, entering.

"Sit down. I'll pour you out a cup." She rose from the

table as he sat down at it, and limped across the floor to one of the two black iron cookstoves. She poured coffee into a chipped mug. "We ain't got any evaporated milk today," she said apologetically, as she carried it back to him.

"I never put anything into my coffee. It's fattening," he said, trying for a light note.

"Oh." She sat down across from him, with the chopped onions between them. She looked down at the tabletop again. There was silence while he took his first sips of strong, hot coffee. "This is fine," he said.

"You come from Chicago?" she asked, raising her head and looking straight at him.

"Yeah. Why?"

"Don't you like living there? Is it on account of all them gangsters that you want to get out?"

"What do you mean, want to get out? I don't want to get out — I like Chicago. I was born there. It's my favorite city in the country."

"Then how come you go off and leave it, and come down to these miserable old mountains? If I lived in a big city up north, there ain't nothing could get me down here."

"Why, it's my job — I go where they tell me. Anyway, what's wrong with the mountains? You're the first person I've heard say anything against them. They look beautiful to me."

"Oh, they're beautiful. So are lions and tigers. But they can eat you up."

He looked at her curiously, his wide slit of a mouth twisted up ironically at one corner. "You don't look like they ate you up."

"There's no way you could know without you was raised here," she said. "They hunch up around you — at night, you can't even see the moon till it's pretty near straight over your

"It's more than that." Their eyes met and held for a moment. "You're somebody, Phoebe Hord," he said simply. "Good-bye."

After he left, she remained standing a while, one hand clasped in the other. Then she resumed her seat at the table, and began chopping onions again.

*

The National Guard left Harlan County on the nineteenth of July. Nothing happened that night, but the next night J. H. Blair's flying squads went out.

Nugent Emory was in charge of one car. He had the names and addresses of four miners, all of whom had been delegates to the NMU Convention in Pittsburgh the week before. The first name on the list was John Y. Tuttle. When Emory's car drew to a stop in front of Tuttle's cabin, the lights were out. The four deputies made the front porch without warning the people in the house. Then they smashed in the door. Tuttle was in bed with his wife and their youngest child; two other children and their grandfather were in another bed in the same room. Staring wide-eyed into the flashlights of the deputies, they showed the brittle helplessness of specimen bugs pinned down for display. Emory told Tuttle he was under arrest for criminal syndicalism and sedition. While the miner dressed, Emory's men tore the cabin apart, searching for "incriminating evidence." They found a NMU membership card, a copy of the *Daily Worker,* a pamphlet entitled "The Secret of the Pay Envelope," and a clipping from a Pittsburgh newspaper that mentioned Tuttle's name. These things they took with them; everything else they piled in the middle of the cabin floor. Then Emory poured a canful of pork grease, a half gallon of coal oil, a jar of honey, and a pot of cold coffee over the family's possessions. "Any of you boys able to work up a good piss?" he asked. Two of the deputies urinated on the pile of clothing. When Tuttle lunged at one of them, Emory knocked him unconscious with the butt of his pistol. The deputies carried Tuttle out of the car, and they drove away toward Harlan. In five minutes Tuttle regained consciousness. Emory stopped the car, and the four policemen took Tuttle out on the shoulder of the road and stomped him. Then they took him on to jail.

Tuttle was the only one of the four men on Emory's list arrested that night. By the time their car bucked up the road toward the second house on the list, the word was out in every mining camp in Harlan County that John Henry Blair had declared war on the NMU, and known leaders of the union were anywhere but home.

That night Blair's deputies bagged seven other NMU members, all of whom were beaten before they were jailed.

The next day the core group met in Evarts, where they were surrounded by the "human wall" Rasmusson had described as their only defense. "Well, we all know what happened last night," the ex-Wobbly said grimly. "I think we got a lot more of the same to look forward to. The question is, will the men be able to stand it?"

"For how long?" asked Wayne Coy. "For the rest of the summer is one thing — when the cold weather comes, and there ain't no grease for the skillet, that's something else."

"Thank God the Guard stayed as long as they did," Rogoff said. "We built up a good head of steam. The NMU's got momentum now. The operators have to slow us down before they can stop us."

Rasmusson nodded, and turned to the two women to explain: "The boys are still signing up at a rate of two or three hundred a week — or anyway they were, before last night. It should take a while to lose that thrust."

"And by the time we do, we should have a majority of the miners in Harlan County signed, sealed, and delivered," said Rogoff.

Rasmusson looked down at his large, misshapen hands, frowning. "Let's put first things first. Right now the most important thing is publicity. We've got to get the story of this Iron Guard terror out to the country. That's you, Ike."

The Labor News Syndicate correspondent was slumped bonelessly in his chair. He glanced up at Rasmusson irritably. "Don't worry — I phoned a story in this morning. It will be in the *Worker* tomorrow."

"We'll need a lot more coverage than that, Ike."

"We'll get whatever coverage the story deserves. The native American fascism angle should get us into the *Nation* and *New Republic*. *Commonweal* is a possibility — so is the *American Mercury*. The editor of *Outlook* is interested —"

"Jesus Christ, who reads those things? I haven't even heard of most of them!" Rasmusson said angrily. "What about the *Post*, or *Liberty*, or the *Literary Digest?* What about something that somebody *reads,* for God's sake!"

Silver's expression was both wary and contemptuous. "Unfortunately, the only thing most people read in this country is the bourgeois press. Don't expect me to get anything placed there for you. Jack Reed himself couldn't get a union story in the *Saturday Evening Post.*"

"Which very conveniently gives you an excuse for not trying," Rasmusson flared.

Silver's eyelids lowered, and he sat up a little straighter in his chair. "If you have any complaints about the job I'm doing, Comrade, feel free to buck them on up the line. I get my orders from New York. I'm not assigned to NMU, and you know it."

"Apparatchik!" growled Rasmusson.

"Bakuninist!" Silver spat back.

Both Rogoff and Liz Craig intervened. "Wait a minute, this is crazy," Rogoff said sharply. "It's the one thing we *don't* need," Liz agreed. Wayne Coy looked at the two disputants expressionlessly, and Jennie Markwell looked away from them with disapproval. Rasmusson gave a curt nod. "You're right. I'm sorry, Ike. I know you'll do everything you can." He paused to allow Silver to reply, but the correspondent shrugged and remained silent, so Rasmusson resumed, "Jennie, what's the legal situation with the boys in Harlan jail?"

"They'll be there a while," Jennie Markwell said matter-of-factly. She had a curiously pleasant bulldog face, and sometimes thrust her little chin forward as small boys push out one knuckle when they make a fist. "Baby Jones has hand-picked himself a grand jury, and they're indicting thirty men for murder, conspiracy, and criminal syndicalism."

"Any chance of a bond? If we could get even one of them out for meetings, it could be a big help — particularly up north."

"Not a chance. They'll be inside until they go to court. The main question is, which court? Jones and the operators want to move the trials to the Bluegrass. We want to keep them here in Harlan."

"That's so there will be miners on the jury? So we can beat the legal frame-up?" asked Liz Craig.

Jennie Markwell smiled very slightly, and Ike Silver raised his eyebrows. "That's right — that's a big part of it," said Jennie.

"This is where it happened, this is where it should be tried," Rogoff said.

"Be a damn shame to make them boys ride all the way

down to Lexington or someplace without there was a good reason," said Wayne Coy.

"Jones wouldn't want to do it, unless he figured it was better for his side," Rasmusson added.

Liz looked from face to face, and then gave a self-mocking grin. "You mean that we can make a bigger stink out of it if we have the trials right in the enemy camp. More publicity — more column inches in the *Worker*. Right, Ike?"

Ike shrugged. "It can't hurt," he said. Nobody else had anything to add. Liz looked around the table, her eyes bright.

"Okay," she said. "So much for legal shenanigans. Let me tell you about Labor Family Relief and the soup kitchens. We're really starting to roll."

The meeting lasted for another hour, and, when it ended, all six participants felt that things could be worse.

*

Two mornings later, Jennie Markwell climbed into her car in Harlan, turned on the ignition, and stepped on the starter. A bomb exploded, demolishing the car. Jennie suffered a number of bruises, but was not seriously hurt.

The next day Ike Silver received a hand-printed note warning him that, unless he left Harlan County immediately, his life would be in danger. He quoted the note in the story he phoned in to New York. The following afternoon, while he was crossing one of the swaying old footbridges suspended over the Cumberland River, he felt a bullet pass an inch from his head and a moment later heard the report of a rifle from somewhere behind him.

That night an associate of Ike's disappeared. The editor of a fellow-traveling weekly published in the West Virginia coalfields, the man was particularly disliked by the Harlan County police establishment. When he was heard from again, two days after his disappearance, he was in Tennessee. He told authorities that he had been kidnaped by deputies and driven to the state border at Cumberland Gap. There he had been severely beaten and forced at gun point to cross the border on foot. He was told he would be killed if he ever returned to Harlan.

High sheriff John Henry Blair began to live in his office, eating and sleeping with guards around him.

Rasmusson and Wayne Coy eluded an unmarked car which pursued them and tried to force them off the road a mile from the Negro settlement of Coxton.

In four days, there were upward of thirty cases of harassment, intimidation, and actual physical violence to NMU members and their families.

Phoebe Hord finished work at the Evarts soup kitchen one night about eleven. She had just put out the coal-oil lamp and stepped through the door onto the porch when a car without lights drove up the dirt track toward the building. Closing the door behind her, Phoebe stood watching the approaching car. *Feller forgot to put on his lights,* she thought. *Better tell him before he runs into something.* She cupped her hands to her mouth and called, "Hey there — your lights ain't on!" As the car passed in front of her, she noticed something from the dark bulk sail through the air toward her. It bumped on the ground a few feet from where she stood. *An empty jar of moonshine, I reckon. Ought to pay some mind where they throw them things — they might hurt somebody.* Then the bomb exploded.

The blast blew Phoebe back against the door, which sprang open, allowing her to fall into the kitchen. The posts holding the porch roof collapsed, and the roof swung down as if it were hinged, blocking the doorway from the outside. The wall nearest the bomb caught fire, and the flames began to spread across the front and back of the shack.

Phoebe was unconscious in the kitchen, but there were people close by who knew she was there. Breck arrived outside less than a minute after the bomb exploded, and Rogoff only a minute or two later. Breck smashed the nearest window and climbed inside. The room was a flickering kaleidoscope of red and black. He could see Phoebe lying in a pool of shadow that lapped over broken furniture, shattered crockery, overturned kettles, cabbage heads, pinto beans, and a chunk of salt pork. The fire was fast and hot, and still relatively smokeless. Breck started across the room toward his sister, but after a few steps he fell down. He continued to crawl on his hands and knees, remembering something he had heard about staying close to the floor in a fire because smoke rises. He reached Phoebe and tried to lift her, but lost his balance and fell flat, with her weight pinning his arms to the floor. He tried to lift her again, but found she was harder to move than before. As he struggled, he drew in a great gulp of smoke and burning air, and the pain was so surprisingly intense he emptied his lungs with a sudden exhalation and sank to the floor. *This here's a son of a bitch,* he thought, closing his eyes against the pain of the heat and smoke, and trying not to breathe.

Outside, Rogoff pushed his way through the first few spectators and ran to a window at the back of the building. It was darker than the other windows, so he concluded that it was farther from the flames inside. He smashed it with his elbow, and shouted, "Phoebe — Phoebe, can you hear me? Are you in there?" He heard no answering voice in the roar of burning wood, so he covered his face with his hands and dived through the window, landing on his knees and elbows on the floor ten feet away from Phoebe and Breck. He scurried toward them like some frightened four-footed varmint, barely touching his hands to the smoking floorboards. He reached Breck and seized him around the shoulders, pulling their bodies together. His face was close to Breck's ear. "Grab her arm!" he screamed, almost unable to hear his own voice. "Drag her! Come on! Breck! Grab her arm!" Breck didn't respond, and Rogoff struck him with his other hand, a weak blow that glanced off Breck's cheek. "Grab her arm, Breck – drag her to the window!" he cried desperately.

Breck looked at him, his eyes round and swimming. Then, awkwardly, he struggled to his knees a third time. He clapped one hand over his eyes, and found Phoebe's wrist with the other hand. Clutching her with a fierce, bruising grip, he dragged her blindly toward the wall of the building.

Rogoff had hold of her other wrist. Seeing that Breck was headed in a direction which would miss the window, Rogoff tugged Phoebe toward the left. The unconscious girl hung between them like a rag doll in a tug of war. Breck felt Rogoff's pull at an angle to his own, and paused to stare uncomprehendingly at the other man. *"Window!"* screamed Rogoff, pointing with his free hand. "Go to the window! *Window!"* He pulled desperately on Phoebe's wrist. But Breck was no longer rational. He responded to the pressure by jerking back, and Rogoff, off balance, fell from his knees to the floor, his cheek hitting the smoldering boards. He felt himself sliding after Phoebe and Breck, toward a windowless corner of the room.

"Window! Window!" he shouted, and then gagged and began a paroxysm of coughing. He kept a grip on the girl's wrist with one hand, while the other clutched wildly for any handhold. His fingers found a leg of one of the cookstoves. It was enough to overcome Breck's impetus; the movement

toward the corner was checked, and the three figures sprawled, immobilized, on the floor.

For a few moments neither man could gain an advantage over the other. Then, anchored by the cookstove, Rogoff began to draw Phoebe toward him. Unreasoningly, Breck tugged against the steady pressure, but could not prevent himself from being dragged after his sister. Rogoff was able to pull the girl to within a yard of the window. He released the leg of the cookstove and clutched the windowsill. Still holding Phoebe's arm, he struggled to his feet. He could feel the cool outside air on his face.

He tried to pull Phoebe upright, but Breck's grip kept her on the floor. Rogoff knew he had come to the end of his resources; he had only seconds left to act. He stepped across the girl's body and stamped down with his heel on Breck's wrist. He had to stamp three times before Breck's fingers opened, and the girl's limp body suddenly surged upward as though she were leaping to safety.

He pushed her out of the window and into the waiting hands of men outside. Then, pausing for a single breath of clean night air that burned in his lungs more sharply than smoke, he turned back to Breck.

Breck was unconscious; when he lost his grip on his sister's wrist, he also lost the need for awareness. Rogoff was able to wrestle the upper part of his body up to the window and push it through; gravity did the rest.

Rogoff fell out after him. The last thing he thought before he lost consciousness was, *I guess this isn't the time.*

*

A week later Rasmusson arranged an NMU picnic. More than two thousand miners, miners' wives, and miners' children attended, for an afternoon of speech-making and singing, interrupted only briefly for food. "They'll get a sight more nourishment for their brains than their bellies," Wayne Coy remarked, as he watched the patient line in front of the soup kettles.

"The important thing is, they're doing something together, as a group," Rasmusson replied. "They're not just being driven. They can see that when they get together like this, nobody can touch them."

"That's right — as long as we've got fifty stout old boys with guns out in the bushes there keeping watch," said Wayne. "But you take them boys away, and see whether the gun-thugs can touch them or not."

Mike Rogoff looked for the Hords. He found them under a tulip tree on the hill overlooking the speakers' platform. Aunt Cloa Burkett was with them, and the seven adults sat in the tall grass as the five children swarmed over and around them. Rogoff wished them good day. Everyone answered him warmly, and Jubal Early got to his feet to make a formal response.

"We're proud to see you, Mr. Rogoff. This family's beholden to you. I don't rightly know what would have happened to them two young'uns without you'd happened by."

"Oh, I imagine they'd have gotten out all right," he said lightly, smiling at Breck and Phoebe. "For a while there, we couldn't decide if I was going to carry Breck or if he was going to carry me."

"I'm obliged," said Breck simply.

"So am I," added Phoebe in a small voice. Her pale face flushed as she spoke.

"We're all obliged to you," said Hannah Hord. "If you didn't come to the speaking with anybody else, we'd be tickled to have you set with us."

"Light and hitch, Mr. Rogoff," Jubal Early urged. He

pointed to a dinner pail on the ground. "There's corn bread and hog jowl there, if you ain't et. Take damn near all!"

Rogoff sat on the grass between Breck and his father. He declined any food, claiming he had already eaten. For twenty minutes he talked with the family. He was respectful to Jubal Early and Aunt Cloa, attentive to Joicy, Hannah, and Bonnie Brae, comradely with Breck, and extremely aware of the quiet presence of Phoebe.

When the conversation came to an easy stopping place, he turned to Breck and said he felt like stretching his legs a while. Would Breck like to take a walk with him? Breck said he would, and the two men excused themselves and began to thread their way through the clusters of picnickers.

"Good crowd," said Rogoff. "Most of these people come from Evarts, don't they, Breck?"

"I seen a lot of them around there."

"I wish we were doing as well signing up men in the camps as we are in Evarts," Rogoff said reflectively. "It's not just the big mines like Black Mountain that are hurting us – it's all those little ones that are still working. As long as they keep shipping out coal, we can't build up enough pressure to force the industry to recognize us. And so far, we haven't had the manpower to shut them down. It's like trying to blow up a balloon with a bunch of little holes in it."

Breck didn't answer. They walked in silence a few moments. Then Rogoff said, "I mentioned you to Rasmusson and Coy the other day, Breck. I told them I thought you could do a job for us organizing. We need organizers who can take responsibility, who can go into the small camps and win the men over, and put a padlock on the gate. Guys who talk the language, who can handle themselves in a fight, and who are smart enough to do the job without asking foolish questions. We think you're that kind of guy." He gave

Breck an intense look, but Breck was staring straight ahead.

"This is the NMU you're talking about me working for? Not the — the Communistic Party?" he asked carefully.

Rogoff's breath exploded in a sound like "Pah." "Of course it's the NMU. Jesus Christ! Do you think the Rooshan Reds have taken over Harlan County, like the newspaper says? And now we're going to elect you Commissar? Hell, Breck, I'm surprised at you!" He watched the other's expression for some trace of embarrassment or chagrin; when he didn't see any, he resumed in a reasonable tone: "Look. In the first place, if I was a Communist, I wouldn't tell you so. In the second place, from everything I know and don't know about Communists, they don't walk up to people and say, 'Hi, friend, great weather we're having, do you want to join the Party?' No, believe me, Breck, that's not the way it happens. When I ask you to take a job as a NMU organizer, that's just exactly what I mean — no more and no less."

"All right. I ain't calling you a liar — not after you saved my life. But listen — I reckon there's some things I'd want to talk to you about, before I give a yea or nay."

"Okay. Do you want to stay where we can hear the speaking, or shall we go where we can talk?"

"I've heard speaking."

"Then let's take a walk down by the creek."

Five minutes later the two men were sitting on a limestone outcropping above dancing white water. Rogoff sprawled back, resting on his elbows, enjoying the rare privacy afforded by the woods around them. Breck sat erect, his arms wrapped around his knees and his forehead wrinkled in concentration.

"I reckon what I most want to know is, what are you and

the union really after?" Breck began. "It don't seem to me it's the same as what the UMW wanted, when my brother Claiborne was working for them. You people don't talk the same way they did, and don't act the same way, neither." He paused. Then, when Rogoff remained silent, he went on: "You all ain't just thinking about the coalfields, are you? There's a lot more to it than that, ain't there?"

Rogoff arranged his thoughts for a few moments, and then began to speak in a quiet, serious tone. "Yes, there's more to it than that, Breck. Not that the coalfields aren't important — they are, they're *damn* important, and not just to the people that work in them, either. But you're right — we think there's more to it than jobs and food in Harlan County.

"You know what's the most important thing in the history of the human race, Breck? It's the fact that a few people took over the riches that God put on the earth for everybody to share, and started selling them to all the rest of the people like they had a right to do it! Back at the beginning of history, I figure everybody shared everything — each person got what he needed, and there was plenty to go around. Some people were good hunters, so they hunted for the whole village. Some people were good farmers, so they planted the crops for the whole village. It was the same with the miners — they dug up the iron and silver the village needed, and each person took what he could use. People *cooperated* — nobody was rich, nobody was poor, everybody had enough to be happy.

"Then some guy — because he was stronger than anybody else, or meaner — decided to make himself the king, the boss. He got other people to help him by promising to make them rich and letting them push around the poor people. He claimed he owned everything — the land, the livestock, the mines, the trees, the rivers and lakes, it was all his, and the common people had no right to any of it unless they worked for him and did as they were told. So they did.

"And all through the course of human history that's the way it's been — a few people claiming to own the earth, and everybody else earning their miserable daily bread by the sweat of their brow when they're lucky enough to eat at all." He sat quietly, letting his words sink in. *As a matter of fact, that's not far wrong,* he thought ironically.

Breck frowned. "I'm not agin folks owning things. A man works hard, it's only right he should be able to buy himself the things he wants. In our family, we never been happy since we give up the house and farm we owned."

"Nobody's against plain people owning their own land," Rogoff said quickly. "If everybody had his own house on his own land, and grew his own food for his family, why, there wouldn't be any need for people like us at all! But that's not the way things are — is it?" He shot a shrewd glance at Breck, his soft brown eyes glittering with unusual brightness.

Breck shook his head. "Not hardly."

"Not by a damn sight! The land's not fit to raise a crop on anymore. The only way a man can feed his family is by mining coal, and the operators own the coal! That's what ownership means today — owning *coal,* not owning your own house — owning a billion dollars' worth of coal, and paying some poor bastards a dollar a day to dig it out for you! Do you believe a man — *any* man — has the right to own a billion dollars' worth of coal?"

"It don't seem right," said Breck.

"You bet it don't seem right," Rogoff cried. "It don't seem right because it *isn't* right! When a man owns coal, or railroads, or factories, then he owns the lives of the people who work for him. He owns their wives and their children. He owns the roof over their heads, and the clothes they're wearing, and even the lousy food in their bellies comes from his *gonif* — his thief in the company store! And if the worker tries to protest, don't forget the operator owns the police and the army, too! You'll never find a better proof than right here in Harlan County!"

"You're sure right about that," Breck replied thoughtfully. "But listen, now. Ain't this true? The UMW, when they was here, all they wanted to do was get better wages for us, and put in checkweighmen, and fix it so as we wouldn't get skinned at the commissary so bad, and things like that. But you fellows, you want more than that, don't you?"

"Yes. I wouldn't lie to you — we want more than that."

"Do you want it to be like it is in Russia, with nobody allowed to own his own house — nor go to church, nor believe in God? Tell you the truth, that's what sticks in my craw the worst — the way you people don't believe in God, and make fun of religion. My people taught me there was nothing lower than to mock the Lord."

Hell, Rogoff thought bitterly. *Here comes the pigeon home to roost.* "I didn't realize you were so religious, Breck," he said lightly.

"It's not so much that I'm religious — it's more that I don't hold with making sport of things that other people put stock in. Why, I've even took advantage of religion myself, using it to get close to gals at the Holiness Church. I'm no Bible-beater — I've lived in sin all my life, I reckon, and it ain't never bothered me a little bit. But I've never made sport of the other fellow's feelings, no matter what!"

"I guess you're talking about some of those booklets we've passed out, and those posters about Jesus being wanted for stealing, and the workingman being crucified, and all that stuff. Is that it?"

For the past few moments Breck had been avoiding Rogoff's eyes, because he had felt awkward about criticizing the NMU's tactics and half expected the other to answer his presumptuousness with an easy and crushing finality. Now he looked up angrily.

"Nobody has any business putting truck like that where believing people are going to see it! Bonnie Brae was raised religious, and when she seen one of them booklets, it about broke her heart that folks she knowed and liked could put out such trash! My Uncle Cawood come over last Sunday with a couple of them booklets, to show my pa what kind of thing the NMU was doing. Pa just shook his head like he couldn't believe it, and Ma started to cry, and then Bonnie Brae got hold of them, and she took on the worst I ever saw!"

Rogoff pressed his hands together in an ecclesiastical manner. "And you blame us. I can understand that. Why not? We bring some pamphlets to Harlan County and hand them out, and they make a lot of nice women cry. What mean bastards we are, right? Destroying the faith of their fathers. We just do it to be rotten — we *like* to make people hate us." His voice had gradually hardened; now he sneered, "You've got it all figured out — that's what makes us such good organizers, getting all the workers to hate us! That's a sample of your realistic organizational mind, Breck? I'm impressed, believe me!"

Breck flushed and turned his head to one side. "Look, don't make fun of me. If I'm wrong, then tell me why I'm wrong. I was honest with you — it's time you was honest with me! How come you to bring them booklets to Harlan County?"

Rogoff was silent a moment, weighing possible answers to the inescapable question. He decided to be as nearly truthful as possible. "All right — the reason we brought in those booklets was because the majority of people in a position to make the decision thought it was a good idea. Maybe it was, maybe it wasn't, but once the decision was made, it was the decision of all of us. That's the way it is in the NMU.

"We knew it was going to bother a lot of religious types, but we wanted them bothered. You've got to understand this, Breck — the church is the natural enemy of the working-man. It's supported by the capitalist class, and its main job is to keep poor people quiet by promising them they'll go to Heaven if they do what they're told. It works against the union every time."

"Aunt Cloa Burkett's a Christian woman, and she works harder for the union than anybody I know," Breck argued. "Her husband, Anse, was an elder in the Holiness Church, and he always spoke up for the UMW."

"Look, I'm not talking about individuals, I'm giving you the overall picture. By and large, the church is antilabor. It's a spy and a pimp for the capitalist system, and our job is to show it up for what it is. Religion is superstition. We're trying to build a world based on scientific fact. Religion lies to people, and we want to tell them the truth. Religion orders them to stay put and do what they're told — we tell them to get off their ass and fight. Every way you can think of, religion is our enemy, Breck! Of course we're going to fight it!"

"There's a lot of folks in these hills that ain't going to take kindly to them booklets, just the same," said Breck stubbornly.

Rogoff nodded. "I know that. Maybe after this is all over, we'll all look back on it and say, 'You know, that antireligious stuff was a mistake — if we'd used our brains for thinking instead of sitting on, we'd have left it all back up north where it belonged.' It could turn out that way; it's happened before.

"But for now, the committee has made the decision, and that's all there is to it. The time for arguing about it has passed. That's the way it is with us. That's what you have to understand about us, Breck."

Breck sat silent and motionless for a few seconds, and then slowly nodded his head — not in agreement, but to acknowledge his understanding of Rogoff's argument. "All right — that's the way you all feel, and once you made up your minds, there ain't none of you going to argue about it. I understand that. But what I asked you before, about what you NMU people want: if you don't let anybody own coal mines or railroads or factories, and if you set folks against the churches too — then you *do* want us to be like Russia. Like I said. Ain't that so?" Breck's expression reflected either hope or fear — or, Rogoff realized, a combination of both.

"No, no, we don't want to do that. Russia's Russia, and the United States is the United States. What we want is for men to be free, like it says in the Constitution — free to work at decent jobs, and raise their families in decent homes, and be able to respect themselves. But to do that, Breck, we've got to go farther than the UMW ever wanted to go. We think that sooner or later the workers will have to own the mines themselves. The coal belongs to everybody, so everybody has a right to be a part owner of the mines. And besides, there's nobody a miner can trust to operate the mines except himself.

"But that's a long time away, Breck," he continued with a candid smile. "For now, the only important differences between us and the UMW are that we work harder, scare harder, and get more results. If you want to work with us as an organizer, that's all in the world you have to worry about."

The two men sat together on the limestone shelf above the sparkling creek, discussing the Party, the NMU, and Harlan County, while the sound of cheers and applause of the spectators at the picnic formed a muted obbligato to their words. Finally Breck tossed a piece of shale into the creek decisively.

"If I was to join up, where would you want me?" he asked.

"Didn't you tell me once that your family used to live in the Excelsior Number Two camp off Poor Fork?"

"Why, yes. I was born there. We farmed the land on Dead Dog Branch before Pa leased it away."

"But didn't you and your pa and your brother Claiborne all work in Dead Yellow Dog mine at one time?"

"Sure. We moved back there from Leslie County after the war, and all of us worked in the mine. Pa got hurt, and they kicked Claiborne out for being in the UMW – but I stayed there up to this year."

"Is your old cabin still standing?"

"I reckon – ain't been out there for a while. We lived along the creekside, in a company house. That old cabin was back up the hollow a ways. It was falling down and pretty well growed over with brush the last time I seen it."

"But you still own it, is that right? Legally, the title to it and the land around it is in your name?"

"Well, in my pa's name." Breck looked at Rogoff curiously. "What's this all about, anyway?"

"We want you to move back to Dead Yellow Dog. We want you to be the NMU organizer there, and take charge of signing up the boys and shutting the mine down. Obviously you can't live in one of the company cabins, but you've got a perfect right to move back into your old cabin up the hollow, and you can let anybody you want camp on your land. There's no legal way the Fairleigh people can get rid of you."

"Well, I'll be dogged," said Breck softly. He thought for a moment. "It's a mite late to go home — but I reckon Ma and Pa will be tickled to death just the same. And Phoebe and Joicy — there ain't nothing holding either of them in Evarts, that's for sure." He gave a single bark of laughter.

"That's another thing," Rogoff went on. "Liz Craig thinks Dead Yellow Dog would be a good place for another Family Relief soup kitchen. Phoebe could set it up. There's nobody in Harlan County that could do a better job, Liz says. If she'd be willing to take it on, that is."

"Oh, I reckon she'd be proud to, if we was to move back there. She liked the work, I know that."

"Good." Rogoff pulled out his bag of Bull Durham, and rolled himself a cigarette. He lit it, and then offered the makings to Breck, who shook his head in polite refusal. Rogoff tucked the tobacco and papers away. "Well, what do you say?" he asked briskly.

"I can't give you an answer without I talk to my pa." He pulled his feet under him and rose. "I expect I better get back now. I'll let you know what he thinks directly I know myself."

They walked back silently through the sun-splashed wood.

*

When Breck proposed to his family that the Hords move back to Dead Dog Branch, everyone accepted the idea with enthusiasm. Hannah was pleased to get her grandchildren out of the filth and congestion of the Evarts shantytown "before they all come down with the bloody bowels." Bonnie Brae and Joicy agreed, and were also excited by the challenges of the move, in contrast to the drab day-to-day sameness of their present life. Jubal Early felt a rare twinge of self-importance at the thought of returning to his own land. And for Phoebe, the twin prospects of a new home and a new soup kitchen were so exhilarating it was all she could do to hide her pleasure behind pursed lips and laconic comments.

It was late August when they moved. Breck and Jubal Early had spent a week covering the largest holes in the cabin roof and floor and patching over the gaping windows, and when the family arrived, their new home was weather-tight.

Hannah's eyes sparkled as she caught her first glimpse of the cabin through the trees. "I declare, there it is!" she said. "Don't it take you back, though?"

The Hords' return to Dead Dog Branch was noted by the management of the Excelsior mines. W. F. Tasker commented on it during a telephone conversation a few days later.

"Oh, one other thing," he reported. "People named Hord moved into a cabin up the hollow a ways. I understand they own it, and used to live there before the mine opened." He paused for the impatient comment at the other end of the line. "Well, there are two reasons. Claiborne Hord, that we fired for being a UMW organizer and who's in jail in Harlan right now, is a member of the family. And the other thing is, there's talk that they're figuring on opening another one of those soup kitchens like was blown up in Evarts. Claiborne's sister, Phoebe, was the manager of that one."

He listened for a few moments, his eyes fixed idly on his gallery of hounds. "The other brother is named Breck. He worked here too. He got into a fight with his foreman over going to a UMW meeting, and we fired him. But that's all I know against him — he's a quiet, hardworking fellow, and never was bit by the union bug, as far as I know."

He paused again, drumming his finger tips on the desk top

before him. "Yes, I'll keep an eye on them, of course, and let you know any developments right away. But I wanted to alert you that we may be needing some more mine guards here. I have no idea what they plan on doing, but it's possible the NMU sent them, the girl anyway . . . Yes, mention it to him, will you? That's all I've got for now. Take care of yourself."

Outside, the whistle hooted. Dead Yellow Dog was busy.

Chapter 11

Predestination and Dumb Luck

J. C. STACKPOOL just wasn't cut out by nature to be a foreman. It hadn't taken the men in his section at Black Mountain long to discover that his threats were empty and his geniality was false — and also that he was too lazy to be an efficient snoop. The company was slower in discovering his inadequacies, but by the middle of July the mine manager knew the truth, and acted accordingly.

Pink slip in hand, J.C. went to see his friend Nugent Emory, who had succeeded Jim Darling as head guard. Emory was sitting at his desk working on the duty roster of the guards assigned to him. It was a hot day, and he had taken off his gun belt and unbuttoned the top three buttons of his shirt. Drops of sweat glistened like sequins among the curly blond hairs on his chest. He looked at J.C. with a frown of irritation. "So they booted your ass out. What you expect me to do about it?"

Stackpool brushed back his shock of tow hair and smiled his boyish, ingratiating smile. "Why, heck, old buddy, I don't expect a thing in the world. I ain't the kind of feller to go asking a friend for favors. One thing nobody can say about J. C. Stackpool — that he goes around asking favors instead of pulling his weight. You know that's a fact, now, Nugent."

Emory gave a neutral grunt. Stackpool took it as encouragement. "It ain't because they fired me for no damn reason, after promising me all kinds of things, and having me move my family here, and all — that's not why I'm here, buddy. I'm not here to ask no favors. I'm here to offer myself to you fellers for a deputy — and you know I'd be a good one. You can't deny it!"

Emory looked at his friend dispassionately. More than most men, Emory was realistic. He enjoyed the time he spent in J.C.'s company, but also was perfectly aware of his flaws. On the other hand, he was equally aware of what qualities were required of a mine guard. On balance, it seemed to him that Stackpool might do very well.

"You've been working with miners — wouldn't it bother you some if you was to have to start leaning on them?" he asked.

J.C.'s smile widened. "Hellfire, buddy, I hate a Red worse than a snake. I'd as soon bust one up as look at him. You just give me a chance to show you!"

"But how about if a miner ain't a Red? How about if he's just a plain workingman trying to feed his family?"

"The way I figure, if he don't want to work, he's a Red. Feller wants to feed his family, he goes to work to do it, don't he? He don't go on strike — that's no damn way to feed a family! Am I right?"

Emory ignored the question. "Being a mine guard ain't no sorghum stir-off — there was four of us killed at Evarts, not to mention all that's been shot at from ambush. You reckon you got the belly for that?"

J.C. replaced his grin with a resolutely unfrightened expression. "One thing that's never been said about J. C. Stackpool is that he ever backed off from a fight. *Any* kind of fight, buddy — fists or feet or knife or gun or whatever. If you're looking for somebody you can count on when trouble starts, you found him here!"

Emory stared at the man before him in silence. J.C. held his intrepid expression, but after a few moments little lines of uncertainty appeared around his eyes. Emory allowed the silence to drag on, wondering how long J.C. could stand it before he was driven to speak again. J.C. stood it for about ten seconds.

"I know you got all kinds of responsibilities as head guard, Nugent," he said in a deferential tone. "I wouldn't have come to you like this if'n I hadn't been sure I could help make your job easier. Way I figure, it's bound to be better for you if you have people working for you you trust. I know if I was you, it would make *me* feel easier, having friends alongside me in my job . . ." His voice trailed off, and silence fell between them again.

Suddenly Emory grew bored. "All right, J.C., maybe we can find a place for you. I'll see what I can do," he said curtly.

"I'll be mighty obliged, old buddy. And you can be sure of one thing —"

"Come see me tomorrow afternoon. I'll tell you then." He looked down at the duty roster on the desk in front of him and picked up his pen. J.C. stood awkwardly, shifting his weight from one foot to the other and trying to think of a politic valedictory remark. But Emory seemed all at once oblivious to his presence, and rather than risk his displeasure, J.C. stepped quietly out of the guard shack.

When he was gone, Emory raised his head and looked at the closed door. *He ain't no Hondell, but he ought to do all right,* he thought. *He might get lucky and kill himself a Red. I'll have to keep an eye on him, though.*

A drop of sweat formed on the tip of his snub nose, and he blew it off with an explosion of breath and went back to work.

*

The next day, when he returned to the guard shack, J. C. Stackpool was hired as a mine guard for the Wolverine-Fairleigh mines, and was also appointed a deputy sheriff of Harlan County. He was furnished with two pairs of khaki pants and two khaki shirts, a pistol, ammunition, and holster, and a badge, and then moved a few personal items into the guards' barracks. His wife and child were now living with her parents, and, when he thought of them at all, it was with satisfaction that he no longer had to go home to them every night.

He enjoyed the barracks life and his duties were undemanding. During August he spent most of his working hours on guard duty, generally at Black Mountain. Three times he was assigned to a flying squad — twice during the day, raiding homes in search of seditious literature and other evidence of "criminal syndicalism," and once at night, to run a NMU organizer out of the county.

The even tenor of his days was disturbed near the end of the month. Nugent Emory beckoned to him in the chow hall.

"Hey, old buddy, what's the good word?" J.C. asked brightly.

Emory deliberately finished chewing and swallowing the food in his mouth, and washed it down with a swallow of coffee before answering. Then he said, "You used to work at Dead Yellow Dog, didn't you, J.C.?"

"Why, yes, for six damn years. Most miserable place I ever seen in my life."

"Well, cheer up — you're going back there."

The smile faded from J.C.'s face, and was replaced by a look of pinch-nosed wariness. "You're joshing me, Nugent — why in the world would they send me to Dead Yellow Dog?"

" 'Cause the rednecks have got in and are trying to sign up the fellers who work there." He buttered a piece of corn bread thoroughly. "They want to shut down the mine, but they ain't going to. They'll get their ass shut down instead." He took a bite of corn bread, licking the butter from his lips as he chewed.

"Well, you know it don't make a hair of difference to me where I get sent," J.C. said seriously. "You could tell me I was to go to Nome, Alaska, and I'd be there tomorrow, Nugent. But Dead Yellow Dog — there's an awful lot of people there I knowed for years, that I growed up with. I don't think they'd take kindly to seeing me in my deputy's suit."

Emory grinned. "Of course there are people you know there. That's why we're sending you."

"Well, I just ain't too sure —"

"Don't worry, you're not the only man going. There's two other deputies, plus Felix Gill, who's in charge. Plus there's already two guards there to begin with. That makes six of you, all told. If six of you can't handle a few draggle-ass rednecks, I got no use for you."

"Oh, there won't be no problem handling them rednecks, I don't mean that —"

"You better check with Gill. There'll be a truck going into town after breakfast, you'll all go over in that. But you check with him right away. O.K.?" Without waiting for an answer he began speaking to the man beside him at the table. J.C. knew he was dismissed.

*

Claiborne Hord had been in the Harlan County jail since the night of the Battle of Evarts, in early May. When he and the other men arrested with him began their incarceration, there were only forty prisoners in cells meant to accommodate two-thirds that number. But as the summer dragged by, a steady stream of new prisoners arrived, and almost none of the original prisoners left. By the beginning of September, more than a hundred men were jammed together there, under the metal roof on the top floor of the courthouse, where the temperature often reached 115 degrees. Union members were allowed no exercise — they stayed in their cells twenty-four hours a day. They stood, or sat leaning against walls, or lay on the floor. Not more than one man in four had a bunk to sleep on at night, and the mattresses were alive with vermin. Sanitary facilities were a half-dozen galvanized iron buckets, which were dumped when they were full, but never cleaned.

The jailer received a dollar a day from the county to feed each prisoner — and spent twelve cents. The invariable breakfast was a smidgen of fatback served with a biscuit and bulldog gravy; dinner was pinto beans and potatoes; supper was pinto beans and cabbage.

One morning Claiborne was exercising his teeth on an unswallowable chunk of fat and gristle he had begun to chew an hour before. A cell mate named Deeter Collins watched him with silent interest, his fat jaws moving sympathetically as Claiborne attacked with his right-hand teeth for a while, then shifted the cartilaginous lump to his left cheek.

"I swear, next time I patch a tire, I'm going to get me a mess of that meat to work with," Collins said.

"You won't need to get none, you can use this," Claiborne answered thickly. "It'll just about be getting limber by then."

"One thing about you, Hord, you sure know how to make

your vittles last. Here I am hungry as a wolf, and you're just chewing away, happy as can be." The plaintive note in Collins' voice was not entirely satirical.

Claiborne prepared to swallow. He took a deep breath, closed his eyes, centered the meat on his tongue, straightened his neck and raised himself on tiptoe. Then, as he drew the lump down his throat, he simultaneously pulled his head down between his shoulders, collapsed his chest, and bent his knees. In spite of these preparations, the meat caught in his throat. His face turned red, his eyes rolled, and beads of sweat appeared on his forehead. Collins pounded him on the back, and after a few moments his windpipe was clear again. He sank to the floor, shaken.

"God dog, that one about had me for sure, damned if it didn't!" he said weakly.

"If you got to go, it's right nice to go while you're eating," Collins replied.

Before Claiborne could think of anything more to say, a sudden awed silence fell over the whole cell area, as the prisoners became aware of a woman's voice, loud and penetrating, originating from the door at the head of the stairs.

"You slimy toads, you foul maggots, go tell your bosses to lock their windows and bar their doors — the people are sitting in judgment on them! Tell them to expect the mercy they gave the widow and the orphan, the justice they gave the convict, the forgiveness they gave the prostitute! No gun-thugs or vigilantes can save them when the workers pass sentence — the workers they have robbed and starved and murdered!"

"Oh, hush up! Don't you never do nothing but talk?" answered an exasperated male voice. As the men behind the bars craned their necks to see, the door swung open to reveal Jennie Markwell, accompanied by two jail guards. They held her by the arms, and pushed her toward the door of the main cell.

"You might as well get used to my voice, you scum — it'll be ringing in your ears when they put you up against the wall and shoot you!"

"You make getting shot sound like a relief, I swear!" The floor guard unlocked the cell door and stood back, and the other two men propelled Jennie into the crowded cell. The door clanged shut behind her as she spun around to face her captors.

"The time will come when you'll beg for that relief like a thirsty man begs for water," she called after them.

"Oh, Lord have mercy!" complained the guard. "I heard enough from her to last me a lifetime!" He and his companion went back down the stairs, closing the door behind them, and Jennie turned to face her cell mates. Her expression was composed, her eyes were bright, and there was a half smile on her bulldog face.

"Hello, boys," she said conversationally. "We're a little cramped for space, aren't we?"

During the next couple of days Claiborne talked to Jennie Markwell at some length. Although they had never met, each recognized the other's name, and they took to one another from the start. Jennie told him such news as she had about his family — that they had returned to Dead Dog Branch, where Phoebe was preparing to open a soup kitchen, and that Breck was organizing the men at the mine for the NMU. The last item of information was particularly surprising to Claiborne.

"Why, I never would have thought it! Old Breck out there signing up boys for the union — him that would never say 'Fire!' if his pants was burning up! What you reckon got him started organizing?"

Jennie shrugged. "Who knows? You being in jail, the gun-thugs pushing his family around, talking to Mike Rogoff—something got through. Anyway, now he's socially conscious, and he's going to close down Dead Yellow Dog or know the reason why."

"If he don't close it down, he'll know the reason why, for a fact," Claiborne said thoughtfully. "I mean, if he gets himself stomped to flinders, he'll figure out that was the reason why. Most anybody would." He pressed both hands together in front of his face as though he were praying in a very restricted space. His long nose was between his fingers. "If he decided to shoot himself any gun-thugs, I surely do hope he keeps down where they can't see him. It's crowded enough in here already."

Jennie laughed. "That's the truth. But don't worry, they can't keep us all in here forever. Sooner or later Blair and Jones are going to have to bring us to trial, or let us out, one or the other. Either way, it'll be an improvement on this." She pushed a damp strand of hair out of her eyes. "Sweet Jesus, it must be a hundred degrees in here, and it's not even noon yet!"

"I heard tell they was going to move us down to the Bluegrass for our trials. You heard anything about that?"

"There's talk about it. The theory is to get a bunch of horse farmers and businessmen on the jury, and they'll be more likely to convict than mountain people would. I wouldn't worry about it. No matter what happens, we'll tell the world about the whole stinking frame-up. The word will go out, never fear. By the time the trial's over, the Evarts miners will be as famous as Sacco and Vanzetti!"

Claiborne thought that over and decided it wasn't quite what he wanted to know. "I was wondering more like, do you think they'll find us guilty?" he said, half-apologetically.

"I mean, I never was too set on being famous—not that I wouldn't appreciate it. But if I had my druthers, I'd as soon be out."

Jennie gave him a look that was both stern and mocking. "Sometimes I wonder if the metal is worthy of the smith's forge," she said.

"Well, if being worthy means getting pounded the hell out of shape, maybe it ain't," he answered.

Jennie's look became more stern and less mocking. "We all have our jobs to do, Comrade," she said firmly. "Some of us are privileged to give more than others."

"I'm not asking any privileges," Claiborne said quickly. Seeing Jennie's expression grow even sterner, he went on to explain. "Look, Miss Jennie—I can see I'm a disappointment to you, and I want to apologize for that. It ain't that I don't want to help you people, but you got to remember I never even joined up with the NMU. I'm still a member of the UMW of A, unless they kicked me out and never told me. I been in this cell since before you all come to Harlan County. So when you talk about me getting famous, and having this great privilege, and all, I feel like I'm here under false pretenses. Like I don't really belong here, don't you see? It makes me feel terrible."

Jennie smiled suddenly, and her face lit up as though a beam of sunlight had fallen across it. "Claiborne, people like you shouldn't be allowed in revolutions," she said. "You screw things up. You never behave the way anybody expects you to. From now on I'm going to tell myself you're a stool pigeon and a scissorbill, so you can surprise me by being the terror of the barricades."

"Maybe after a while you might want to try it the other way 'round, just for the variety."

Jennie snorted. "If you want to do something useful,

Comrade, step over to that slop bucket there by the wall, and stand in front of it with your back turned. I hear the call of nature."

*

Breck worked as quietly as he could signing up the men at Dead Yellow Dog, but, almost immediately after he arrived, Felix Gill reported to W. F. Tasker that the NMU was organizing the miners. "It's that Hord, all right. He's got a couple men inside the camp here working with him."

"Who are they?"

"Atkins and Combs. They've been talking to the others, getting them to go meet Hord at his cabin up the hollow. That's where he signs them up."

"Fire them. And anybody else you know has joined up." The sour-faced mine guard nodded and turned to leave. "Wait a minute," Tasker said. "That soup kitchen the Hord girl's messing with — is it open yet?"

"No, sir. I heard around that she figures to start feeding folks tomorrow."

"Well, I want you to pass the word that anybody going up there to eat anything just might as well stay there, because they won't be working for Excelsior when they get back. People want to work here, they get their food here, right at the commissary. You make sure they know that — the women, especially."

Gill nodded and left. Tasker got to his feet and walked to the window overlooking the driftmouth. *Somebody always wants to bitch things,* he thought. *Why couldn't they just let well enough alone?*

After Atkins and Combs and five men they had recruited had been fired, Breck abandoned any attempt at secrecy. Every day he waited on the road outside the gate to Excelsior

No. 2, flagging each car that entered or left the property, and handing a mimeographed leaflet to every driver who would take one. Some of the miners wouldn't accept the leaflets, and some took them and then threw them out on the road. Many of the men looked frightened and a few scowled and cursed. Occasionally an approaching car would speed up instead of slowing down, and Breck would have to jump for his life.

But — the leaflets got inside. And at night men continued to come through the woods, avoiding the creekside road where they might be seen, and tap on the door of the Hord cabin as cautiously as a stray dog making friends.

Tasker and Gill continued to fire anyone they suspected of NMU membership, but they realized that there must be many new members who had escaped their suspicions. Vacancies were filled by strikebreakers brought in under police escort — and even one or two of the strikebreakers were recruited into the union. Tasker was outraged when he heard about this. "Jesus Christ, Gill, it's getting so you can't trust anybody!" he exploded.

Gill's five deputies realized the union's organizational drive was succeeding, and it made them apprehensive and angry. J. C. Stackpool was particularly upset. When he had arrived at the mine and learned that Breck Hord was responsible for the situation, his first reaction was incredulity, and his second, pride. It was only after he thought it over for a few moments that he reached his third reaction: the shock of betrayal.

My old buddy, my playfellow, he thought, *how in the world could he do something as low-down, no-account rotten as this? And after we was such good friends, and all!*

Some nights J.C. lay in his bunk, thinking up things to say to Breck when he saw him through the wire the next morning. The next day he would try them out: "Say, Hord, how does it feel to sell out your own people to the Rooshan Reds? They going to make you a Commissar after the Revolution, Comrade?" Or, "Breck, when I knowed you, you used to have good sense. What are you doing in with them Reds and Jews and nigger-lovers? Some things, buddy, the more you stir them, the more they stink. Why don't you come back on your own side?" Or, "I reckon there's something wrong with the Hord blood. I always did figure old Jubal Early was simple, and that girl Phoebe's so crippled up she can't hardly walk, and your brother Claiborne's going to have his neck stretched like he deserves — but none of them are a patch on you, old buddy! You got them beat six ways from Sunday for pure crazy orneriness. I can't wait till they put a bullet right through your belly!"

It enraged J.C. that he couldn't seem to provoke a reaction from Breck, no matter what approach he used. Whether he attacked with sarcasm, calumny, or sweet reason, Breck accepted his words with a level gaze and the slightest hint of a smile. And when he looked into the other's unblinking eyes, J.C. was reminded of the shivaree on Dead Dog Branch, and he could feel remembered soreness in his body. He was reduced to shouting profanity — "Goddamn you to hell, you son-of-a-bitching bastard!" — that had no more bite than a benediction.

During September and early October Breck kept signing up miners. Roughly half those he signed were fired soon after, and moved from the company cabins they had occupied, to tents or lean-tos on Jubal Early's property; the other half remained at work in Dead Yellow Dog, undetected by Gill and his deputies. Finally the day came when Breck believed he could close down the mine.

He told Rogoff, and Rogoff agreed. The two men were

sitting on the porch steps, enjoying the murmurous, moonless night. Breck sat upright, hugging his knees, looking out past the flimsy cloth and tarpaper housing to the black loom of the hill beyond; Rogoff lay back with his head cradled on his arms, staring up at the glittering stars.

"Pull them out," Rogoff said. "They're as ready as they'll ever be. Get the word out tomorrow — call the strike for the next day."

"All right."

When Breck didn't say anything more, Rogoff raised his head and looked at him. "There are going to be problems, Breck. You know that. But you'll have the union behind you all the way."

"All right," said Breck again. For a moment Rogoff was irritated that Breck didn't ask for advice or encouragement. He opened his mouth to point out some of the troubles sure to lie ahead, but then thought better of it and lowered his head onto his crossed wrists again.

"*Oi vay,* will you look at all those stars," he said, stressing the Yiddish phrase drolly, as he sometimes did with goyim. "You wouldn't see so many in a whole month in Chicago."

"I reckon," said Breck absently. He was silent a moment. Then he said, softly, "You're sure as sunup we're going to win this strike, ain't you? I wish I could be as sure as you fellers are. Sure about anything, I mean. Sure about water always being wet, even — sure about trees always growing up, instead of down. Sometimes I get to thinking, I ain't hardly sure of my own name. It'd be easier, if a man could be sure."

"And you think *we* are sure — Rasmusson, and Coy and me?" Rogoff shifted his position, propping his head up on one elbow. "I'll tell you what we're sure of, Breck. We're not sure of winning *this* strike. What we are sure of is *winning*, period. We know history is on our side. We know that sooner or later there will be justice in the world. We don't believe there's any power strong enough to stop it. It's coming. Maybe not this year, maybe not this lifetime, but it's coming just the same."

"If you're so sure it's coming anyway, why stick your neck out and maybe get it chopped off? Why not just wait for it to come?"

"Because there's always a chance we can make it come sooner, and we wouldn't be men if we didn't try. Poor people have terrible lives, dirty, hungry, hopeless lives. If we can help to push history along so even one generation of people who would have been poor can be saved that, then it's been worthwhile."

"But it ain't going to be this generation — and it ain't going to be in Harlan County."

"Listen. In church, when a little baby dies before it's even had a taste of life, or when some awful, unfair thing happens to some good person, while the bastard right next to him is making a fortune screwing people, the preacher says it's God's Will, it's Predestination. And when some drunk falls down three flights of stairs and gets up on his feet without a scratch, we call it Dumb Luck. Well, I say Predestination and Dumb Luck are two ways of saying the same thing — that our destiny is out of our hands, and there's no point in getting our bowels in an uproar about it. Whether some God with a long beard is handling things, or whether everything works out like billiard balls bumping together and pushing each other around the table, it doesn't make any difference to us. All we can do is just do our jobs."

Breck said sadly, "That ain't much to lean on."

Rogoff grinned mirthlessly. "What did you have before? The American Dream? Look, where I grew up on the West

Side of Chicago, I was a dirty kike, and if I didn't want to spend my life in a sweatshop going blind twelve hours a day, with a wife and six kids I couldn't afford to feed, drinking soda water because my gut was rotted out, then maybe I could go into the rackets, selling niggers policy numbers! But whichever, I was a billiard ball, believe me! Click, click, click, and into the side pocket. Have you ever heard of a billiard ball deciding what direction to go?"

"How's that so different from now — if you don't even know how this strike here in Harlan is going to turn out?"

"Because now I *know* I'm a billiard ball, and I don't care," Rogoff said earnestly. "I'm doing what I'm supposed to do, and it will all work out by some kind of higher mathematics, some kind of physics of history. It's got to — and by working to make it happen, I'm *proving* that it's got to. And maybe I'm making it happen a little sooner! Can you understand that?"

Breck was silent a moment, then he sighed. "I guess I can understand it for *you* — but it ain't all that much help to *me*. I mean, winning a strike in Detroit, Michigan, in the year two thousand ought ten is fine for the people who'll be living there then — but I guess I care more about Dead Yellow Dog right now. I kind of hoped you'd help set my mind at rest."

"No, I can't set your mind at rest. All I can do is promise you it means something."

"And what if that ain't enough?"

"Then I'm sorry."

Breck didn't answer, and Rogoff tried to think of something to say that would raise his spirits. He was still rummaging through his mind when Breck spoke again.

"That time by the Evarts bridge, before you come down, when we shot Darling and them other gun-thugs — all I can remember thinking was, killing is an important thing in a man's life; it ought to mean something bigger than just getting a feller you don't like. A friend of mine named Sam Troutman was just a few feet away from me, and his body was all tore up with machine-gun bullets. Every so often, it would jump and twitch when another bullet hit it. And I lay there asking myself was it enough reason for Sam to be dead, just because we hate the gun-thugs?"

"It wasn't just the gun-thugs you hated. It was the men behind them."

"Then how come we didn't shoot the men behind them?"

"That's what the strike is, Breck — a way of shooting the men behind them. A better way than with bullets. You can't reach them with bullets, and, if you could, you'd only kill the human part of them. But that's not the important part; it's the money part that's important. The strike hits them in the money part, the big fat money belly where all their power comes from. If we can get enough good solid licks in there, we've moved history along a few inches."

"I reckon." Breck realized he wasn't likely to get an answer from Rogoff that would satisfy him completely, and it was getting late. He sighed and got to his feet. "I'll tell the boys about day after tomorrow. They'll be glad to hear we're ready."

Rogoff rose also. "Do that. And, Breck." He put his hand on the other's shoulder, and gave it a squeeze. "Don't try to nail everything down in your mind overnight. Ride with it."

"Ain't much else I can do, seems like." Breck said with a small grin.

*

The next day Felix Gill found out Breck's plans before noon. He told W. F. Tasker, who immediately called Black Mountain, where he talked to Nugent Emory. Emory asked for Gill to be put on the phone.

"Listen, Gill — are your boys all right? Are they up to a little work tonight?"

"Why, sure. It'll be good for them — they've been jumpy lately, with nothing to do but watch the goddamned union grow."

"All right, tonight we'll lean on the rednecks a little. You be ready about midnight. I'll bring over four or five more boys from up here, and we'll take a run over to Hord's place."

"What we aiming to do?"

Emory chuckled. "Why don't we just wait and see what happens when we get there? Only I wouldn't plan on no bowl of soup at the soup kitchen, if I were you!"

That night Phoebe and Joicy were closing the kitchen when Francis Duffy came by for a cup of coffee. The old shotfirer was as spruce as usual. His clean white shirt, threadbare at the collar, was meticulously mended and smelled of lye soap; his face was as pink and scrubbed looking as if it had been laundered at the same time.

Duffy had lived in an old army pup tent on the Hords' land ever since he was fired from Dead Yellow Dog for "sedition." He was a lonely man, with few friends, but the Hords had always been kind to him, and he reciprocated by helping out at the soup kitchen. He was an insomniac, and often would leave his sleepless bed in disgust and walk to the kitchen in hopes of conversation and coffee to make the night pass faster.

He sat over a mug of black coffee, with his blue-veined hands wrapped around it to keep the welcome heat from dissipating. Phoebe and Joicy were completing their work for the night. In a few moments they would be through, would turn out the lamp, and lock the door, and Duffy would have to return to his twisted blankets. To delay the moment, he was arguing with the women about their recipe for bean soup.

"Disputing with a man from Schuylkill County about bean soup is like disputing with a beaver about building bridges," he said aggressively. "With McClure not twenty miles from where I grew to manhood, and the bean soup they make there famous throughout the civilized world!"

"Well, this ain't McClure bean soup, this is Harlan County bean soup, and that means we make do," Phoebe retorted briskly. "If you don't look at your spoon through it, it won't seem so thin."

"I've seen thicker *water,*" Duffy said.

"Then you should have et it when you seen it," Phoebe snapped. Joicy giggled, and Phoebe flashed her a smile of ackowledgment; since Claiborne had been in Harlan jail, Phoebe had risen above her dislike of her sister-in-law, and the two women had arrived at a friendly, if not intimate, relationship.

"If there was any bacon, wouldn't nobody mind putting it in, Mr. Duffy," Joicy said. "But I can't remember the last time I seen any bacon. Miss Craig and the Labor Family Relief people, the only meat they send in is fatback and jowl. Most of it, if it ain't fat, it's gristle."

Duffy took one hand from his coffee mug and rubbed his smooth pink chin. "It's the difference of night and day, what a handful of fried-up bacon bits can do." He licked his lips in reminiscence, and his eyes looked back down a corridor of years to a remembered soup so thick, so dark, so pungent, so steam-wreathed and nubbly-textured on the tongue, no other soup had ever overlaid its memory.

Emory entered the room quickly, four deputies behind him. Five others waited in the darkness outside. All had their guns drawn. Emory's eyes flicked from Phoebe, to Joicy, to Duffy, then back to Joicy again. "Well, if it ain't Big Tits. I ain't seen you since we put your man in jail, Big Tits. You been getting enough, hon?"

Joicy stared at the intruders in shocked surprise, for a moment unable to understand their presence in the kitchen. But Phoebe's reaction was instantaneous. She flung the nearest object at hand, a small saucepan, at Emory's head, and simultaneously began to scream, "Fire! Help, fire! Gun-thugs gonna set fire to the kitchen!" Emory struck her on the temple with his pistol barrel, and she fell backward over a chair and sprawled on the floor, unconscious. Joicy began to scream then, and Emory slapped her across the mouth. "Get her in the car and keep her quiet," he ordered J. C. Stackpool, who was closest to her. "Gill, you get that coal oil slopped around, now! The rest of you boys, you fix up them stoves and this other truck — I don't want no more meals cooked here, ever!"

Francis Duffy stood up slowly, his hands half-extended toward Emory. "You can't do this, man — you've burnt down one kitchen around their heads already," he cried in a shaking voice.

"Shut up and get out if you don't want your own ass fried," Emory snapped. He poked the old Irishman in the belly sharply with the muzzle of his pistol.

"So help me God, you'll pay for your crimes," Duffy shrieked wildly. "The hawks will have your eyeballs, and the dogs will be nosing out your guts!"

Emory lost his temper and knocked the old man to the floor, then began kicking him toward the door. "You old fart, I told you to get out! Out, goddamn you, out!"

His face transformed by sudden fear, Duffy scrambled crablike ahead of the heavy work shoes that arched toward him and exploded in his chest and side. He scuttled over the doorsill, rose to his feet, and ran toward the dark hill. One of the deputies tripped him as he passed, and he sprawled full length on the ground. He heard laughter around him as he pulled himself to his feet and began to run again. He didn't stop until he was deep in the shadow of the trees.

Emory dragged Phoebe out of the shack by her ankles, as though she were a sack of meal, and slung her from the porch. "You fix them stoves and all?" he called into the kitchen. One of the men inside shouted an affirmative. "Then touch her off!" A match flared in the darkness, and the flare spread into a serrated strip of flickering orange, silhouetting the deputies as they ran through the door onto the porch. In a moment the thin bright line exploded into a swirling ball of flame pushing at the thin dry walls that compressed it. The sound was like firecrackers exploding among a flock of geese, with a waterfall in the background.

In the sudden flickering brightness, Emory could see the two cars of his command clearly. He trotted to the one in which Joicy sat in the back seat, held silent and motionless by a guard on each side of her. He opened the right front door and climbed in beside the driver, slamming the door behind him. "Well, I reckon breakfast's going to be a mite delayed tomorrow," he said comfortably. "But don't you worry, Big Tits. We'll figure out something for you to eat." He smiled at Joicy as the engine roared and the car jerked forward away from the burning cabin. His good humor, briefly threatened by Francis Duffy, was completely restored.

*

It was false dawn when Joicy walked back along the creekside and up on the porch of the Hord cabin. Breck and Jubal Early were at the scene of the fire; Hannah and Bonnie Brae sat with Phoebe, who tossed restlessly in her sleep. Aunt Cloa Burkett was with them.

Joicy walked with a heavy step, and held her body stiffly. She brushed a lock of hair back from her forehead, and with her other hand idly poked the hem of her shirtwaist into her skirt and smoothed it down. The only expression on her face was fatigue.

"The gun-thugs took me off. When they burnt the kitchen," she said simply.

Hannah and Bonnie Brae rushed to her, pressed her down into a chair, patted her, gave her a cup of coffee, and kept up a steady hum of solicitous and loving phrases. Aunt Cloa sat unmoving through thirty seconds of this, her eyes as bright and hard as the points on new fishhooks. Then she interrupted: "Did they do it to you?"

"Yes, they did."

"How'd they do it?"

"They helt me down. One helt my feet, and another helt my hands pulled up over my head. I fought hard as I could" — she paused for a moment, and then innate honesty forced her to finish the sentence — "for the first two or three times."

"Who was it? What ones could you recognize?"

"Nugent Emory, him that's the head gun-thug. And that J. C. Stackpool. I don't recollect the others."

"You sure? You sure you ain't seen them over to Dead Yellow Dog or someplace? You sure you can't remember anything that can put a name to them?"

Joicy shook her head hopelessly. "No'm — I didn't even look at their faces any more than I had to. Poor Claiborne, it's going to be a worry and a shame to him, when he finds out."

"Don't you fret about that — there's a lot can happen 'twixt now and then." She patted her fat little hands together decisively. "All right. Bonnie Brae, you make sure no menfolks come in that door. The first thing we want to make sure of is, there ain't going to be no new gun-thugs born into this world. Joicy, honey, you just sit back in your chair and put your feet up on the edge of the table here . . ."

Rogoff heard about it early the next morning, and came directly to the Hords' cabin. Breck wasn't home and Joicy was asleep, but Phoebe had just awakened, and Rogoff sat with her a few minutes. They were alone in the room.

"It don't seem possible people could be so low-down mean," Phoebe said. "Just to try to give a little food to hungry folks who don't have nothing else to eat — is that so bad you'd burn a house down to stop it?"

"If you wanted to stop the strike, *yes,* you'd burn the soup kitchens down. Of course you would. Because the kitchens do more to keep the workers going than anything else." He took Phoebe's hand in his. Her eyes widened, and her fingers trembled on the verge of flight, then settled back warily in his clasp. "Phoebe, don't you know you're more help to the NMU than a roomful of new organizers?"

She looked at him for a moment, then turned her eyes to the window. "Pshaw. There ain't nothing to cooking up a kettle of soup."

"There's a lot more to it than that. And you know it, or, if you don't, you're the only person in Dead Yellow Dog who doesn't." He squeezed her hand, but her cold fingers gave no answering pressure. "How do you feel, Phoebe? How's your head where he hit you?"

"Oh, I been worse off and lived. It ain't *that* that hurts so much. It's that anybody, even a low-life gun-thug like Nugent Emory, or a sneak like that J. C. Stackpool, would want to take food away from hungry people, from old women and little babies — the only food they had! That's what hurts!"

"Do you think you'll be able to start over — set up another soup kichen? If we could find you a place for it? I mean, would you feel up to it?"

She turned her face toward him. Her eyes brightened, and the pale skin over her cheekbones was suddenly flushed. "Of course I'd feel up to it! Somebody's got to feed them people, and I already got the hang of it."

Why, she's beautiful! Rogoff thought in surprise. "Aren't you afraid?" he asked gently.

She reflected a moment. "I reckon I am, in a way. Only I'm more afraid of something else."

"What's that, Phoebe?"

"Going back to like I was before the soup kitchens come. Going back to when I didn't even like living with myself."

"Don't worry — you'll never go back to that. You never could now, Phoebe." Slowly, his face moved toward hers. Her eyes were so wide they looked almost round. "Phoebe," he said again, almost inaudibly. His lips touched hers. Her mouth trembled like sweet berries on a branch stirred by the wind. He put both hands on her shoulders and pulled her body gently against his. After a moment he felt her hands cross on the back of his neck. The kiss lasted many seconds, and when he withdrew his mouth from hers, he still held her tightly in his arms. "Phoebe. You're somebody. You're really somebody," he said.

Her eyes were shut tight. "Oh, yes," she whispered joyously. "Oh, I am!"

Breck came back to the cabin a few minutes later, and he and Rogoff went outside to talk. As he left the room, Rogoff turned to look at Phoebe. "Now you take care of yourself, you heah?" he said, goodhumoredly mimicking the speech of the mountain people.

"I hear," she replied. "You too." The two men left and the door closed behind them. Phoebe sighed and pressed her hands tightly together. She didn't feel sorry for herself at all.

Rogoff had come to see Breck to assure himself that his lieutenant at Dead Yellow Dog wasn't about to undertake a private vendetta which would jeopardize the shutting down of the Excelsior mines. He soon discovered he had nothing to worry about. Breck was determined on revenge, but he intended to enjoy it his own way, the mountain way — without having to pay a price for it at law. In a month, or in a year, Nugent Emory would die and nobody in the world would be able to prove that Breck Hord's finger pressed the trigger.

Francis Duffy didn't feel that way.

The old Irishman had received a near-mortal blow to his self-esteem. The image of himself scuttling away from Emory's flying boots was clamped immovably over the lens of his memory; he could think of nothing, remember nothing, hope for nothing that wasn't double-printed with the picture of his humiliation.

From the burning soup kitchen he had returned directly to his tent, keeping to the trees and shadows. He crawled inside and felt underneath his blankets until he found his rifle. It was the same .22 bolt-action, single-shot Remington he had carried at Evarts, when for a thrilling moment he thought he had killed Jim Darling. Since that time he had taken it hunting often. His marksmanship was respectable.

A box of .22 long rifle ammunition was wrapped with the rifle in a sheet of oilcloth. Duffy opened the box, counted out ten cartridges, and put them into his breast pocket. He closed the box, neatly folded the oilcloth around it, and tucked the parcel under the blankets, at the rear corner of the tent. Then he hesitated, squatting in the musty darkness with the rifle across his thighs, feeling that there was something he should do before he left. Some final thing. But he couldn't think what it was.

He intended to go to the Black Mountain camp, headquarters for Nugent Emory's mine guards. He also intended to get there without being seen, which meant avoiding the road through Harlan Town and cutting straight across country, up and over the crest of Big Black Mountain, down to the valley of Clover Fork, up and over a second crest, and finally down behind the armed camp on Schoolhouse Branch. By crow-flight line, it was a distance of five miles. Duffy knew it would take him most of the day to travel it.

The climb over Big Black Mountain was hard on him. As he approached the crest, he stopped often to catch his breath. *Twenty years ago I could have taken it at a dead run,* he thought. *It's a shame to sit here blowing like a leaky bellows.* The trip down the south side of the mountain was much easier. The sun was well up, and birds were singing in the trees. He found that his thoughts turned lovingly to his childhood and young manhood in Pennsylvania half a century before. He remembered one girl with braids and freckles, another who smelled of peppermint and young sweat. He thought of a good girl, who had seemed too virtuous to approach, and a bad girl, about whom he had compared notes with his friends after the fact. He tried to recall the name of a girl he had thought he loved, and who had married another, and after a few moments succeeded.

Young women they run like hares on the mountain, he sang to himself with quiet irony. *If I were but a young man, I'd sure go a-hunting, To my right, follow-dee-yo, to my right, follow-dee.*

When he reached the bank of Clover Fork, he sat down under a yellow-leafed maple and took off his shoes and socks. *They say if you get your foot wet in Clover Fork, you'll spend the rest of your days in Harlan County,* he remembered. He grinned suddenly. *I wouldn't be at all surprised if that was true.*

He forded the creek and started up the second rise. It was nearly noon, and the air was still. He began to perspire, and breathing became difficult again. He had to stop and rest often, and when he walked, he held on to tree trunks to steady himself. After an hour he was still midway up the slope, and for the first time wondered if he would be able to reach the summit. The memory of his humiliation at the hands of Nugent Emory gave him the strength and stubbornness to keep going. The last hundred yards up, he fell three times; the third time, he lay on the ground for a full minute before he realized he must look just as he had the night before, when the deputies had tripped him outside the soup kitchen. He struggled to his feet and reached the crest.

Below him and a mile away stretched the thin silver ribbon of Schoolhouse Branch. Beside it lay Black Mountain camp. He could see the barracks buildings, the slag heap, the tipple, the cluster of cabins on the creekside, the management houses higher up the hill. *Glory be, it looks as though I could toss a rock down on it and squash it entirely,* he thought.

He worked his way down the hillside, careful to keep out of sight from the camp below. By three in the afternoon he had taken up a position less than fifty yards from the barbed-wire perimeter, and had settled down to watch and wait for his quarry.

There was a continual flurry of comings and goings around the barracks. Cars arrived and departed, men lounged on the front steps of the buildings or briskly went about their business, and a game of work-up baseball was in progress. Duffy lay behind a tree and observed it all, his wise turtle's eyes hooded against the late afternoon glare.

Nugent Emory drove up to his office in the guard shack, and entered the building. He parked his car in such a position that its left side was facing Duffy. From where he lay concealed, the old shot-firer could look down through the open car window to the seat where Emory would be sitting when he started the engine again.

He had an excellent shot; no more than seventy-five yards, a downward angle of twenty-five degrees, and no wind. All he had to do was wait until Emory came out of the guard shack and put his head into the sights. Duffy raised the rifle butt to his shoulder and maneuvered the car window, the blade of the front sight, and the vee of the back sight into alignment.

Then, with consternation, he realized he could not hold them there. His hands were shaking so much the front sight surged above the car's roof, then sank below its running board. And worse, as he held his breath waiting for the three-point alignment to return, his eyes misted, and he seemed to be looking out from under a foot of sloshing water.

God strike me, I can't do it! he thought in anguish. *Will the bastard get away with it then, after all?* For a moment he could think of nothing but the humiliation he would have no way to expunge, and he was nauseated by his feelings of futility and self-contempt.

But in a few seconds he regained control of his emotions.

He realized that if he could not trust his own hands and body to provide a stable gun platform, he could nevertheless construct one from the rocks and fallen branches around him. With extreme caution, he began to assemble flat stones and straight pieces of wood until he had enough to begin using them to angle and steady the rifle. He worked slowly, only adding a rock or stick when he was sure it would reinforce the alignment rather that weaken it. He was afraid Emory would reappear before he had the weapon firmly sighted in on the piece of air one foot above and one foot to the rear of the center of the steering wheel.

But the gun platform was completed before Emory climbed back into the driver's seat.

Duffy's finger rested as lightly as thistledown against the trigger. It was the only part of the gun he touched. His pale blue eye gleamed behind the rear sight, the third point in the alignment. When Emory settled into the car seat, his left temple became the fourth point. For a second, Emory's head was absolutely motionless; Duffy pressed back the trigger, and the gun made a flat *plop* of a sound.

But nothing happened. Emory's head moved again, the car's engine came to life, Emory shifted to reverse gear, turned his face toward Duffy, and put his head out of the car window, preparing to back away from the wall of the guard shack. The shot had missed. For a moment Duffy was so shocked he couldn't move. Then, wildly, he wrenched the rifle from the framework of rock and wood he had worked so long to construct, jerked open the bolt, pushed another cartridge into the breech, slapped the bolt closed, swung the butt to his shoulder, and instantly fired again.

Below him, Emory continued to back away from the shack, unaware of the two tiny lead pellets which had just passed within a few inches of his head. After he had backed twenty feet or so, he shifted gears and began to move forward toward the dirt road that led out of the camp. He leaned forward over the steering wheel.

In desperation Duffy loaded the rifle again, and, as Emory's car passed slowly before him, fired a third time without even pausing to sight. Incredibly, a neat, round hole a little smaller than the diameter of a pencil appeared in Nugent Emory's temple. His smooth, firm chin sank to his breast, and the car's engine stuttered, and its forward motion ceased. It coasted quietly to stillness.

Francis Duffy stood clearly visible on the hill, his rifle held theatrically above his head, any idea of concealment either forgotten or rejected. *Ah, if the Mollies could see me now!* his heart cried. *Ah, if they could see Francis Duffy, with the blood of his enemy watering the poor ground of Harlan County! Ah, Mother! It's your son Francis that has done this!*

Five mine guards fired simultaneously, and Duffy was dead before he hit the ground.

expected. Breck had achieved considerable support and control, and the miners were content to look to him for direction. He had never made them unrealistic promises and had always pointed out the difficulties that lay ahead, so they were better able to face the approach of cold weather than some of their more optimistic union brothers.

Dead Yellow Dog was almost completely shut down. A maintenance gang kept up power for necessary services, but W. F. Tasker didn't try to go beyond that. He was sure the strike would collapse with the first snow, if not before, and was content to bide his time. His reading of the political realities within the Fairleigh-Wolverine empire led him to believe that there would be a reaction against the violence ordered by the Coal Operators' Association, and that the man whose record showed him to be both moderate and far-sighted would come into increased favor with management during the months ahead.

He argued his point of view with his head guard, Felix Gill. "Goddamn it, Gill, all this union crap will be forgotten by Thanksgiving. Why, buddy, at the big camps on Clover Fork and Martin's Fork, the miners are coming back three, four, six a day, and the colder it gets, the faster they'll come in! It just stands to reason! What you reckon they'll live on if they don't come back to work?"

"How do you know the union won't open up more of them soup kitchens, and bring down all kinds of food from up north?" the head guard said stubbornly. "How do you know them bastards won't still have their picket line across the gate this same time next year?"

"Because they won't be able to get through the winter, can't you understand that? Food's only one thing — but where are they going to live? In those spit-and-paper shacks of theirs? Why, hell, Felix, every one of them'll be down with the bloody flux, or influenza, or pneumonia, or some other damn disease the first day it snows! They'll either come back then, or they'll be lined up as stiff as pokers, waiting to be buried when the melt comes next March."

"Mr. Tasker, all I know is your mine's shut down, you don't know when it's going to open again, and we're just sitting around on our ass and not doing nothing about it. Why don't we lean on somebody?"

"Because I say not, is why!" Tasker glared at Gill angrily for a moment, then, his native caution drawing him back from an unnecessary clash with his head guard, he continued in a reasonable tone: "Look, buddy, all I'm saying is I don't want your boys out gunning for any Harlan County folks. I don't want any of our people dead. I don't give a damn what you do to any New York Jew Communist you get your hands on."

"How about Breck Hord? He's worse than the Communists."

"Felix, I said no Harlan County folks! Don't forget that I'm going to — that *we're* going to be living here long after the last Communist is back in New York City! We don't want to poison the well! Remember what I say, now — leave our own people alone. You need some exercise, get it off the foreigners."

Gill glared at the mine manager in bristling disagreement. "That ain't the way John Henry Blair wants it. That ain't the way they think up at Black Mountain."

"Well, that's the way I think here, and it's me that does the thinking at Excelsior. And that's all there is to it." The two men looked at each other measuringly for a second, and then Gill nodded curtly and turned to leave. Searching for a subject which would end their meeting on a happier note, Tasker called after him, "Oh, Felix. I hear one of your boys is beating my time. Now, that's a hell of a thing to do to a poor old cocksman like me."

Gill turned, and his thin white lips flexed in the hint of a smile. "That right? Somebody dipping his wick into your lamp oil? Well, I declare!"

"You bastard, you know that goddamned J. C. Stackpool has been screwing Amy Herron! If *I* know it, every other damn soul on Dead Dog Branch has known it for weeks! Don't play dumb with me!" Tasker said, feigning indignation.

Gill grinned more broadly. "One thing I don't worry about is who's getting what pussy, Mr. Tasker. You worry about it, I guess it's up to you to do something about it. Only I sure hope you don't make a damn fool of yourself!" The head guard's eyes sparkled maliciously. "Every man gets the horns put to him once or twice, so they say." He turned again and left the office.

Tasker relaxed, and his aggrieved expression changed to one of satisfaction. He had decided to relieve himself of Amy Herron's favors months ago. He had begun a new relationship with the sixteen-year-old daughter of one of the men on his maintenance crew, and had been anxious for his former mistress to find a new lover so she would stop searching for opportunities for private recriminations. He was only surprised it had taken her so long.

It won't hurt for the boys to think they've got it up old W. F., he thought comfortably. *It ain't easy to hate a man when you're plunking his gal.*

*

Mike Rogoff's last day in Harlan County began before dawn, when he awoke suddenly in his bed in an Evarts boarding house. One moment he was dreamlessly asleep, and the next he was wide-awake as if he had been up for hours, lying flat on his back with his eyes open and staring up at the ceiling. *It's here,* he thought briskly. *Whatever it is, this is the day for it.*

Since he had come to Kentucky, Rogoff had often remembered that terrible night in Chicago when he had discovered the fear of death. Remembered, not relived; the crawling terror had not returned, only the memory of it, the surprise at its intensity, and at his inability to cope with it.

This morning was something different, neither the original terror nor the secondhand recollection, but a new thing that was close to acceptance. But acceptance with no sacrifice of the will to resist, no fatalism, no boneless slide toward Predestination or Dumb Luck — for, regardless of his words to Breck Hord, he had never really considered himself a mindless billiard ball bouncing off the rails of economic determinism. *So if it's coming, let it come. A man does what he can.*

He lay in his bed, calmly watching the ceiling turn from black to gray, and then to its normal daytime color of mottled dun. His mind was empty, so empty that occasional random thoughts seemed to give off echoes in its depths. After a half-hour he sat up and threw the blanket back. *It's a day like any other day, and it's time to get up.*

He had coffee and corn bread for breakfast, then walked to the NMU office on the main street of the town. There was a message asking him to meet with Rasmusson and Coy in Harlan Town at noon, and he called back and made an appointment. He looked through an envelope of press cuttings from northern liberal magazines, sent by Ike Silver. Three representatives of a local on Black Joe Branch came to argue strategy for a meeting, and he sided with one of them against the other two. He took a minute to jot down a list of immediate expenses, for which he would need more than sixty dollars within the next five days. Liz Craig called, asking if he could spare four or five men to ride shotgun on a three-truck convoy of food coming in from Lexington, and he agreed to have the men waiting in Manchester by mid-afternoon. He heard reports of violence the night before in three coal camps off of Poor Fork. He decided there was nothing to be done about two of them, but, in the case of the third, he called in one of the men who lounged outside the union hall all day long and gave him some instructions. The man, who was armed with a cheap .32 caliber pistol, then left.

From ten to eleven, Rogoff wrote a report for Comrade Brown in Chicago. It demanded the utmost in concentration, not only because he was a poor typist, but because he was determined not to give Brown any information he could use against anyone, any time — not an easy job, considering the unpredictable changes of direction the Party line was likely to take in the future.

He finished the report, sealed it in an envelope, and placed it in the desk drawer where it would remain until picked up by the courier who would take it out of the county before mailing it. Then he leaned back in his chair and rolled his first cigarette of the morning.

So — if today's the day, what then? he thought calmly. *Any final conclusions, do yourself a favor and draw them now — there may not be time later.* He struck a match and pulled a mouthful of harsh smoke into his lungs. He released his thoughts from the necessities of time and place and found they carried him swiftly back to his youth. He remembered: a gang fight on a West Side El platform, and the annihilating desperation he had felt when two Irish kids tried to push him onto the third rail; the rat he had captured in his younger brother's crib, where it had come to gnaw the milk-stiffened blanket that half covered the baby's head; the smell of wet wool and sweaty bodies in the Jewish school after a rain; riding on the 39th Street streetcar (it wasn't called Pershing Road then) past the Campbell's Soup plant, and smelling the boxcars full of ripe and overripe tomatoes; the Lake Michigan beaches in summer, where he went to look at the shiksas and the fear he felt because he knew it was wrong and would probably be punished for it by the muscular Wops and Polacks and Micks and Lugans and Krauts who lolled around their girls on the sand like young Charles Atlases. He remembered hs sister's loveless marriage and his father's agonized death. He remembered the icy snowballs kids would make from the gray snow that covered the ground like filthy bandages over a wound, and the exploding pain when one of them hit him on the cheekbone. He remembered a summer Sunday at Lincoln Park Zoo, when he had a bag of peanuts to feed the animals. He remembered his hoarded three-inch stack of Haldeman-Julius Little Blue Books — Marx, Freud, Havelock Ellis, and Jack London — that had turned the doorknob and opened the door of the world a crack for him. He remembered much fear and anger and despair, and very little joy.

Tentative final conclusion: the mass of men lead lives of quiet desperation. Or anyway, this one did. Or would have, if he hadn't done something about it. Another tentative final conclusion: nobody should be poor. Still another tentative final conclusion: the kind of a God who would create something like this — who needs Him? Or would keep Him around on a bet?

His cigarette burned his fingers and he crushed it out in his tin ashtray. His thoughts arranged themselves in a kind of catechism, which he recited to himself, playing the roles of both questioner and respondent: *Is hope possible? Yes. How may one hope? By working for the Party. Will hopes come true? Eventually. For us, and for the people we know? Irrelevant. Then what have we to give the people today, in their own lives? The certainty of progress toward socialism. That's all? That's all. But that's not enough to promise them, is it? No. Then we must lie to them? Of course. And lying, can our conscience still remain clear? Yes, and in no other way.*

He was surprised to find his fingers rolling another cigarette, although he had made no conscious decision to do so. *All kinds of things happen without anybody deciding to do them. That's the inevitability of the historic process, and I'm a part of it, as long as I exist. But when you've stopped existing, what's it like then? How does it feel not to feel?*

Oh, no you don't! he told himself firmly. *That kind of foolish question we don't waste time on — no matter what day it is!*

He sat motionless, and willed his mind blank. He was successful for a few moments, but then shapes and words began to form again. "I know what I'll do," he said aloud in a cheery voice. "I'll write Ruth." He rolled a blank sheet of paper into the typewriter and pecked out the words "Dear Ruth" on it. Then he stopped to think what he should say to his sister in the first letter he had ever written her.

"How's tricks, Sis?" he typed, trying for a light, brotherly tone. "I hope you had a nice summer in Rogers Park. How's Morris, the Julius Rosenwald of Morse Avenue? Did you get in plenty of swimming? How are the kids? I calculate it's about time for Martin's bar mitzvah — wish I could be there to celebrate. Give a hug and a kiss to Sarah —" *Shit,* he thought disgustedly, and tore the paper from the machine and inserted another sheet. "Dear Ruth," he wrote, "You'll be surprised to see a Kentucky postmark on this letter. Well, Sis, therein lies a tale. I came down here five months ago to help the local coal miners organize a union, and it's been something less than a tea dance at the Edgewater Beach, believe me. I mean these mountain boys are *rough!* Half the people in the county are deputy sheriffs, and they'll try anything to stop the union – you name it, they've done it. The Iron Guard in Europe has nothing –" His typing slowed and then stopped. *What am I telling her this for?* he thought wryly. *If she'd cared about the revolution, would she have married Morris the Moneybag Myerson?* He pulled the second sheet from the typewriter, crumpled it, and threw it into a wastebasket to lie beside the first.

He wrote the third draft slowly and deliberately, with the trace of a smile on his lips. "Dear Ruth. I'm writing to wish you and Morris and the children well. We took different routes in life when we left home, and who is to know which of us was right, if either of us was? One thing we agreed on, neither of us was going to settle for the West Side ghetto. You wanted to get out of it, I wanted to get rid of it – *shalom,* an end to argument. You traded it for an eight-room apartment with a lake view, and I for a rooming house in Harlan County, Kentucky. Both good trades, and who knows which was the better?" *I know which was the better,* he thought. "I want an end to resentment and hostility between us, Ruth. I know the last time we saw each other I said terrible things to you and to Morris. I wish I could unsay them, sincerely. I hope you will try to put them out of your mind, just as I will try to forget some things you said at the same time. Nobody has enough brothers and sisters to afford to lose one."

Ah, Ruth, I remember you after Papa died, in your prim white shirtwaist and black skirt, your eyes so dark and scared looking, your mouth so soft when you didn't remember to press your lips together. That was before you graduated from the business college, and got a job in the Loop, and began to wear ambition like make-up on your face.

"My wish for you and your family is a better world, a goal we can agree on even if we disagree on ways of reaching it. Tell Martin and Sarah their Uncle Mike loves them. Your affectionate brother —" He pulled the paper from the typewriter and scrawled his signature on it, *"Michael."*

Reading it over, he felt it had a fatalistic tone about it, so he wrote under his signature in longhand, "With any luck, I may be able to see you for Hanukkah. Mazel tov!" Then he addressed an envelope and sealed and stamped the letter.

He pushed his chair back from the desk, rose to his feet, and left the office, beckoning to another of the men who lounged on the street outside. "Henry, are you busy?" he asked unnecessarily. "Can you take a ride into town with me?" Henry nodded, pleased to be singled out for duty. "You're heeled, aren't you?" Rogoff asked him in a low voice. Henry looked blank, and Rogoff said patiently, "That means you have a gun, don't you?" Henry grinned and nodded. "Good," Rogoff said, and walked down the street to his car, with Henry following. They both got in, and Rogoff headed toward Harlan.

He met Rasmusson and Coy in a house a mile from the city, and they talked about the probable future of the strike. There was no doubt that union membership had peaked and was now declining. The question was whether to undertake some dramatic action which might either speed up or slow down the decline, or to try to continue into cold weather with things as they were. Rasmusson had heard that a group of well-known writers and educators was expected to visit Harlan County shortly, and felt that nothing uncertain should be started until the celebrities had concluded their investigation and left the coalfields. Coy argued that unless the erosion of members was stopped now, the strike was lost anyway — he suggested dynamiting some of the larger mines. Rogoff refused to take a position, and pointed out that, as field organizers, their job was simply to acquaint the NMU home office with the facts; Pittsburgh would tell them what to do. The meeting ended on an inconclusive note. Rogoff collected Henry and drove out along the Poor Fork road. He had two other stops to make before Dead Yellow Dog, and it was dusk before he reached the Hords' cabin. While he was there, he said two things that were remembered later.

The first was while he was talking to Breck Hord. "You've got an instinct for leadership like a hound has an instinct for hunting, Breck. Trust it. Don't bother yourself with questions — there are enough intellectuals in the struggle already, believe me. You just follow your nose. Fight when you feel you should fight, lie low when you feel you should lie low, tell the truth when it seems right, and tell lies the other times. Sometimes you'll be wrong — but not often, and not far wrong."

The second was just before he left. He was alone with Phoebe for a moment on the porch. It was dark. He touched her lightly on the elbow with his index finger. "I'll tell you something, if you won't get mad."

"I won't get mad."

"Some day a man is going to make love to you, and it will be the best thing that ever happened to him. It will be like all his birthdays were squeezed up together into one perfect time." She opened her mouth to answer, but couldn't say a word. "I wish I could be the man," he went on. "I *hope* I can be the man. But if I'm not — somebody will."

Rogoff was less than a mile from the safety of Evarts when

he was forced off the road by a car full of deputy sheriffs. Felix Gill was in charge. Henry would have tried to use his gun, but Rogoff told him not to be a damn fool. The two men climbed out of their car and stood with their hands in the air. Gill smiled thinly. "Well, if it ain't a New York Jew Communist — just what we was looking for," he said. "Mr. Tasker won't have no call to be upset at all!"

Rogoff and Henry were crowded into the back of the deputies' car. They sat on the floor, squeezed in among legs and feet. One of the guards amused himself by poking them with the barrel of his pistol. Rogoff sensed that Henry, stripped of his weapon, was panic-stricken, and tried to offer him reassurance: "Well, I suppose we'll take a few lumps, Henry. That's what you get for bumming a ride with a dangerous person like me. Next time you'll know better."

"What do you mean, next time?" asked the guard with the pistol. "You don't mean you think there's going to be any next time!"

"Look, this boy just happened to be along in the car. You've got nothing against him," Rogoff said reasonably.

"Sure, he's just a poor innocent hitchhiker out looking for a ride on a back road in Harlan County in the middle of the night," said Gill from the front seat. "That's why he's carrying a pistol."

"Where are we going, or should I ask?" said Rogoff.

"To the good-bye place," Gill replied. "So you can start thinking of all the people you'd like to say good-bye to. We'll give them your message."

The car passed through Harlan and then proceeded up the Poor Fork road to Cumberland. From there Gill ordered the driver to take the dirt road leading to Lynch and the Virginia state line. The car bounced up the west face of Big Black Mountain, twisting through one hairpin turn after another.

Above the dense loom of the mountain the stars were intensely bright; from where he sat, on the floor, they provided the only light Rogoff had to see by. The men in the car were quiet, for it was difficult to talk over the screech of the gravel under the tires. Once Gill burst out, "Jesus Christ, watch what you're doing, boy! You want to put us all down there at the bottom of the hollow?" After that, everyone was quiet again until the car reached the top of the mountain.

"This'll do," Gill said, and the car stopped. "Okay, everybody out." Hands grasped Rogoff and Henry, pulled them over the running board and deposited them on their hands and knees outside. Rogoff rose to his feet. He felt a pair of arms slip under his own, and then a moment later two hands locked at the back of his neck. As the pressure of the full nelson increased, his head was forced forward, his chest collapsed, his belly and crotch arched upward. Gill stood in front of him, his thin, malevolent face only inches away, and cursed him in a shrill, flat voice for five or ten seconds. Then he drove his bony knee into Rogoff's groin. Rogoff would have fallen, but for the man who held him. "Keep him up, now!" Gill ordered. Rogoff's feet dangled futilely in the air, his knees half-bent in an instinctive and pointless gesture of self-protection. Carefully and deliberately Gill began to strike him on the face — twice on the nose, then once on the mouth, then on the side of the jaw, then on the temple, then on the nose again. Gill was not a powerful man, but he was lithe and fast, and could hit with whiplash force. Rogoff knew his nose was broken, and probably his jaw as well. He might also be blind in one or both eyes. He tried to twist his head from side to side, but the iron grip behind his neck kept his chin pressed tightly against his breastbone. He raised his arms straight over his head, hoping to slide out of the wrestler's hold that immobilized him, but the man behind simply increased the pressure. Blood roared in Rogoff's ears, and Gill's voice seemed to be a great distance away as he cautioned, "Watch out you don't break his neck, now! We ain't ready for that yet."

The stunning blows continued, although Rogoff lost any sense of continuity between them; each seemed to occur as an individual phenomenon, exploding into his mind without cause, instantly disappearing without any relation to the blow to come. The only thought he could hold to as the beating continued was, *how much of me will there be left that works?*

When Gill got tired of hitting him, he stomped him, kicking him in the head, chest, ribs, pelvis, and groin. Meanwhile three of the guards were working Henry over. Both men were unconscious. Gill, breathing heavily, said, "All right, that's enough. Let 'em alone a minute. We're going to have to wake them back up. Somebody, get that whiskey out of the glove compartment, hear?" A deputy reached into the car and produced a pint Mason jar full of moonshine. Gill took it from him, unscrewed the cap, and raised it to his lips. As he swallowed, his eyes remained on the motionless bulk of Rogoff's body by his feet. "Goddamn, but if there's one thing I hate, it's a New York Jew," he said reflectively. "It's a damn shame to waste good squeezings on one." He bent over Rogoff and lifted his head, sloshing an ounce or two of the rank corn liquor into his mouth. Rogoff coughed, and Gill began slapping him, alternating the slaps with more swallows of whiskey. "Listen, boy, you hear me? It's all right, it's all over now. You can leave now. Just get up on your hind legs and walk away, that's all you got to do. Just walk down the mountain, find yourself a big, soft bed, climb in, and go to sleep — how does that sound, buddy? Here, have another swallow of this good 'shine — it'll put the blood back in your pecker." Rogoff drew a noisy breath and began to cough convulsively from deep in his lungs. Gill helped him to a sitting position. "Wake that other boy up, now," he said over his shoulder. "But don't use up more of that whiskey than you need to!"

In a few moments Rogoff and Henry were on their feet, supported by two guards apiece. The guards turned them so that they were facing down the winding dirt road toward Virginia. Gill told the guards to let them go. Rogoff said, in an unrecognizable voice, "I can't walk — can't stand up. All — broke."

"Sure you can, old buddy," Gill said soothingly. "You can do anything you want to, if you'll just try — you know that? It's the God's truth."

Henry suddenly began trying to run. He ran for five steps before he fell to his knees, then he struggled up and began to run again. Gill let him get almost twenty feet away before he drew his revolver and shot him. The bullet hit the stumbling man high in the back and rolled him forward down the hill.

Rogoff stood motionless, staring ahead of him down the road. He couldn't see anything.

"You ain't going to get into that big, soft bed without you start walking," Gill said. "Don't worry about that other feller — he was trying to ex-cape. Nothing like that ain't going to happen to you. Just start walking down the road, that's a good boy."

Rogoff took an experimental step forward, then another. Gill's pistol hand inched upward to bring the weapon closer into alignment. Rogoff stopped, and, as if in sympathetic motion, so did Gill's hand. For a moment nothing on the mountaintop moved.

Then Rogoff dived off the road into the underbrush.

Instantly Gill fired. His target was moving so quickly, perpendicular to his line of sight, he was unable to be sure whether he had hit Rogoff or not. "Son of a bitch is getting away! Turn them car headlights on, quick! And spread out — we're going to go into that bresh and find him!"

Rogoff drove forward in the darkness, crashing into bushes and trees, sprawling, recovering, clawing himself to his feet again. He was as blind as a mole in his tunnel. Every bit of strength, of intelligence, and of will that remained was concentrated in the single task of getting away from the voices behind him. It wouldn't have been enough, if he hadn't been lucky and fallen over a cliff. One moment he was scrambling along on hands and knees, and the next he was falling freely through the air. He fell ten feet before touching ground, then ten more feet before touching again, and then ten more feet after that before rolling to a stop against the trunk of a fir tree.

Above him the flashlights of the deputies zigzagged through the underbrush for fifteen minutes, before Gill decided to call it a night. From where he lay, drifting in and out of consciousness, Rogoff could hear the slam of the car doors and the throb of the engine. The car headed back down the other side of Big Black Mountain, and the sound of the motor dwindled to silence.

And Rogoff was alive. Beaten, crippled, never to return to Harlan County, the taste of defeat as bitter as his own bile in his mouth — but alive.

Chapter 13

Comic Relief

IN LATE OCTOBER, the NCDPP, in association with the International Labor Defense, compiled a list of attacks on the rights of miners in Harlan County by agents of the Coal Operators' Association; it included eleven murders, plus numerous cases of battery, dynamiting, and other illegal acts.

The NCDPP was the National Committee for the Defense of Political Prisoners, which shared many of the names on its letterhead with the ten or twelve other Communist-controlled committees operating from New York City that fall. The NCDPP presented its list to Mr. Theodore Dreiser, the well-known novelist, in the hope that he would take the lead in investigating and publicizing the situation in eastern Kentucky.

Dreiser had written no fiction of importance since *An American Tragedy,* but had recently visited the Soviet Union and recorded his impressions in *Dreiser Looks at Russia.* Since his attitude toward Communism was more sympathetic than otherwise, he was considered by Party strategists as the leading literary fellow traveler in the United States.

Everything about Theodore Dreiser, now sixty, was formidable — his vices no less than his virtues. His passion for the underdog was towering, and so was his monumental egotism. His rages were huge, his prose style massively clumsy, his politics made up of vast, featureless stereotypes. He was totally without humor, and his sex urge bordered on satyriasis. Even his personal appearance seemed excessive — he was well over six feet in height, narrow-shouldered but wide-hipped, with a horse face and a big, loose mouth that seldom completely closed over his yellow buck teeth. He was generally dressed like a Broadway bookmaker.

Dreiser eagerly accepted the assignment, and immediately sent telegrams to a number of leading writers, lawyers, and academicians — including Senators La Follette and Norris, Felix Frankfurter, and Berea College president William Hutchins — asking them to join him on his Harlan County investigative committee. Not a one of them responded. Then Dreiser asked the NCDPP for volunteers. There were seven respondents, the best-known of whom was John Dos Passos, author of the trilogy in progress that would later be called *U.S.A.* The chairman arranged with his fellow committee members to meet them in Kentucky, and then wired the governor of that state demanding protection for the group while within its boundaries.

A few days later, when Dreiser met his associates at Boone Tavern in Berea, Kentucky, he was accompanied by an attractive brunette with a demure manner and a voluptuous shape, whom he introduced as "Marie, our stenographer." Several of the committee members were startled, and Dos Passos privately expressed forebodings but stopped short of communicating them to Dreiser.

From Berea the committee went to Pineville, in Bell County. They registered at the Continental Hotel, where they were met by the city's mayor, together with Judge D. C. "Baby" Jones of Harlan. They were promised complete cooperation by the authorities of Bell and Harlan counties, but, from the time they arrived in eastern Kentucky until they left four days later, they were under surveillance by the deputies of John Henry Blair.

That night the group was further augmented by the arrival of a representative of the ILD and a reporter from the *Daily Worker.*

The next morning the taking of testimony began. NMU organizers had lined up most of the witnesses, who all had bitter and pathetic stories to tell. Dreiser and the other committee members questioned them sympathetically, and Marie, her legs splendidly crossed, took notes.

At the end of the first day's testimony, it was obvious that the evidence was conclusive and damning. Whether or not the committee was partisan; whether or not the testimony was selective; whether or not the union leadership was Communist — the Coal Operators' Association in Harlan County was guilty of a calculated policy of terror and oppression beyond the belief of most of their fellow citizens in the United States of America.

Another two or three days' worth of the same kind of material — and then all that was necessary was to get the facts back to New York, and tell the whole story to the Congress, the press, and the American people. Or so it seemed.

The next day Samuel Ornitz, a member of the committee, was red eyed from lack of sleep. He reported that he had been kept awake half the night by a drunk spy in the next room, who kept giggling and whispering, "I can see *you,* but you can't see *me!*"

Herndon Evans, editor of the Pineville *Sun,* came to the hearings to interview Dreiser. Believing this was an opportunity to expose a member of the Coal Operators' establishment, Dreiser turned the tables and began to interrogate Evans. He demanded to know what Evans' income was, and, when told it was $240 a month, pointed out that that figure was six times as high as an average miner's monthly paycheck. He administered a brief tongue-lashing to the editor and began to move on to other subjects, but Evans stopped him. "And how much money did you make last year, Mr. Dreiser?" he asked pleasantly. Dreiser backed and filled a few moments, mumbling about the uncertainties of a writer's income, but Evans persisted, and finally Dreiser admitted to receiving something over $35,000 the previous year.

"And how much of that did you give to charity, Mr. Dreiser?"

As the other committee members looked at their scratch pads, or out the window, or at the ceiling, Dreiser replied that he did not believe in private charity. He believed that the responsibility for charitable activities should lie with the government, and furthermore that acts of individual charity were degrading to both the giver and receiver. When he paused, Evans asked again, "So how much did you give, Mr. Dreiser?"

Gruffly, Dreiser admitted he had given nothing.

"Isn't that surprising," Evans said wonderingly. "With an income only one-twelfth as large as yours, I gave better than two hundred dollars to charity last year. I guess there's not much doubt which of us degraded folks the most."

But this was a side show. The main event was the accumulating evidence of the brutality and avarice of the strong toward the weak, of the rich toward the poor. Dreiser moved the hearings to Harlan Town, interrupting them to attend a NMU meeting and visit a soup kitchen. On November 7 the committee returned to the Continental Hotel in Pineville. The mood of the investigators was one of satisfaction and confidence. After dinner in the hotel, they separated and retired to their individual rooms for the night.

A little after midnight the desk clerk in the lobby received a call from Dreiser's room. The novelist asked to be connected with his secretary. The clerk made the connection and listened to the ensuing conversation, which was brief. "Marie?" "Yes." "Get it down here." "All right." Marie hung up, Dreiser hung up, and the room clerk left his chair and walked quietly up the fire stairs to the second floor, where he joined the deputy standing in the shadows at the end of the hall.

"What's going on?" asked the deputy.

"That black-haired girl from the third floor — she didn't just go into Dreiser's room, did she?" the clerk whispered.

"Which one's Dreiser?"

"The ugly one — the boss one."

"Naw, ain't nobody gone into his room since I been out here."

"Then she'll be here directly. Hush up, now, and squnch back against that door, there, where they can't see you."

The beautiful Marie, dressed in a robe and slippers, appeared outside Dreiser's door a minute later. She tapped her finger tips against the wood, and the door opened. A whispered exchange followed, and the secretary entered the room and the door closed behind her. Silence descended on the dim hallway, broken only by the rhythmic chomping of the deputy's teeth on the toothpick that jutted from his mouth.

"You reckon she come down to take some dictation? I didn't see her bringing no books or pencils," the clerk said quietly.

"Only thing she was bringing was underneath that bathrobe. There was enough of that, though."

The desk clerk's rodentlike features were suddenly brightened by a smile of pure delight. "You reckon that famous man is in there screwing that little old girl?"

Kentucky; to those who did, the Harlan coalfields became the background for a dirty joke.

When he published a book on the facts the committee had uncovered, it went almost completely unread.

The Coal Operators' Association had vaccinated the public with an injection of farce, and so prevented it from coming down with a bad case of truth.

Chapter 14

The New Year

As ice began to form over the pools and shallows of Poor Fork, and the winter wind sliced down from Pine Mountain like a rusty scythe, there were many miners who went back to work on any terms they could get. The number of mines closed down by the union dwindled to a handful. In the others, men worked where and how they were told, dumbly, without protest; their wives queued up in silent lines, to exchange their scrip for overpriced food in the company stores. In their homes, the NMU was never mentioned; it was as if one of the conditions for reemployment in the mines was a kind of voluntary collective amnesia – as though, by acting as if the Communist union had never existed, the miners and their wives could expiate their sin in having joined it.

The NMU's core group had, for practical purposes, ceased to exist. Rogoff had been the first to go; within a month, both Rasmusson and Wayne Coy were also beyond the borders of Harlan County – Rasmusson in a jail, Coy in a hospital. Pittsburgh sent another organizer to Harlan to pick up the pieces, but he never had a chance. John Henry Blair's deputies hounded him so efficiently it was all he could do to maintain a tenuous contact with the few small locals still functioning. Jennie Markwell was gone; she had been offered the choice of being transferred to the jail in Hyden, a backwater where she might have remained indefinitely, with no effect whatever on events in Harlan, or of leaving Kentucky voluntarily. She chose the latter, but not until she had indulged herself in a farewell blast of purple oratory. Liz Craig was also gone, for Family Relief had given up on the soup kitchens. Ike Silver and the *Daily Worker* reporter were gone; even propaganda papers can't manufacture news without action, and the action in Harlan County had dwindled to the chattering of chilled teeth and the rumbling of hungry bellies.

But the strike still continued at Dead Yellow Dog. Every morning Breck got together a picket line of silent, hungry, shivering men in front of the gate of Excelsior No. 2. He kept a fire going in an empty fifty-gallon oil drum beside the road, and brewed ersatz coffee over it — a drink made from burnt pinto beans, dried roots, nuts, herbs, and bark, cornstalks, and sometimes charcoal — anything to make it taste dark, strong, and bitter. The pickets took two-hour shifts, but Breck stayed on the line all day long, which was probably the only reason most of the others stayed at all.

Inside the wire Gill and his guards watched the thin rank of scruffy, pale-faced men who presumed to besiege them. Sheepskin coats, real coffee, and heated bunkhouse notwithstanding, the deputies were becoming more irritable with each passing day. Gill brought the subject up regularly to W. F. Tasker. "How much longer you figure to wait before you bust them damn Reds? You let us go over to Hord's cabin tonight, I guarantee you there won't be no picket line here tomorrow."

Regularly, Tasker would answer, "Nugent Emory figured that way when he went over and burnt out their soup kitchen. I didn't notice that ended the strike. Only thing I noticed it did get one girl raped and one head guard shot down dead. I don't think we need much more of that on Dead Dog."

Gill spat. "I can't understand how anybody would let their whole business be closed down by one man. That's all it is, one damn man! We lean on him, and the rest of them will fall over their feet running in here to go back to work tomorrow!"

"You heard what I said, Gill. This foolishness is all over but the shouting — all Breck Hord can do is string it out for a couple of weeks extra, and the rest of them aren't going to thank him for that, once they're back on the job. No, you leave him be, hear?"

"You're the boss."

"I'm tickled you know that, Gill," Tasker said curtly. Then, to be sure his head guard didn't go away mad, he changed the subiect with a sly smile. "By the way — that old J. C. Stackpool. He still gigging frogs in my pond?" Gill answered that, as far as he knew, he was. "Son of a gun," said Tasker, shaking his head ruefully, "that sure is a good one on me."

*

Amy Herron was sick with fear. Her hands trembled on the cold steering wheel, and she couldn't seem to pull enough air into her lungs to satisfy her heart-pounding need. She lowered her head between her shoulders, so she could feel the soft silkiness of her mink-dyed rabbit-fur collar against her cheeks. The doors of the car were locked, but that fact gave no reassurance; outside the breath-steamed windows, in the cold darkness, stood a crowd of women, silent and implacable.

She had been a fool to decide to drive into Harlan that night, she knew. J. C. Stackpool had been on duty, and she was fed up with spending her nights alone at home inside the wire fence at Excelsior No. 2. In high-heeled shoes and a shiny dress with yellow chrysanthemums on it, covered by a good green cloth coat with a fur collar, she climbed into J.C.'s Chevy and drove out the camp gate. She headed toward Harlan Town. But the road was slimy with frozen mud and new ice, and she had gone less than a mile when her car wheels skidded off the road on a curve and mired themselves in the ditch. Amy's attempts to extricate the car were fruitless, and, swearing sullenly, she settled down to wait for a passing car she could flag down for assistance.

Few cars ran at night on the Poor Fork road. She waited twenty minutes before she saw headlights approaching. She jumped from her car and, tottering on her high heels, ran into the middle of the road, waving her arms. The approaching car stopped. "Can you give me a hand — my car's stuck in this damn mud!" Amy called. After a few moments both doors of the car opened, and two figures emerged. Amy was half-blinded by the headlights in her eyes, and it was only when the two figures moved ahead of the car and into the light that she recognized Aunt Cloa Burkett and Phoebe Hord. Her reflexes were fast; instantly she turned and dashed toward the Chevy in the ditch. She slipped on ice and sprawled painfully, feeling sharp rocks rip her stockings and scratch her legs. She clawed herself up again and leaped into the car, slamming and locking the door behind her, and then the other door as well. The windows were tightly closed. "Now what?" she said aloud. "Now what, you bitches? Try to get me now!"

Aunt Cloa was on her way from one miner's cabin where a child had just died to another where the children had, their mother said, "just a-give up trying." Her lumpy round face was set in stiff outrage. Phoebe, limping awkwardly beside her over the irregular road surface, felt more tired than anything else. Since Family Relief's decision to close the one remaining soup kitchen and not reopen the others, Phoebe had spent her days with Aunt Cloa, assisting the old granny-woman on her calls and studying her methods. It was tiring and heartbreaking work, but it helped her keep hold of the good feeling that had been born in the kitchens.

"It's Amy Herron, the gun-thugs' whore," Aunt Cloa said with satisfaction. "Psalms, seventy-two, nine: 'And His enemies shall lick the dust.' " She raised her voice in a piercing shout. "Floyd Isom! Hey, you, Floyd Isom! Maryjane! Maryjane Isom! This is Cloa Burkett. You get out here now!" Lowering her voice, she explained to Phoebe, "The Isoms don't live more'n a hundred yards away. We'll get one of them out down here, and send him to tell the women living over by your place."

"What you want to tell them women for?" Phoebe asked.

"Why, we got us a treed coon here, child. I reckon there's a mess of womenfolk got plenty of reason to want to see it knocked down."

A light came on in a cabin nearby, and a few minutes later one of the older Isom boys left to carry Aunt Cloa's message to the tents and lean-tos along Dead Dog Branch. In half an hour cars began to arrive, and then women appeared on foot. Newcomers joined the group that encircled the mired Chevrolet, until there were more than twenty gaunt and ragged women cursing and jeering at the terrified captive inside. Aunt Cloa let them work themselves up for a while, then took charge of the situation.

"This ain't doing us no good. We could freeze to death out here, while that whore stays as warm as lamb's wool inside that car. Get some big rocks! We can bust out these windows in no time!" When a five-pound chunk of limestone was brought, she took it herself, and smashed it against the side window nearest the steering wheel. The glass shattered; jagged shards glittered in the air, flying in all directions. A fragment struck Amy Herron, scratching her cheek, and she began to scream; another piece ripped along Aunt Cloa's fat wrist, opening a bloody two-inch gash. Unheeding, the old midwife thrust her arm through the hole in the glass and grasped the inside door handle.

"Watch out, Aunt Cloa, you'll cut your fool arm off!" Phoebe cried. Aunt Cloa grunted and turned the handle, and the door swung open. She stepped to one side, and pointed dramatically to the figure huddled against the opposite door.

"There she is, shining like a mackerel in her fancy furs!" she trumpeted. "Take her out of there!"

Eager hands seized Amy by arms, legs, hair, and soft fur collar, and dragged her out of the car, where she was held upright by the press of bodies around her. Like the Furies, the women clutched, jabbed, scratched, tore, and spat at her, as she screamed in hopeless hysteria. Piece by piece, her clothes were ripped off. First, her warm coat, with the collar hanging by a thread, looking as defeated as the dead animal it had once been. Then the dress with the yellow flowers. Then the slip. Then the underwear. Then the garters she wore on her heavy thighs on the nights when she expected a man to raise her skirts. Finally she was naked except for the high-heeled shoes, and the torn stockings which sagged on her legs like shedding skin. Through it all, her voice keened in mindless terror, above the snarls of the pack around her.

"Stop them, Aunt Cloa! Stop them before they kill her!" Phoebe cried suddenly.

The old woman stared at her as if she were crazy. "What do you care? 'Judgment is mine, sayeth the Lord.' This here's the Lord's judgment upon her!"

"It ain't no judgment — it's a plain murder! You don't stop it, they going to kill that woman before your eyes!"

Aunt Cloa's eyes narrowed until they almost disappeared in the doughy lumps around them. "So be it. The whore of Babylon shall be made desolate and naked, and they shall eat her flesh, and burn her with fire. Revelations, seventeen, sixteen." She folded her arms, satisfied and immovable.

Phoebe spun away from her and threw herself into the surging crowd of women around Amy. She tugged and elbowed and twisted her way until she reached the center of the crowd, where the pressure from behind squeezed her against the naked woman. She wrapped her arms around Amy protectively. "Stop it!" she screamed to the others. "Stop it now, that's enough! You hear me? That's enough!" Hands thrust toward her face, and she freed one arm and struck out at the women nearest her. "Stop it! Stop it! Stop it!" A foot kicked the ankle of her crippled leg, and it collapsed under her. She started to fall, with one arm still wrapped around Amy Herron. Fists pounded against her back as she slipped toward the ground, pulling Amy down with her.

The two of them would have died there in the frozen mud if Aunt Cloa hadn't decided that, whether Amy Herron was worth saving or not, Phoebe Hord was. With a baritone rumble from her chest, she leaped on the backs of the Furies and began peeling them off one by one, like the leaves of an artichoke. Punching, butting, and kicking, she arrived to stand spraddle-legged over the fallen women. "Anybody think she's stout enough to come up against Aunt Cloa, you just come on, now!" she challenged, her eyes moving from side to side like smooth-rolling ball bearings. The blood from the cut on her wrist had blackened the sleeve of her coat, and her hair had come loose from its bun, and stuck out at all angles.

None of the women accepted her offer. They stood, mumbling or silent, as she helped first Phoebe to her feet, and then the shivering, whimpering Amy Herron. Aunt Cloa shepherded them to her car, pushed the naked woman into the back seat and Phoebe into the front, and then turned to the other women watching her. "Go on home now," she ordered. "We done enough. We put the fear of God into this here whited sepulcher, so she won't never be able to think of sin again without remembering the vengeance of decent women. That's enough for now. Any more, and we'd be as bad as the gun-thugs." A grumble rose from the surrounding women. "Go on home, I told you!" she said, in a louder voice with an edge to it. "I mean it!" After a moment two or three of the women turned away and began to walk down the dark road. Satisfied, Aunt Cloa climbed into the car, slammed the door, and started the engine.

They drove a mile without speaking. Then Aunt Cloa snorted and said, "What in the world got into you back there, child? You acted like you didn't have good sense."

"I didn't want them to kill her, Aunt Cloa."

"Why not? Can you give me even one good reason why the world wouldn't be a better place if they had made cat meat out of her?"

"I guess I don't think it's that low-down a thing to make love. Not low-down enough to get killed for," Phoebe said quietly.

"Not even when it's with a murdering gun-thug—a treacherous, cowardly wretch who forced your own sister-in-law?" the old woman cried incredulously.

"Not even then. It seems to me that loving ain't really a

bad thing itself, even if it's with a bad person. I mean, not like stealing, or killing, or burning down soup kitchens. The person may be ornery as he can be, but loving with him don't mean the orneriness rubs off him and onto you. It's not as if it was soot."

From the back seat Amy said through chattering teeth, "It's cold back here! I got to put something around me, or I'll freeze to death!"

"There's some burlap sacks on the floor you can use. Now hush up!" Aunt Cloa glanced at Phoebe through narrowed eyes. "Are you saying it's all right for anybody to fornicate with anybody else, and decent people should just forget about it, and pay no nevermind to the Seventh Commandment?"

Phoebe closed her eyes and leaned her head back against the seat. "No, ma'am, I'm not saying that. All I'm saying is that breaking laws out of love isn't the same as breaking laws out of hate. And if God says adultery is wrong, then I guess God will punish it when He's ready."

"I'm still cold — you want me to freeze right here in your car?" whined Amy from the back seat.

"Either that or I'll warm you up till you think you've been setting in a fire. Shut up, whore." Aunt Cloa lowered her voice as she spoke to Phoebe. "All of a sudden you've got a mess of brand-new ideas about lovemaking. You're still a good girl, ain't you, child? You ain't gone and forsaken the ways of righteousness, have you?"

Phoebe gave a little laugh. "I haven't forsaken anything, except maybe looking down on folks as much as I used to."

"Well, see that you don't. Lust is an abomination. Try not to think about it." She drove on in silence. Once or twice she cleared her throat as though to say something, and then thought better of it. In a few minutes the gate of Excelsior No. 2 appeared in the headlights. J. C. Stackpool stood inside the wire, one hand resting on his holstered pistol, the other shading his eyes in a vain attempt to see into the glare. Aunt Cloa stopped the car with a jerk. "Out, you," she snapped.

"I can't get out like this!"

"Oh, yes you can." The old woman turned to look at the passenger in the back seat, and the smile on her face looked like a crack in a stone. "Now. Out." Amy grabbed the door handle and turned it, stepped quickly out of the car, with her burlap bags clutched around her, and kicked the door closed. Immediately Aunt Cloa reversed the engine and backed twenty feet down the road. Amy was pinned in the headlights, her bruised, muddy flesh gleaming whitely around and between the two brown sacks she pressed against her body. Her shame made her more naked than Botticelli's Venus.

"Well, I'll be dogged!" breathed J. C. Stackpool in astonishment. "What you been doing, Amy?"

*

A letter arrived from Claiborne. He was in the jail at Mount Sterling, on the edge of the Bluegrass, where he and nine other defendants in the Evarts murder trial had been transferred:

Dearest wife, childern, and family

Im writing this in the Mount Sterling jail, where our trial is finalley going to start, unless they change it again, which I hope they dont, as Id just as soon get it over. The food is better than in Harlan, soups and hameburgs, etc., and there is a bed for everboddy. The lawyer says dont worry, well get out all right, only I dont know. People here in the Blue Grass, they dont care so much for mountain people.

How are you, honey, good I hope. How are the childern? How is Ma and Pa and Breck and Phoebe? Is Breck still working for the union? It tickles me, old Breck being a union man, when he never paid it no atenttion for so long. Hes a good boy. Tell him to do a good job or his brother Claiborne will pin his ears back (ha ha).

There is a boy in here from Leslie county who knows some of the Allardyces. He says there so lazy they wouldnt take a lick at a snake ifen it was fixin to bite them. Tell that to Pa.

Well hon I guess thats all for now. Give everboddy a kiss for me, and tell the fellers to keep backin up the union. Your lovin husband

Claiborne

Joicy cried for half an hour after she read the letter, while Phoebe sat beside her and comforted her. "He don't know nothing about them gun-thugs, or he would have said something," Phoebe assured her sister-in-law. "There's no sense you plaguing yourself, because it sure isn't going to start bothering him until he hears about it first. There's time enough after he gets out of jail for you to start worrying."

"He'll hear about it 'fore he gets back home – he's bound to! How am I going to look him in the face? How can I add to his trouble?" Her handsome, high-cheekboned face was flushed in splotches, and her coarse black hair lay limp and sweat-dampened on her brow.

"Why, I don't reckon you'll be adding all that much to his troubles, Joicy. When he finds you and the family still got your health, and when he's safe out of jail and looking forward to a good new job and a big fat paycheck, why I reckon this other truck won't cause him five minutes' bother. You see if I ain't right."

But to her brother, Phoebe was more realistic. "It don't look good for Claiborne and them others in Mount Sterling, does it?" she asked Breck a few minutes later.

"Not so's you'd notice it," he answered.

"You reckon they'll hang them?"

"They'll try. They'll send them to jail a good long spell, more than likely."

"What about the strike? There ain't but six or seven mines closed down in the whole county, and it's four months till the spring melt. Is there any chance left to win, Breck?" When he didn't answer, she put her hand on his sleeve and leaned toward him. "Christmas is coming, and we've not even got grease for bulldog gravy. What are we going to do? What in the world are we going to do?"

He looked straight ahead, his face expressionless except for the tiny lines that fanned out from corners of his eyes, suggesting hidden pain.

"We hold on," he said.

*

In late December, Pittsburgh made an incredible decision. The executive committee of the NMU decided to attempt to shut down Black Mountain coal camp by means of mass picketing on January first.

Not only was Black Mountain the headquarters for one division of John Henry Blair's mine guards, it was also one of the largest and busiest mines in Harlan County — and during the six months of its activity in eastern Kentucky, the NMU had never succeeded in closing it for a single day.

It was two days after Christmas when Breck received his orders. He couldn't believe them. He stared at the young NMU organizer who had brought the message. "You want me to bring my boys to Black Mountain on New Year's Day to picket?" he asked incredulously. "Are you crazy? Why, there ain't twenty men on Dead Dog Branch who could climb to the top of that hill yonder! You know what the families here had for Christmas dinner? The union sent one twenty-five-pound bag of pinto beans, some flour, and ten cans of lard! That was for all of us together, and nobody knows when any more food's coming in! The woods is hunted out — there ain't a squirrel for twenty miles around. Half the young'uns are sick in bed with the flux, and the others stay in bed beside them 'cause it's the only way they can keep warm! It's all I can do to get ten men outside the gate to picket for two hours — and you say bring my boys to Black Mountain!" His voice rose in desperation. "Can't you understand it's crazy? If there's a single car left that runs, which I don't think there is, where would we get the gas for it? You think it would run on hot-air speeches? Or do you think we'll all just mosey over the mountain, through the snow, and have us a picnic on the other side?" Realizing that his excitement was running away with his tongue, he caught himself until he could reassert his usual taciturnity. Then he said bluntly, "It ain't sensible."

"Well, sensible or not, Comrade, it's what the committee has decided," the young organizer said stubbornly, "I know you've got problems — everybody has problems. But you've also got your orders."

On the first of January Breck and five other Dead Dog miners arrived outside Black Mountain camp before sunup, with a gallon and a half of gasoline left for the return trip.

The wind was rising, and snow stung their faces. While the others walked in circles stamping their feet, Breck found the young organizer and reported their arrival.

"How many did you bring?" the organizer asked, raising his pencil and clipboard expectantly in mittened hands. When Breck told him five, he marked down the number beside the typed words "Excelsior No. 2," and then gave Breck a reproachful look. "Is that all you could manage to scrape up?" he asked.

Breck thought of two or three things to say in reply, but only answered in a simple affirmative. "I don't know," said the organizer, shaking his head worriedly, "I just don't know."

As the eastern sky lightened to a dull putty gray, Breck was able to make out individual figures in the dark line of silent men who watched them from inside the barbed wire. He began to count them. *Lord Almighty, there's a hundred gun-thugs if there's a one,* he marveled. *And there's some of them with machine guns.*

By eight o'clock it was as light as it was going to be, and the wind had risen to gusts of almost gale intensity. The organizer had gotten a fire going in a ditch below the wind, and the men had formed themselves into a picket line and were shambling past the main gates in single file. Breck stayed in line for fifteen minutes, then ducked out and stood by the fire toasting his bare, numb hands. The organizer was there with his clipboard, checking over the list of mining camps still unheard from. "I don't know what's keeping them," he said for the third time.

By nine o'clock it was obvious to everyone that all the pickets who were coming had come. The guards behind the wire relaxed and began joking with one another, and calling pleasantries to the miners outside: "Hey, boy, you better watch out you don't get trampled to death in that crowd out there!" "See that feller whistling? He's so lonesome he's trying to keep his courage up!" "You all sure do have your buddies behind you — about ten miles behind you!" Breck held his place in line, his head down, his eyes fixed on his broken shoes, his stomach queasy with the nausea of hunger or defeat, both of which feel the same. *If this is all, why, I been made a fool of!* he thought grimly. *It's all been for nothing! Has it? Hasn't it?*

A column of five trucks approached the gate, which the guards opened for them. The leading truck moved slowly into the picket line, nudging men out of its way gently, like some large herbivorous animal. The pickets stood on both sides of the road, dully watching the trucks move past. When the trucks were inside, the guards closed the gate again, but the men didn't bother to reform their picket line. There didn't seem any point in it.

Of the twelve thousand miners in Harlan County, less than seventy-five had answered the NMU's call for mass picketing of Black Mountain mining camp. It was a final and irrevocable defeat for the union.

In the car on the way back to Dead Dog Branch, Breck told the others that as far as he was concerned, the strike at Dead Yellow Dog was over. "I reckon Tasker'll put you to work right away — he ain't never had no bad trouble to hold against you. He'll be glad to get knowing men back working the face."

"How about you, Hord? You think he'll take you back, too?" asked a man in the back seat.

"I wouldn't hardly think so," Breck answered evenly.

"No, not hardly. It might be you'd do better somewheres else, Breck." The man's solicitousness was a little insincere.

"Don't see how there'd ever be much for a feller living on Dead Dog Branch to do, if'n he couldn't get a job at Dead Yellow Dog."

"I expect you're right," said Breck.

*

The next day Breck went for a walk to think things over. It had snowed the night before, and in the bright, cold morning light the ground looked downy-soft, and the spruce and fir trees on the hillside bent their branches under their cottony burden. Breck walked along the road that ran toward Excelsior No. 2, watching his feet kick up little puffs of powdery snow at every step and leaving a raw human trail across the unbroken surface. *Once you take a step on it, it don't never look the same,* he thought. *Until the next time. Then it's brand-new again, like you'd never walked on it at all.*

There were two things Breck wanted to think about. One was how he was going to support his family. The other was how he was going to kill J. C. Stackpool. The first presented the more immediate problem, so he gave it the larger part of his thought; because he was absolutely certain he would kill J.C. in time, he could afford to let the event come at its own pace.

There was no work for him in Harlan County, he knew. Or Bell, or Leslie. The Coal Operators' Association controlled all the payrolls. But what about Perry County? The Hords had kinfolk there, the Cleggs. Maybe they could help. And Hazard was in Perry County, there surely were jobs in a town as big as Hazard. Or what about farther away — Lexington, or Louisville, or even up north to Detroit or Chicago? It stood to reason a willing man could find something to do in places like them, even if times were bad.

But he'd have to go alone, he couldn't take an old man,

four women, and five young'uns on his back, with no money and not even a sure job to go to. He'd have to leave them where they were, on Dead Dog Branch. *At least the house is stout,* he thought. *God knows what we'd find somewheres else.*

If he was to leave, then, the sooner the better. As long as he stayed in Harlan County, he was nothing but another mouth to feed. The quicker he could get where he was going, the quicker he could find the money to move the family. Besides, without him around, maybe the others could get food from the Red Cross or somebody.

He was walking with his head down, so the first thing he noticed about the approaching car was the sound of its engine. He looked up to see a two-year-old Chevrolet coupé approaching over the untracked snow. It was driven by a man whose face, the little of it that showed between cap and muffler, seemed familiar.

The car stopped close to Breck, and the driver put his head out of the window. At close range, Breck saw wiry red hair protruding below the man's cap, and recognized Sizemore, the organizer for the United Mine Workers of America.

"Mightn't you be Breck Hord?" Sizemore asked politely. Breck nodded, and Sizemore said with a smile, "I kind of thought you were, the way you looked, walking along there, like your thoughts was a million miles away. I've seen you look that way before. I'm a friend of your brother Claiborne. My name's Sizemore."

"I know. You was in Evarts, up till the fight."

Sizemore's left cheek and eye jerked in a startling involuntary wink. "That's right. I represented the UMW. Your brother Claiborne was working with me. He was practically my right-hand man."

"He's in jail now, down at Mount Sterling," said Breck.

"I know. We've got a union lawyer there, defending him."

"Oh? What does he reckon Claiborne's chances are? They ain't going to hang him, are they?"

"Not a chance. The first fellow they tried was charged with murder, and the jury found him not guilty. Now the prosecution has changed the charge against your brother and the others to conspiracy to commit murder, which is even harder to prove. Even if the jury finds them guilty, they won't give them the death penalty."

"They might lock him up for a good long time, though."

"Chances are he'll be out in two years at the most – either with a pardon from the governor, or on parole," Sizemore said positively. "But look – it wasn't your brother I came here to talk about. It was you."

"Me?" said Breck in surprise. "What would you want to see me about?"

Sizemore opened the right-hand car door in invitation. "Come on and get in here and I'll tell you. There's no reason we've got to freeze to death while we talk."

Breck kicked the snow off his shoes against the running board and got into the car. The inside air was warm and smelled of tobacco and old upholstery, with a faint underlying suggestion of moonshine whiskey. Breck stretched out his legs while Sizemore drove a hundred yards farther down the road and stopped under a stand of trees. The UMW organizer switched off the ignition and turned to look at him. His expression was purposeful.

"First off, there's some stuff for you and your family in the rumble seat," he said. "Flour, cornmeal, beans, some side meat, coffee, Karo syrup – I reckon it's enough to hold you all for a week." "That's handsome – that's mighty handsome," Breck said slowly. "We're beholden to you."

Sizemore waved his hand impatiently. "The UMW takes

care of its own," he said, as if dismissing the subject. "We'll drive up to your place and drop it off directly. But that's not what I really came here to Dead Dog for. I came up to have a talk with you, Breck. About the union."

"The union I'm in is a different one — the NMU."

"I know all about the NMU." He took out a pack of machine-rolled cigarettes, offered one to Breck, took one himself, and lit both of them. He inhaled deeply, and coughed. "I know all about the NMU," he repeated. "The whole thing was a mistake. It never should have happened. They never should have got into eastern Kentucky to begin with."

"When they come in, they was the only union here," Breck said quietly. "They done what they could. If they made any mistakes, it wasn't from running away."

"I'll give them that. They fought, all right. But they had no business in Harlan County. Basically, they were outsiders, Communists, come down to cause trouble and try to start a revolution. They didn't think like mountain people think. They didn't understand our loyalties, or believe in our religion — they acted like we were immigrants right off the boat in some New York sweatshop. It takes a mountain man to understand another mountain man — those flatland Reds never had a chance of winning their strike."

Breck answered carefully, aware that he might be ruining an opportunity which somehow seemed to be opening to him. "I won't fault the NMU, Mr. Sizemore. I worked for it, and I believed in what we done, and I reckon I'll be proud I was a member for the rest of my days. You might as well know that."

"I do know that — if you felt any different, you wouldn't be the man I drove out here to talk to." The two men looked at each other in silence a moment. Sizemore's pale blue eyes were shrewdly appraising, and Breck's returning gaze was straightforward and slightly defiant.

"All right, Breck, I'm going to be honest with you," the UMW man said abruptly. "Last year the UMW made a hell of a mistake, pulling out when it did. In fact, for quite a while now the UMW has made more mistakes than anything else — it's developed what you might call a real genius for mistakes. There are reasons, naturally — John L. has been fighting for control against the racketeers and labor-fakers, and sometimes the fighting has gotten pretty dirty. Maybe we haven't been too willing to put our necks out to organize any new fields until we had our own house in order. Maybe we've allowed some locals to fall away because we didn't control the steering committees. Maybe some of our people have worked out an occasional sweetheart contract with a mine operator, and maybe" — his lips twisted as if the words he was speaking had a foul taste — "maybe we've even tucked our tail between our legs and run like a goddamned rabbit, right when the rank and file needed us the most.

"I'm not denying any of it, not to you, Breck, because I'm being absolutely honest with you. It's true, it's all true. But it's past history now. It's all over, because John L. is in control, and the grafters and the porkchoppers are on the way out. The UMW has slimmed down and toughened up, and we're ready to come back into east Kentucky and do the job right. And to do it, we need men like you helping us."

"You want me to work for the UMW, organizing here in Harlan County?"

"That's right. We want you on the payroll."

"How much pay would I get from the payroll?"

"Twenty dollars a week, for now. More, when the union treasury can afford it."

Lord God Almighty, I forgot there was that much money

in the world, Breck thought. "How do you know I'll be worth it?" he asked.

"Anybody that could close down Dead Yellow Dog for three months, and then bring a carful of pickets over to Black Mountain besides, is going to be worth it," Sizemore said flatly. "Don't worry, we're not giving you any charity. We plan on working your ass off, if it don't get shot off by the gun-thugs first."

"How come you figure to win, if the NMU couldn't? The operators are strong as they was last summer, John Henry Blair's got more guns than ever, and most folks been hungry so long they ain't about to risk whatever jobs they got going out on strike again. How you figure to beat that?"

Sizemore snubbed out his cigarette deliberately. His hand was large, square, and freckled, with wiry red hairs on the back. "This is nineteen thirty-two, Breck. It's been four years since the bad times started in coal, and more than two years since they spread to everywheres else. People are tired of it — not just here, but all over the country. They're moving. You can feel it. They're moving toward something different, something better. They don't believe it when some politician tells them prosperity is just around the corner. They know if they're ever going to see prosperity again, they have to organize and go out and grab it for themselves — no Detroit car builder or Harlan coal operator is going to give it to them.

"Mark what I say, now, Breck — there's good times and bad times for unions, the same as for anything else. I been in long enough to know. I'm telling you, we're starting the best time the UMW's ever had. I want you to be a part of it. How about it?"

All Rogoff could promise me was that the strike would mean something, Breck thought dryly. *Sizemore's got him beat all hollow.* "I reckon I'd like to take a try at it," he replied.

"Good – you won't be sorry!" Sizemore said with a smile. "Here, let me give you your first week's pay." He dug into his pants pocket and counted out two crumpled fives and ten ones. "There's a meeting this Thursday at headquarters in Middlesboro. You be there and you can draw your next week's pay then."

Breck thanked him, and Sizemore asked a few questions about Claiborne and the rest of the Hords. Then he started the Chevy and drove up the road to the path that led to the cabin, the tracks of his wheels straddling the footprints Breck had made less than an hour before. He stopped the car and opened the rumble seat, handing Breck a large bag of groceries. "I'm tickled to death you're going to be with us. See you in Middlesboro," he said. He got back into the car, waved his hand in farewell, and maneuvered backward and forward until he was headed down the road toward Poor Fork. Then he drove away.

Breck stared after the car until it disappeared over a rise, and continued to listen to the diminishing sound of its engine until it became inaudible. He hugged the bag of groceries to his chest, feeling the shape of the slab of meat and the can of syrup through the brown paper. The cold, dry air around him was absolutely silent, absolutely still.

Then, from half a mile away, the steam whistle at Dead Yellow Dog cried out like a hound with its foot caught in a trap.

Breck turned and started to walk up the pathway.

We'll see, he thought. *We'll see.*

Bonnie Brae met him at the door to take the food.

Author's Note

THE "VOLUNTARY COLLECTIVE AMNESIA" I mention at the beginning of the last chapter of this book still exists in Harlan County. Very few residents seem willing or able to remember the brief existence of the National Miners' Union. Coal miners prefer not to recall their membership in an organization led by Communists; the United Mine Workers of America perpetuates the myth that it unionized the coalfields single-handed; the coal operators would rather not dwell on a period when they hired gunmen in droves to establish a reign of terror in eastern Kentucky.

But the printed record is clear for anyone who cares to consult it, spelled out in eyewitness articles in *The Nation, The New Republic, The American Mercury,* the labor press, and the Dreiser committee's *Harlan Miners Speak.*

Personal recollections are harder to come by, for Harlan County residents aren't likely to open up to outsiders. It was only due to the intercession of Dexter Collette, a Berea College student whose father had worked in the mines in 1931, that I was able to talk frankly and at length with a number of veterans of the struggle.

A dissertation by Paul Taylor, "Coal Mine War in Harlan County" (University of Kentucky Library), answers many questions. So also does the Oral History collection at Alice

Lloyd College, containing valuable first-person tapes on coal mining and coal mine violence during the thirties.

I want to thank Harry Caudill and Herndon Evans for their sympathy and helpfulness. My point of view in this book, like the responsibility for any errors that may have crept into it, is my own — but these men helped me to know the mountains better by looking at them through their eyes.

J.S.